THINGS TO DO BEFORE
THE END O

Emily Barr worked as a journalist in London but always hankered after a quiet room and a book to write. She went travelling for a year, which gave her an idea for a novel set in the world of backpackers in Asia. This became *Backpack*, a thriller that won the WHSmith New Talent Award. Her first YA thriller, *The One Memory of Flora Banks*, has been published in twenty-seven countries and was shortlisted for the YA Book Prize. Emily's third YA thriller, *The Girl Who Came Out of the Woods*, was published in 2019 and nominated for the Carnegie Award. *Things to Do Before the End of the World* is her fourth YA novel. Emily lives in Cornwall with her husband and their children.

Follow Emily Barr
on Twitter @emily_barr
and Instagram @emilybarr01
#BeforeTheEndOfTheWorld

Books by Emily Barr

THE ONE MEMORY OF FLORA BANKS

THE TRUTH AND LIES OF ELLA BLACK

THE GIRL WHO CAME OUT OF THE WOODS

THINGS TO DO BEFORE THE END OF THE WORLD

THINGS TO DO
BEFORE THE END
OF THE WORLD

EMILY BARR

PENGUIN BOOKS

PENGUIN BOOKS

UK | USA | Canada | Ireland | Australia
India | New Zealand | South Africa

Penguin Books is part of the Penguin Random House group of companies whose
addresses can be found at global.penguinrandomhouse.com.

www.penguin.co.uk
www.puffin.co.uk
www.ladybird.co.uk

First published 2021

001

Text copyright © Emily Barr, 2021
Cover image copyright © Shutterstock
Emoji (page 204) copyright © Shutterstock

The moral right of the author has been asserted

Set in 10.5/15.5pt Sabon LT Std
Typeset by Jouve (UK), Milton Keynes
Printed and bound in Italy by Grafica Veneta S.p.A.

A CIP catalogue record for this book is available from the British Library

ISBN: 978–0–241–34527–6

All correspondence to:
Penguin Books, Penguin Random House Children's
8 Viaduct Gardens, London SW11 7BW

For Seb

12 December

You know when you worry about everything all the time? Sometimes it turns out that it's the thing you haven't bothered to think about – the thing that's too outlandish, even for you – that turns out to be the one that's going to get you. That was what happened that day.

It was a cold afternoon, a Thursday. There was a Christmas party going on at college and everyone else was there. I never went to parties, so I had slipped out of the building and melted away (knowing no one would notice), and now I was walking round the park to kill time. Mum worked at home, and I didn't want to see the pity and frustration on her face when she realized I hadn't gone to the Christmas thing. I was planning to wait it out for a bit and then pretend I'd had a lovely time.

The grass was still crunchy underfoot in the shade. I crisscrossed the park to stomp on the crispest leaves, telling myself that I would need to be braver than this in future, because I had promised myself I would audition for the play, and a girl who couldn't walk into a dining hall to eat a handful of Quality Street and listen to the student choir singing 'Jingle Bells' wasn't going to be very good at standing on a stage and declaiming Shakespeare.

Whenever my stomping took me close to the children's playground I looked at the toddlers running and climbing and tried to remember if I had ever felt so carefree and un-self-conscious.

I wished afterwards that I could go back and recapture that ordinary boredom and mild self-loathing, but it turned out that nothing feels the same when all your assumptions about what might happen next have been ripped away, and you've discovered you don't have a future at all.

It changed slowly, and then fast. A man was staring at his phone. Then half the adults in the park were doing the same. Someone cried out. The atmosphere changed (appropriately), and I took my phone out of my pocket to see what had happened.

A newsflash had been delivered to my lock screen, even though I had settings that definitely didn't allow them.

The United Nations, in conjunction with a coalition of the world's governments, has confirmed that an accelerated atmospheric shift is underway and that it will have 'profound consequences' for the Earth and its population. Click for more details.

I clicked, but there were no more details because the network had crashed. I didn't need to see those details anyway, because I'd seen the rumours over the past few months, and had happily ignored them while worrying instead that I couldn't speak to the girl I liked, and that I wasn't sure if I was brave enough to audition for Juliet. That proves that even if you try to keep yourself safe by dwelling on all the bad things you can think of, something huge will always manage to slip through. I knew what the story was: the thawing of the permafrost had unleashed such an unexpectedly massive load of carbon dioxide, laced with various toxins, that it was fast becoming impossible for humans to live here. We didn't have time to evolve to thrive in our new atmosphere. That at least was what the rumours had said.

Later, when I did get to read the detail, I discovered that it was all true, and a date had been calculated for the definitive change of the air: September the seventeenth. Less than a year away.

Anyone with existing breathing difficulties would probably die before that. So would the birds, and some of the animals. We had done this to ourselves, and to the creatures, and there was very little we could do about it. It was the catastrophic breakdown of everything.

In the park everyone was just staring, like I was. Even the children, who couldn't possibly have understood, seemed to be frozen, mid-jump, mid-climb, mid-shout.

If the robins in the trees had had phones, they would have been looking at them too (and tweeting: 'The birds die first?'). The squirrels in the branches ('And the small animals?'). The dogs on the leads. The cats. The rats. The ants and the mice. The newsflash beamed across the world in a moment, invisible until it landed, and then everywhere.

The world paused. I watched the other people. Everyone had taken something out of a pocket. Everyone was staring. There was a hiatus, because it was not a thing you could understand at first.

Then things continued. A discarded burger wrapper was the first to move. The wind blew, the children jumped, the birds flew, and everyone apart from me started to talk. A man started crying. I watched people trying to make phone calls. The rumours had been around for months and it shouldn't have been a surprise – and yet it was.

I walked to the nearest bench and sat down. There was a woman already there, who was old enough to have been my grandmother and I wished she was (my grandmother had died last year), and we looked at each other, then quickly away.

'Well,' she said. 'How about that?'

I couldn't answer.

'OK for me really. I've lived my life and I'll take all my pills before this happens. This isn't the way I'm going to go, thank you very much. It's you young people . . . I mean, look at them, the kiddies. And you. A pretty girl like you. So much ahead.'

I wished she would stop talking. I followed her gaze to the children in the play park, and thought of Sofie and Hans-Erik. I pulled my hair round my hand and nodded.

I wrote a text to my mum that just had a couple of words in it (*Oh, Mum*) but it didn't go through. I wanted to see Zoe, and I wondered what the scene was like at the Christmas party. I pictured it: happy, noisy, and then frozen, as everyone realized that there wouldn't be a next Christmas. I sat still for a while and just stared at the park. The grass was scrappy at this time of year, and I wondered whether the worms were going to be all right.

I didn't realize I was running, but when I looked down I saw that my feet were slapping over cold grass, and I was heading for the street. I bolted down the pavement, ignoring everyone, swerving on to the road when I needed to. We lived two blocks from the park, and as soon as I was running downhill towards home, the door swung open and there was my mother, on the threshold, waiting. I ran straight into her, and she grabbed me and held me, and even though I was taller and chunkier than she was, I wanted to be her baby again.

When I stopped trembling we sat on the sofa. Mum made us both sweet tea, handing me the mug with a hand that wasn't quite steady. She had somehow gathered together all the chocolate in the house and laid it out on the coffee table.

'Right,' she said, when she'd settled down beside me. She handed me a Twix. I opened it. 'OK. So it seems I was wrong.'

My parents (all four of them, but particularly Mum) had insisted that the stories were rubbish, and I'd happily believed them. Teachers said it was scaremongering, and that we were being hysterical by believing it. Mr Baxter, my drama teacher, had given us a whole month of lessons themed around doomsday cults and mass hysteria, to give us what he called 'much-needed perspective'. Everyone had come together to push the view that these rumours were what happened when you allowed anyone to say anything they wanted on the internet anonymously.

My mum – the person I looked to for reassurance above everyone else – had insisted so hard that there was no truth in it that I had been a tiny bit suspicious of what she really thought. She'd called it 'laughable' and 'stupid'. She said science didn't work like that. She did big laughs out loud to show how ridiculous it was. She agreed that there were lots of things to worry about, but insisted that we weren't all heading for a mass extinction in the immediate future at least, that if there was something like that on its way, scientists would have sorted it out by now.

She said we should take it as a wake-up call and clean up our act.

Now, of course, she was struggling, but, still, she was trying to be brave. I had chosen to believe her, and Mr Baxter, and everyone else, because it seemed too outlandish even for me to spend too much time worrying about this. It had barely made my top-eleven worries until now. I knew that I would have to scribble over the other ten because this was now the only thing.

I pictured the permafrost. I imagined it thawing out, and a green cloud coming from it and spreading across the planet. There was a reason that that stuff had been locked away, and we had undone it.

I dropped the Twix and grabbed Mum's hand and gasped for breath. Thinking about it made me panic and fill my lungs with all the air I could, as fast as I could, while it was still there.

She held me and muttered into my hair. 'Oh, Libby,' she said, and then she whispered something about violence, but I didn't stop to ask what she meant. I supposed there would be violence, but I had no capacity to think about that. Not yet.

There was, of course, a caveat, and when Mum found it in the small print she seized upon it. 'Look!' she said. 'It might be all right. They might be able to sort it out.'

I didn't understand how, but there was a chance that things might be OK. There was an operation underway to minimize the effects, to recapture the carbon and neutralize the other stuff. Meanwhile, finally, we *were* cleaning up our act, for all the good that would do. All fossil-fuel plants had been closed, all flights had been stopped, and forests were being intensively planted in an attempt to try to push the genie back into the bottle. I didn't read the science: I just looked at the numbers. Seventy per cent, they think. Seventy per cent we all die. Thirty per cent, somehow, life continues, though it might be through gas masks.

Seventy per cent was a lot. If I got that in a test at college I would be quite pleased.

One minute you're walking in the park, pretending to be at a party. Then you discover that the next nine months will probably be your last. Everyone's last: a reverse gestation. You realize that you happen to be alive at the time when your species becomes extinct, and you wonder whether any part of you could come to find that quite interesting.

You have to decide whether to go with it meekly like you usually do, or to do something brave, to live your last months with all the energy and bravery you can muster, to rage against the dying of the light.

PART ONE

WINCHESTER

Things to do Before the
End of the World . . .

1. Audition for Juliet

January

In the weeks that followed I stayed in my room and unravelled. I kept the curtains closed and put on the music that spoke to my mood. I didn't read, didn't write, didn't draw, and I certainly didn't look at the internet. I just shut down. My music rewound time, from Billie Eilish to Kate Tempest to Radiohead to Deftones to Leonard Cohen to Rachmaninoff.

I carried on eating because Mum knew that if she put a plate of honey toast beside me I would eat it, and if she put a cup of hot chocolate next to it I would drink that without even noticing.

I had, of course, known that I was going to die one day. Everyone works it out once they get to the age of about three and discover that even their beloved parents can't promise otherwise. Parents have to admit that, yes, you *will* die but it will be a long, long time in the future, and, yes, admittedly, they will die too but you'll be grown-up by then and probably have children of your own. I (along with everyone else in the world) just needed to come to terms with the fact that it was going to happen sooner than I'd planned, and also that it would be horrible in a way I couldn't imagine, even though I thought about it all the time.

Merry Christmas!

The further out I zoomed my perspective, the calmer I became. I was born: that is an incredibly unlikely fact, right there. My life, in cosmic terms, would be over anyway, almost before it began, whatever happened. The whole of the human race was insignificant, if you looked from a wide enough distance. It took me a long time to get to that, and it was hard work keeping it up as a perspective, but it was the only thing I could do. Around me the world burned and rioted and fought and cried. Christmas came and went, and then, somehow, things carried on.

When I emerged in January, ready to go back to college and see what the remaining months might hold, I discovered that most people had found ways of dealing with what was happening. While I had been shut away, my mother had, in an unlikely turn of events, started going to church. It had started on Christmas Day; now, after a few weeks, she had decided the C of E was 'too woolly' in the face of oncoming catastrophe, and was going to look further afield. My stepfather, Sean, declared the whole thing was a hoax and wouldn't happen ('And if it's not a hoax, it's best to act as if it was'), and was carrying on as normal. Dad and Anneka had also opted to ignore it because they had small children and their days were busy enough to allow them to shut out that kind of thing. Most people, it turned out, were just getting on with it while making extravagant plans for the summer.

The coming summer was the last summer we would ever have. It was going to be filled with festivals and parties and trips and holidays and everyone doing the things they'd always wanted to do. It had been renamed the 'end times' by one magazine, which had stuck, and now it seemed that the whole planet was going to have a huge desperate party.

Not me, though, because I didn't go to parties.

My tiny win turned out to be that I did find the courage to sign my name on the audition sheet for *Romeo and Juliet* on the first day back at college in January. If there were only a few months left, I felt I could at least try to use it for something. Even if that something was trivial to everyone else, it would be meaningful to me.

The changing of the atmosphere had, when I wasn't looking, been named 'the Creep', and the term had been adopted by everyone. Similarly, the day the news broke was universally called twelve-twelve. I pictured the Creep day and night: that green cloud creeping across the planet, over land and sea, poisoning everything and everyone in its path until it was the only thing there was.

At college they said we still had to sit our summer exams and carry on as if things were normal. We had to leave all thoughts of impending doom at the door; and the oddest thing was that we did. We just carried on and hoped for the best, because you can't panic for long before you run right out of energy and decide to do something normal instead to give your mind and soul a break.

I did, however, have one thing I needed to do. As soon as I got home from my first day back at college, I went to my room and tapped an email into my phone.

Dear Zoe,

Hello! I know we're barely really 'friends'. I know you don't really notice me. If you were trying to lull yourself to sleep by naming all the people in your drama class (or is it just me that does that?), I'd be the one you forgot. In the morning you'd wake up and say: 'Olivia Lewis! That's the one.'

But I am more interesting on the inside than I am on the outside. Am I? Is that a terrible thing to say? I'm not going to send this so it doesn't matter. Yes, I think I'm more interesting inside than my boring outside would make you think. I'm just too shy to speak, even though we're sixteen and I should have the world at my feet. What's left of the world. At what will soon be the decomposing remains of my feet.

Oh God! I'm terrible at this! Shit. That was not romantic. I'm trying to throw caution to the wind and make a heartfelt declaration of love, but instead I'm talking about my feet rotting.

Zoe Adebayo, I have known you since we were four, and I'm in love with you. I know you're with Elisha and that even if you weren't you wouldn't be interested in me, but I'm going to be brave and say it anyway. Zoe, I love you. It started in Year Eight, and here we are now in Year Twelve. You do the math! (Four years.) I love how kind you are, how confident. I love the way you dress – the vintage men's jackets, the tea dresses, the clompy boots. I love your hair. I . . . am going to stop now before this sounds too weird. I love you. I do. That's all.

I don't expect this to change anything, but I wanted to tell you anyway. I'm not going to send this so it doesn't matter, but I'm glad I've written it down. Maybe one day, perhaps in September, I'll be able to tell you.

Love, proper love,

Libby xxx

I saved it to drafts. I started another one.

Hey Zoe,

Are you auditioning for the play? I've just signed up for it. I don't usually dare to do this kind of stuff, but as times have changed I'm thinking what the hell.

Do you fancy meeting up and looking at the script?

Libby xxx

I saved that to drafts too.

Zoe,

Fancy a coffee?

Libby xxx

I saved them all, and figured that one day I would find a way to write one that I might actually be able to send. I knew she was auditioning for the play. I had written my name underneath hers a few hours ago, had stroked her name with my fingertip when no one was looking.

I would just have to turn up and see what happened.

2. Die in front of an audience

March

'Let me die.'

I said those words. I spoke them, and my whole heart was in them. The person I loved was dead, right in front of me, and I had nothing to live for. It was hopeless. There was no future. I knew for sure that I wasn't going to live. I was not going to face these consequences, this left-behind world.

I lay down next to him and held him. This was it: our plan had failed. Time to die. And so I did die.

I died slowly, in agony.

I had never been happier.

I tried not to breathe, not to twitch, not to move, only half listening to the things that were going on around us. My body vibrated with the footsteps as Friar Lawrence and the others ran across the stage. Next to me, Zoe didn't move either. My arm was thrown across her ribcage, and I gave her the tiniest squeeze. She answered by changing her breathing to do some sharp huffs of acknowledgement. I loved the smell of the dust and the make-up and the theatricality of it all. I was on the floor, and the ground beneath me made me feel safe. I just lay there, as close to Zoe as I could possibly have been, holding her, until I heard the words:

> 'For never was a story of more woe
> Than this of Juliet and her Romeo.'

Then the audience were applauding, and I stood up and pulled her to her feet, keeping hold of her hand for as long as I could, using my other hand to put the dagger into the pocket of my dress. We bowed, and everyone bowed, and the audience seemed to have enjoyed it (they were the world's friendliest audience, made up of parents, bored siblings and indulgent grandparents). I looked out and saw Mum and Sean, and, right on the other side of the room, Dad and Anneka. Mum was crying, and even my dad looked as if he hadn't hated it.

This was probably the last time I would act on a stage, and when I thought about the fact that it was over I felt the panic and horror threatening. I was clinging to the thirty per cent, and the belief that 'they' wouldn't 'let it happen', but I didn't really believe it. I believed in the seventy. How could you not? It was maths.

I wished I could keep my Juliet self for the next six months. I longed to be this Juliet-Olivia until the Creep came. The applause picked me up like a gust of wind and it blew me to a different place, a hillside where the sun was shining, where I could speak, where everyone was looking at me and clapping because I had done something good. I had been a good Juliet; I knew I had. They were telling me so. Life on this hillside was simple and wonderful, and perhaps, this time, I might be able to stay here, just until the end of the world.

I wanted to be like Juliet because she knew her own mind and did her own thing. I wanted to be her, apart from the bit where she died, far too young and unnecessarily.

But then Zoe pulled her hand out of mine, and we had to walk off the stage. If there had been a curtain it would have gone down for the last time, but there wasn't, so everyone just shuffled away while the audience picked up their bags and looked at their watches.

Backstage everyone was saying things like 'well done' and 'you were brilliant', and all the cast were hugging each other and riding the adrenaline and trying to hang on to the feeling. Lots of people told me I had been awesome, and I made an effort and looked them in the eye and smiled and thanked them. I had to keep hold of this. I needed to stay this way. It was my only wish: to be someone different.

Zoe wasn't my Romeo. I was Olivia Lewis rather than Juliet Capulet. But I could make Olivia Lewis into someone different. Someone better. Someone a bit more *Juliet*.

When I looked around it turned out that we were at college. The changing room was the music classroom behind the stage. The Montagues and Capulets were wearing jeans and hoodies, and hugging each other goodbye. The caretaker wanted us to leave because she needed to lock up. She was being indulgent, but there were only about another ten minutes, I was sure, before she would kick us right out.

I didn't want to be the last to go because, it seemed, I was teetering on the verge of being the other Olivia, the one who was terrified of standing out for any reason. I shoved my stuff into my bag and walked, with Zoe, into the entrance hall where the parents were waiting. We walked in a crowd of friends. I knew that there was going to be an after-party tomorrow, but I also knew that although I was invited I wasn't going to go to it.

'Bye then,' I said to Zoe, and even though my voice came out very quietly she heard, and turned and gave me a huge hug. I loved the smell of her. I loved the fact that she had cut her hair short for the play, to embody Romeo properly. I loved everything about Zoe. I held her as tightly as I could.

'Bye, my Juliet,' she said. 'And – speak again, bright angel.'

'Olivia!' said Zoe's dad, Chidozie, looking at me. 'Well, you were immense! It's like quiet Libby – gone! Juliet Capulet – present and correct! Astonishing actor in the house. Amazing. Bravo, my dear. I hope . . .' He paused. 'Well. I hope we'll get to see you pursue a career on the stage.'

'Thank you.' My voice came out so quietly he could probably only tell what I said by the shape my mouth made, and by the fact that I wouldn't, really, have been saying anything else.

I thought about Zoe's words. They were from the play, but she knew. She knew I needed to keep speaking. She understood.

'Darling.' Mum was there, and there were tears in her eyes and mascara on her cheeks. 'Oh, darling. You were amazing.' She pulled me in for a hug. Sean rubbed my shoulder. I wanted to stay like this for as long as I could, because the magic was still there.

I could see Dad over Mum's shoulder. He tapped his watch and mouthed, *Babysitter*, then waved and turned away. Anneka blew me a kiss and the two of them left in a blur of tweed jacket and stilettos.

It seeped away as I said goodbye to Zoe, who would never again be my Romeo and who would go back to barely being my friend. It melted further as I sat in the back of the car, like a child, while Mum and Sean talked about other things as we drove home through the night. By the time I took off Juliet's make-up and got into bed it had gone. I wrote a long email to Zoe, full of love, secure in the knowledge that I wouldn't send it. Then I cried myself to sleep, and woke up as boring-as-hell Olivia Lewis, the girl everyone forgot.

3. Don't give up on your education

I woke late on Saturday, and I knew that the play was over and everything was bad. I didn't want to get up and be in the world; I was terrible at it. I wondered whether I would feel more secure if I tried some meditation, or found some rules to follow.

In Year Seven and Eight I'd had a low-key friendship with a girl who had an obsessive-compulsive disorder. Shayla. It was thanks to Shayla that I stayed away from the kinds of behaviours that people would casually call 'a bit OCD', just in case, for me, they might be a sliding slope to actual OCD. Shayla had scrubbed her hands raw, had been tormented by visions of horrific things that would happen to her parents and brother if she didn't complete her rituals in the right way at the right time. It had been awful for her. At the end of Year Eight her family had moved away and I didn't think anyone from our school had stayed in touch.

I hoped Shayla was all right. I tried to imagine how she was dealing with what was happening right now.

I wasn't Shayla, and I knew instinctively that I shouldn't clutter up my world with ritual in case it became too important. My main way of getting through the days was by being unnoticed. Invisibility was my superpower.

I pulled on a big sweatshirt over my pyjamas, tamed my hair into a ropey plait and went downstairs to make some toast.

I would say I was born quiet, except that Mum said I cried the whole time as a baby and she thought I was going to be the noisiest child ever. But from my earliest memory (screaming and clinging to her when she tried to leave me at a nursery) I couldn't interact with people I didn't know. I never worked out how to be myself in a way that I could bear. I never knew how to trust the world when it was outside my control.

Now I was studying for A levels in drama, English and Spanish (exams scheduled for beyond the end of the world). And I still couldn't speak. I had picked two subjects that involved talking, but that was because I could wear them as a disguise. English was fine because I could just read a book and then write down what I thought about it. I loved drama. And I was taking Spanish because I knew I was good at languages, and because most of it didn't involve actually speaking: I could get through the parts that did by acting a character who lived in my head. Her name was Carmen and she was immense. She didn't flinch at the prospect of having a long conversation with a stranger about deforestation in the Basque region; she just got on with it.

Somehow, though, I couldn't manage to channel Carmen, or Juliet, or anyone but myself in the rest of my life. I had tried and tried and tried, but it didn't work.

I walked my usual way to college on Monday. I put my head down and walked, alone, through the rain, with my hood up and a scarf wrapped twice round my face and shoulders. My bag was heavy on my back. I wondered what would happen if I just carried on walking, past the college, out to the main road, and on and on and on. Eventually I would reach the sea, where the bad stuff was happening to the Earth, and then I would see what happened to me.

When I passed Zoe's house I slowed down: occasionally I managed to time my walk to college in such a way that she would come out as I was passing, and we would walk together. I thought Zoe barely noticed me when we weren't in drama, but she would walk beside me companionably enough if we met by accident, or 'by accident'.

Her house was smaller than ours, and there were more people living in it. I'd never been inside, so I didn't know much more than that, but I knew that her parents were lovely. Her dad, Chidozie, was Nigerian, and her mum, Sam, looked like a classic Winchester Tory but was actually very funny, and their family was always smiling. I wasn't stalking them.

The door opened and Hector, her little brother, came out. I heard him yell 'Bye!' back into the house, and I saw him slam the door and fast-walk down the pavement, with no coat on, his body braced against the rain. I watched his afro heading away from me, in the direction of our old school, and I knew he hadn't seen me at all.

At college it turned out I was still someone, residually. It seemed that there had been a lot of our fellow students in that *Romeo and Juliet* audience; they were there, I supposed, to support their friends. (Can I break off here to say that I wasn't completely friendless? I'll come to my friend in a minute.) There was a bit of a buzz as I walked down the corridors. Perhaps I was imagining it, but I was sure I heard someone say 'Juliet'.

A couple of people turned to look at me and I stuck my head down and pretended not to notice. I had unwound my scarf when I got indoors, but I pulled my hair across my face and used it as a shield instead. My college was a massive sixth form, with thousands of people in it, and I had liked it as soon as I arrived last September because it felt anonymous. It was far better than school had been, and also there were lockers in hallways so I could ghost through it pretending I was in one of those American high-school movies.

This morning was the first time I had felt like an actual character rather than an extra.

The corridor smelled of polish. It always did on a Monday morning. My first period today was tutor, and I was nearly there when a boy stepped in front of me.

'Hey,' he said. 'You're Olivia, right?'

I hesitated. 'Yes,' I said, but the word stuck in my throat and I ended up swallowing it back down. This happened a lot. Luckily for him, I was nodding my head at the same time.

'Right,' he said. 'Knew it. Saw you in the play. You were epic.' He started walking with me. He thought I was *epic*. This was my moment to step out of myself. I needed to say *thanks*. That would have been a starting point at least. This was the person I needed to be, just until September. That was how I would hang on to a little bit of Juliet.

'Thanks,' I said (whispered). Triumph!

'Yeah, it was a great production. I love it that you did it all female. Was that, like, your take on the fact that it would originally have been done all male? So Zoe Adebayo as Romeo was the equivalent of Richard Burbage?'

Yes, I wanted to say. Exactly that. The fact that the people who had signed up were eighty-four per cent female had set us off on that track, and we decided to go for it. We researched the original all-male production as best we could. It happened sometime before 1597, and every single character was played by a boy or a man. We had decided to do the opposite.

I was pretty sure my new friend already knew this, though, because all that had been in the programme, including the bit about Richard Burbage. Still, it was nice of him to want to talk. I was pleased that he'd actually read the programme notes. Zoe had been a wonderful Romeo: impulsive, sure of herself, romantic. Devoted to me.

That was all the stuff I said in my head. When I opened my mouth to join the conversation in reality, it turned out my stupid brain condensed it to 'yep'.

He waited for me to say more. He was, I could see, a nice-looking boy, even if he did have a man bun. I tried to say more words, but then I saw that we were outside my tutor room.

'Tutor,' I said, motioning to it with my head, and I went in without saying goodbye.

I heard him laugh, behind me. 'Enigmatic,' he said. His footsteps walked away.

I went to sit with Max. One of the reasons I liked Max was because he never really wanted to talk either. He found social things as impossible as I did, and he spent all his time drawing.

'All right,' he said, looking over the top of his glasses at me. Max had been born in Singapore and had lived here since he was six. I considered him my best friend, even though we barely exchanged six words a day. We wrote messages to each other – that was our medium. We said quite a lot by email and WhatsApp and text. We said hardly anything through speech.

I nodded.

'Play went well then.' He didn't look up from his notebook. I looked over, and saw that it was covered in a comic strip of aliens performing on a stage out in space. I tried to read what they were saying, but it was too far away.

'Did.'

'I wanted to come.'

'S OK.'

We smiled at each other.

'Hey, Libby Lewis!' said a girl called Esme. 'You were, like, *amazing* in the play. So cool!'

I felt Max looking at me. I drew up all my talking strength, and I smiled and turned to look at her, and I said, 'Thank you very much.' I said it clearly, and I looked her in the eye and I smiled.

'Who knew you had it in you?' she said, and then she lost interest and turned back to her friends.

4. Share your chocolate

On Saturday evening, with the magic of the play thoroughly gone, I went out to babysit for my tiny half-brother and -sister. There was nothing Dad and Anneka liked more than a babysitter, and I was happy to do it because there was little that made *me* happier than being climbed all over by my half-siblings (it sounds sarcastic, but it was true). Anneka had asked me by text:

> You were so wonderful in the play.
> We've got you a little present. And
> the kids can't wait to see you.

> > Same. I can't wait to see them.
> > And you didn't need to get me
> > anything!

> Well, we did. See you at seven?
> Your dad has some news too.
> He'll tell you on Saturday.

We hadn't talked about whether the kids would get to grow up because Anneka refused to address the subject at all, though I supposed she and Dad must have spoken about it together. The babies were brilliant, because whenever I saw them I was sure that they would have long and happy lives. They were like seeds beginning to unfurl; it was unthinkable that they wouldn't carry on. As far as I was aware, they knew nothing about the Creep, and I hoped that when they grew up they would look back and be amazed at how blissfully ignorant they had been of such a huge thing.

I didn't give my dad's news a single moment's thought.

It was Anneka who answered the door, with Hans-Erik and Sofie dashing up behind her.

'Wonderful,' she said. She kissed me on the cheek. She smelled amazing, as she always did, like moisturizer and make-up and expensive perfume, and I could see that she was ready to go. Her straightened hair brushed my face.

It was cold outside: it had rained all week, and the daffodils in their front garden had collapsed under the onslaught. I took my coat off and hung it up next to all the other coats of the household, watching it drip on to the floorboards. I took my boots off too; this was a strictly no-shoes household.

Sofie and Hans-Erik flung themselves at my legs.

'Libby!' Sofie shouted. 'Libby's here! Libby's here, Hans!'

Ever since Hans learned to walk they had become a bundle of eight limbs, a squishy spider made of toddler. There was only a year between them, and they were sticky and blond and incredibly hard work and gorgeous. I was pretty sure they loved me, and I loved them right back.

At least they were both ready for bed, for once, and they looked like the cosiest little people in the world, in onesies with feet, with fleecy dressing gowns on top. Anneka had a passionate hatred of gendered clothing and had never put Sofie in pink or Hans-Erik in blue. They were both wearing green today, and their cheeks were rosy and they smelled of baby bath product.

I crouched down and let them climb me.

'Hey, you two,' I said. 'What have you been up to?'

'We got you choclit,' said Sofie, who always spoke for them both. Hans only managed the odd word here or there (I felt a particular kinship with him).

'Thank you!' I said. 'I love chocolate.' I stood up and carried them, with difficulty, one on each hip, into the living room. Each of them took a handful of my hair.

Dad was in there, already wearing his shoes and his jacket.

'Olivia,' said Dad. 'Well done the other night. It was excellent.'

'Thanks.'

'Yes,' said Dad. 'Thanks for tonight. Here. We got you these. Don't share them: these two have had their teeth brushed already. Take them home and have them there.'

He handed me a huge box of posh chocolates. Right in front of the children: I could hardly *not* share them – I smiled at them both.

'Thanks,' I said again. I was pretty sure I'd got my social skills from my dad, except that he was able to hold down a relationship so well that this was not his second or even third but his fourth marriage. He was pretty much Henry the Eighth. I had no idea how he'd managed to convince a beautiful Swedish woman to marry him and have his babies; I thought it must have been her idea. He wasn't ugly, my dad, but he was a fifty-year-old man who always looked exhausted. I supposed that anyone would have looked tired if they were half a century old and spent all their time running around after giggling toddlers.

I sometimes wondered whether his four wives would meet one day at his funeral, and what it would be like if they did. I had never met wife number one, Margaret, and I didn't know anything about her. As far as I was concerned it had begun with my mum, wife two. Number three had been evil Patsy; I had been so delighted when they divorced that I wrote her an email to tell her so and actually sent it, then blocked her so I wouldn't see her reply. Now there was lovely Anneka. I was pleased there were no children from the odd-numbered marriages.

'You're welcome,' he said.

I looked at the children. 'Bed at eight?' I said.

'It should be seven thirty. The routine. You know. But yes, eight would be fine this once.'

Most people didn't like my dad, I had noticed. He fell out with people easily, and lapsed into silences that could last for days (hello, pots and kettles). But he still knew how to get a woman to marry him. Four women. And that was a skill I could not imagine possessing.

Anneka swept back into the room. She was wearing a silky blue dress and, as ever, she looked stylish and beautiful. She handed me a carrier bag.

'Some clothes I don't need any more,' she said. 'Take anything you like and then do whatever you want with the rest, OK? Charity shop, whatever.'

'Sure,' I said. 'Thanks.'

'Right,' she said. 'They should go to bed at seven thirty, so that's now really. Can you read a couple of stories? No television for them, though of course watch whatever you want once they're in bed. Their milk's on the hob ready to warm up. Don't let it boil. Have fun. We should be back by eleven.'

They were out of the door in a whirl of coats and scarves and my stepmother's perfume and I knew they wouldn't be back at eleven, because they were always at least an hour later than they said. The door closed, and for a few seconds the house was silent. Sofie and I looked at one another.

'*Could* we maybe have telly?' she said in a tiny voice after the door had clicked. She was cautious at suggesting such a thing.

'OK,' I said. 'Why not? Telly's fun. As long as you don't tell. But *really* don't tell. And if you have to tell someone, tell Daddy not Mummy, OK?' Sofie was terrible at being discreet.

'And could we maybe, *possibly* have *one* of your choclits?'

'If we make sure we brush your teeth again afterwards.'

33

I sat on the sofa with my tiny siblings leaning against me and watched old episodes of *Pingu* with them until it was nearly nine o'clock. The three of us ate every single one of my Hotel Chocolat chocolates. I brushed their tiny teeth again and put them to bed and hoped that they wouldn't tell on me, or be sick, and then tucked the empty chocolate box into my bag to throw away at home.

'Night-night, Libby,' said Sofie. 'Love you.'

'I love you too.'

'Love,' said Hans-Erik.

I kissed his little forehead. They shared a room, and it was the sweetest little room in the world. Everything in it was small. The beds were little. The chairs were little. Even the chest of drawers was tiny, because it only held tiny clothes.

I left their night light on and crept downstairs, where I looked through the bag of clothes. It was all sequinned and chic, the wardrobe of a glamorous forty-year-old woman rather than a teenager, but there were some things in there that I thought I might wear one day, if I was feeling brave.

Much later, at one in the morning, Dad walked me home. It only took fifteen minutes, but it was always a bit agonizing walking with him. This time, however, he had been drinking wine all evening and so he was relatively chatty.

When we reached the end of the road he said, 'Actually there was something I was going to say.'

I remembered. 'Anneka said you had some news.'

'Yes. Not that it matters in any material way, least of all now.' He paused for a long time. I waited it out, and in the end he carried on. 'Do you remember that I had a brother? Andy?'

'Oh yes.' My dad's brother hadn't been mentioned for years and years. Barely ever, in fact. I knew he lived far away. 'Is he in . . . Australia?'

'America.'

'That's right.'

'Well, he's died, I'm afraid.'

'Oh. Sorry.' I tried to get my head around this. I had forgotten my uncle existed, and now he didn't. It was a strange arc. 'Were you . . . in touch?'

'We argued long ago,' he said. 'Before you were born. We hadn't spoken for decades and now we never will.'

'I suppose not,' I said. 'Right.' We walked for a bit in silence. This time it was him that waited it out. 'I'm sorry he died,' I said when the silence became too much. 'And I'm sorry you couldn't have made friends.' I wanted to ask whether my unknown uncle had panicked about the Creep and killed himself, but I didn't have the words. As it turned out, Dad told me anyway.

'I heard from his lawyer,' he said. 'He was in a car accident. I never expected to see him again. But it does make one . . . Well, we should have got over it, years ago. Silly really. Ridiculous. Grown men holding a grudge.'

'Where did he live?'

'New Jersey, I think. Princeton. He'd lived there for years. He has a widow and a daughter.'

'A daughter? How old?' I tried to imagine such a thing. I had cousins on Mum's side, and Sean had a sprawling family, but I'd never thought there was anyone else related to Dad.

'I didn't know about her until the letter arrived. Around your sort of age, I think. There's another thing. It seems Andy regretted our falling-out, as I did too. He worked in finance, and we're going to inherit a . . . substantial amount of money. Life-changing. Which under other circumstances would be . . .'

'Wow.'

It was cold, and the only people around were drunk. We walked side by side. I wanted to ask why they had argued. This was probably my only chance; knowing Dad, we would never speak of his brother again.

'You know the college fund,' Dad said, 'that your grandparents set up for you? Well, Anneka and I think you should have that. Use it to do whatever you want over the next few months. Because if . . . well, you know. If things pan out so you need money for college, we'll have Andy's inheritance now. You'll be fine. You should do whatever you want this summer, under the circumstances.'

'OK,' I said. 'Thank you.' I wished there was something I wanted to do. This was where I should have said: *Brilliant! I'll catch the Trans-Siberian Express and see all I can of the world.* 'What happened between you?' I said instead.

'Oh,' said Dad. 'Well, it doesn't matter any more.'

We walked to the outside of the house, and I said goodbye.

I wanted to hug him, because his brother had died, and because he had just given me thousands of pounds and told me to do whatever I wanted. It was an amazing thing to happen. But I didn't.

5. Contact family you never knew you had

I couldn't shake the thought of that cousin, of around my sort of age. The fact that she lived on a different continent was the thing that drew me in, because it meant that, now there were no planes and almost no time, we wouldn't meet. I thought that if I could get Dad to find her email address I might write to her, saying I was sorry that her dad had died.

I went to sleep thinking about her, and woke up still thinking of her, and in between I had fragments of dreams of the New Jersey Turnpike and a man who looked like my dad, in a car accident, dying. I knew I could have got to the States on a boat now that I had money, but although an odd part of me wanted to see what it was like, I knew I wouldn't do it.

I woke earlier than I usually would on a Sunday. The sun was coming in round the edges of the curtains, and I wasn't going to go back to sleep even though it was only half past eight. I went downstairs and found Mum measuring coffee into her AeroPress. She was dressed for church, in a sensible knee-length skirt and a brown jumper.

'You look like Maria von Trapp,' I said.

'A girl can try.'

'Are you still Catholic?'

She fiddled with the coffee, pushing it through the filter. 'Well, not really,' she said. 'I never was. But I'm still going to their church. A bit of certainty, you know? Nobody's more sure of things than the Catholic church. I'm kind of in a mental place for a nice binary outcome. Up or down.' She indicated the directions with her head, as she said them.

I sat down. 'The Catholic church has baggage,' I said. 'And also, Sean and me would definitely go to hell. Is that what you want?'

I was smiling, but she wasn't.

'Of course not. But Sean was brought up Catholic, so he can just do a deathbed conversion and he'll be fine. And you too. I was thinking: if you come to Mass on September the twelfth, that should do it.'

'If you're still a Catholic on September the twelfth,' I said, 'I'll do whatever you like.'

'Thank you, darling.' She kissed me. 'That means a lot. Heaven wouldn't be heaven if you weren't there.' She looked at her watch. 'Right. I've got ten minutes. How was babysitting? Didn't hear you come in.'

'It was nice. Did you know Dad had a brother?'

She looked at me quickly, and then looked away. 'Andy?' she said.

'Yes.'

'Jesus. I mean. Wow. That's a blast from the past. Have they made up at last?' I shook my head. 'What then?'

'He died.'

'Andy died?'

'That's what Dad said. In America.'

'Oh,' said Mum. 'What a shame. They never made up. How ridiculous and pointless that was. Honestly. Men.'

'That's what Dad said too. Not the *men* bit. And he said Andy has a daughter. My cousin. He thinks she might be about my age.'

'Oh gosh. Poor girl. Do you know what happened?'

'Car crash.'

Mum shuddered. 'Coffee?'

'Yes please.' I had taught myself to like coffee over the past six months. I thought if I was going to be an actor I'd need to like coffee, and if the world was going to end I would still like it to end with me liking coffee. The drama group had got into a routine when we were rehearsing: someone would go out to Nero's and bring it back for everyone. That was how I had learned to appreciate a flat white. 'He left Dad lots of money,' I added. 'And Dad said I can spend my college fund this summer.'

'Wow!' said Mum. 'How amazing. That could change your life, Libby.' I nodded, but I didn't want to talk about it. 'Think about doing something with it at least. I never met Andy. He was in America before I came on the scene. Your father hated him. So, a cousin? Are you thinking of contacting her, because she's far away and you won't have to meet?'

I smiled and took the cup Mum handed me. She had given me the one she'd just made for herself.

'You know me,' I said. 'Yes. Since we won't have to meet, I'll just email.'

'Invite her to stay,' Mum said at once.

'Mum!'

'Sorry.' After a few seconds she said: 'Do, though. Poor girl. Anyway. I'm off. See you later.'

'Say hi to God.'

I took the coffee upstairs and opened my laptop. It turned out that it was, not surprisingly, difficult to track down someone whose name, age and address I didn't know but whose father was probably called Andy Lewis. I had to give up. I had a shower, then stalked Zoe's social media until Mum came back from church.

'What do you think my cousin's name is?' I said as soon as she walked through the door.

'Darling,' said Mum, 'I didn't know she existed until you told me, so how could I possibly know that?' She pulled her hair out of its bun and took off her jumper and became herself again. 'I've obviously got no idea.'

'No Christmas cards when you were with Dad? From Andy and someone and little cousin . . . Jenny?'

'No. That was the whole point. They were dead to each other.'

I was deflated. 'So how was church?'

'Text your father. He'll know her name by now. Oh, it was fine. A lot of baggage, like you said. Patriarchy. I felt a bit judged, to be honest.'

I looked at my mother. She was so much cooler than me, and that, I thought, was both brilliant and a bit annoying. She dyed her hair blonde these days, and it was shorter than it used to be. We looked alike, but she was more polished than I was. Much more polished, I thought, than I would ever be.

I wished I had a sibling. Some days I wished that so hard that I thought I would explode. I hated being an only child. If I'd had a brother or sister with the same parents, my life would have been completely different. We would have been together, whichever house we were at. He or she would have looked out for me like Sofie looked out for Hans.

As it was, the main person who looked out for me was Mum. She had millions of travel stories from her youth. She had been everywhere, done everything. Her stories would begin with 'When I lived in Japan' or 'When I was in India', and I wished I could be more like her, while knowing that there wasn't a single bit of me that would have dared to have had any of her old adventures. Nothing was stopping me from having my own adventure right now apart from the fact that I didn't want to.

I wondered whether Mum was fighting an urge to run away from it all. I knew she was up to something. She had a project that she worked on, on her laptop, late at night. Sometimes I would come downstairs and find her typing, and she would always minimize the screen and pretend to be reading the *Guardian* instead. That meant it wasn't work.

I wondered whether she was writing her life story, just in case someone was around to read it one day. That seemed like a supremely pointless thing to do, but millions of people all over the world were doing it for the imaginary 'future archaeologists'. Or maybe she was making travel plans, lining up trains and boats and trains and boats, and one day I would wake up and find she had gone.

She wouldn't go without me and Sean. I was sure she wouldn't. Mum and Sean had been together for years, and he was brilliant. They worked as every couple should, and although it was a lovely thing to live with, it was also a bit intimidating. I couldn't imagine myself in a position where I could have any relationship with anyone, ever, let alone one that was actually good.

I texted my dad.

Do you know my cousin's name?

By the time he replied I was writing an essay about *Othello*, and I'd left my phone downstairs. Later, I picked it up and saw his text:

**Natasha Lewis. Oddly enough
I've been exchanging messages
with her. She's very effusive.
Turns out she's eighteen. She**

wants to know all about you.
Would you like her email?

I said yes, and a minute later I had it. It was that easy. I knew that if I stopped to think about what to say I would never send it, so I just wrote:

Hello Natasha.

This feels very strange, but I'm your cousin, Olivia (Libby).
I live in Winchester in England and my dad has just told
me about your dad. I'm so sorry. I wish I'd known about you.
I just wanted to say hello anyway, and that I'm sad to hear
about your loss and I hope you and your mum are OK.

Love, Libby xxx

I sent it without reading it through. Then I waited. While I waited I wrote another email, because these messages were my way of relaxing at the moment. They were my therapy, more of a diary than anything else.

Hey Zoe,

Just another email to check how you are. Don't worry, I won't
send it. I've just discovered I have a cousin and I never knew
about her. In a sense it doesn't matter now, but it's a strange
thing. My uncle died; I never met him and no one ever talked
about him. He left my dad lots of money but we won't get it
until next year so that doesn't mean anything either.

This feels like a time when the family secrets all come out. Who knows what else there is?

Anyway, as you know I have always felt alone. More alone than I should have felt. I've always wanted a brother or sister, even though I now have one of each (they're too small). And to know that there is someone my own age in my family is a huge thing. It makes me so happy to think of cousin Natasha, and I particularly like it that she's thousands of miles away. She can't come over here so I won't meet her. Which makes it safe for me to write messages to her and ACTUALLY SEND THEM.

Anyway. That's me. How are you, my Romeo?

xxx

Mum and Sean were at the gym, so I watched the news for a bit (computer simulations of possible futures, from the full extinction to a kind of dystopian horror in which I, for one, wanted no part, and millennia of re-evolution that would be completed just in time for the sun to turn into a red giant and vaporize the Earth). Then I watched three episodes of a horror series on Netflix, which was less scary, and sent a WhatsApp message to Max:

> So, I had an uncle I'd forgotten about.
> I never met him and now he's dead.

Sux! He might have been the best uncle ever. All the presents you missed!

I know! But it also means I have a
cousin I never knew about, and she's
alive.

??

Yeah. She lives in New Jersey. She's
18.

Noo Joizy!

Shut up. I've sent her an email.

Written or sent?

Both.

Bet she won't reply. Anyway you won't
get to meet her.

I know!👍👍 That's why I wrote.
How's your weekend?

Or if she does reply the world will end
before you can read it. Weekend OK. You?

Weekend boring except for new
cousin excitement.

I kept checking my phone. When nothing happened I decided to go out before Mum and Sean came home, so I went into the diluted sunshine and walked over to Zoe's house just in case she was around, but she wasn't.

I walked past, then took out my phone and frowned at it, to give me a reason for turning round and walking back again, but there was no sign of anyone there and no email on my phone. I did it again, but still nothing happened. I went to the park, and walked across it by myself, and then I went home. I was extremely bored and very grumpy.

I was dreading the day when Zoe and her family would move to Nigeria by boat or train so she and Hector could get in touch with that side of their heritage. So far they hadn't, but I thought they would, probably in the summer. People were doing a lot of that kind of stuff. Even without aeroplanes, it was surprisingly possible to get to places. Zoe might leave for the summer and never come back.

I missed the play so much. I wanted to cry. I missed the structure it had given to my life, the illusions of friendships.

When I got home, however, I had an email. It was from Natasha Lewis, and, as Dad had said, she was effusive. She had changed my subject line (hello) to OH MY GOD.

Wow!!!! Thank you SO MUCH for contacting me! You are my cousin, Olivia, and I never knew you existed. I NEED TO SEE A PHOTO OF YOU. So where do we begin? We need to meet ASAP.

I guess we start by saying that our dads must have been assholes to each other but there's nothing we can do about that because that ship has sadly sailed.

And then we say that we should do it better. You and me, healing the rift. How about that?

Here is a photo of me. This is my Insta. Tell me what else!

47

Thanks for being sad about my dad. It sucks, all of it. But now I have a cousin. Tell me ALL ABOUT YOU. And send a photo so I can imagine you.

(Where are you on the Creep? I vary but am currently on Team 70 and ready to embrace it because I don't trust humans to pull things back. I know there's going to be an afterlife so I'm OK with that.)

Natasha xoxoxoxox

I read it three times, trying to catch my breath. Then I opened the photograph and looked at her.

Natasha looked older than me, like the kind of eighteen-year-old who has grown up properly, who could be twenty or twenty-five. Her black hair was in a sharp bob and she was smiling. She looked extremely chic. I fiddled with my plait even though I knew she wasn't actually looking at me. I was scruffy and dull, my hair too long and too tangled, and I knew it would take me a long time to get a selfie that I didn't hate. I found a photo from a few weeks ago instead, when I'd been getting ready for the play and I was all excited.

I clicked on the link to her social media, and saw photographs of New York, and then, further down, a photo of her standing with my Uncle Andy.

I knew it was him because he looked like a shinier version of my dad. He was even wearing the same kind of glasses, and his hair was the same: like Dad's it was a bit long just because he was pleased he still had hair. He looked like Dad but more together. I wondered which of the brothers was older.

He had his arm round his daughter's shoulders. They looked closer than my dad and me. They looked like parallel-world versions of the two of us. They were people who could talk to each other, who had a close relationship, while my dad and I struggled to say a single word.

However, mine was still alive and hers wasn't. I felt my eyes fill with tears. I wondered when it had happened, and whether she had witnessed it, and whether I could ask her without being insensitive.

It turned out I couldn't. Not yet anyway.

Hi Natasha! Thank you for writing back to me.

I stared at the words. I didn't really know what to say in the face of her excitement. I chewed a strand of hair and tried to carry on.

Here's a photo of me. It's when I was getting ready to be in a play. I agree with you about Team 70. What do you mean about the afterlife?

I didn't know what else to say, so I just wrote: Love Libby xxx and sent it before I could second-guess myself. It wasn't a very good email, but at least I'd said something. Now it was her turn again.

6. Try not to be shy

Over the next few weeks something changed. Natasha and I exchanged messages (sometimes every couple of days, sometimes every hour), and, gradually, it felt different.

> What I mean by the afterlife is this: I don't think that death is the end. I think it's just the beginning. I know that people live on after death. Spirits. So I'm a bit excited to find out what it feels like when that happens.

I stared at those words for forty-eight hours because I didn't really know how to reply. I knew lots of people believed in life after death in various forms, but I'd never heard someone of my own age say they believed in spirits. That was the same thing as ghosts. Everyone knew ghosts weren't real. Didn't they?

She wrote again.

> Hey, Libby! Write back! Don't freak out about the afterlife! It's fine. Tell me what you believe! Every idea is valid. And

'nothing' is a valid idea too. Here's a thing I was reading about the other day: human brains have an inbuilt thing that stops us being able to think about our own deaths. It's like the ends of magnets. If we try to confront it head on, we just swerve away and think about something else. It's kind of self-preservation.

That feels true, doesn't it? So maybe I can only look at our upcoming extinction and feel OK about it because I believe that death isn't the end. Otherwise I wouldn't be able to focus on it at all.

I thought about that for a bit. Then I took a deep breath, reminded myself that I was never going to meet her, and wrote:

That makes sense. About the not being able to think about it. The magnets. I think that's what's happening with my dad and stepmum actually. Because they have the babies they just can't think about the Creep. They don't talk about it unless they have to and then they just say things like 'what might happen' as if it probably won't. I guess if you can't think about your own death, you certainly can't think about your children's.

She replied at once:

Exactly. You can't. And that's why it's kind of an amazing time to be alive. I mean, how lucky are we? How incredibly privileged to see the most enormous thing that will ever happen to the human race? People have lived for hundreds of thousands of years, and we get to be the ones here at the end. We actually get to witness something immense. I mean, if you were a dinosaur, you'd want to be the one looking at the sky and seeing the meteor, right?

I wasn't sure quite why, but that perspective changed me. It gave me a new way of looking at things, and I found I was able to open up and argue back:

It's not really a privilege because we made it happen. If we'd treated the planet better, we'd get to stay here. I'd prefer that TBH. I don't know if there really is a Chinese curse that goes 'May you live in interesting times' or if that's just a bit of a racist myth, but it would be quite nice to live in boring ones, don't you think? My mum says the nineties were like that.

— — —

Well, sure. But the thing with the nineties is that all the crap was just round the corner. This is the dinner we've been served, so let's grab it with both hands and eat the fuck out of it. Right? You in?

I smiled as I sat in my cosy bedroom, thousands of miles from her, and wrote:

Yes. I'm in. Here's the thing, though. I haven't wanted to say this to you before. But in real life I'm incredibly shy.

I stared at those words. I waited to see what she would say. But when she did respond, she just said:

Hey, I used to be shy too. I got over it by pretending I wasn't, and then suddenly I wasn't any more. I can totally help you fix that if you'd like me to.

Then she went back to talking about the dinosaurs.

After that I could write much more to her. She told me all the wild and wonderful things she was doing in New York, and I told her about my daily tiny dilemmas. I told her about Zoe. I told her about Max. She encouraged me, and never laughed at me, and she made me feel better than I had for a long time. Soon I couldn't imagine my life without her in it.

And then one morning I read a message from her.

I want to help you get the girl, you know. I've been you. I can't stress that enough: I know how it feels. Do you want me to talk you through it until you're not shy any more?

I thought about that for ages and replied:

I think I do. Please.

Natasha said:

It's easy. I'm going to give you a list of tasks. I need you to do each one of them, and come back with photo proof

that you've done it. Ten things. When you've done them
I guarantee you'll feel different.

I waited for the list, but it didn't arrive. It wasn't going
to be that neat and ordered. She said she would send the
tasks one by one, when I was least expecting them.

7. Make travel plans

April

It was a Thursday night in spring and Sean was sprawled on the sofa. He did a great sprawl. All his limbs went in different directions, and he managed to take up the entire space.

He was good at talking, so we rubbed along well when it was just the two of us. He talked, and I listened. And sometimes I talked too, and when I did he listened.

We were waiting for Mum to come back from yoga. Sean was sprawling and chatting, and I was making dinner. It was just pasta and tomato sauce, but I was doing the tomato sauce properly, following a recipe from a massive Italian cookery book, and it was taking ages. Right now I was cooking onions in butter and also waiting for the skins to start peeling off some tomatoes that I'd put into a bowl of boiling water.

It was strange how normal things felt. Here we were, five months from the end of human life on Earth, and I was making pasta sauce. Mum had given up on church, and moved on to Buddhism and hot yoga, which felt much more like her. She meditated for ages every day, and went out to classes every morning and evening. She was still nominally running her proofreading business, but she had scaled it right back, because what was the point?

'Smells incredible,' Sean said. He had wiry black hair and a beard. 'I'm so hungry. Would we have any crisps?'

'No,' I said. 'You'll spoil your appetite.' There was no way he was eating crisps when I was cooking a sauce from a book.

'Fine. So.' He paused, then spoke fast. 'Look – can I run something by you, Libs?' he said. 'This is a bit out there, but what isn't, you know? Your mum and I were thinking how awesome it would be to get away for the summer. Particularly, you know, under the present circumstances.'

'Going away in the summer is not *out there*,' I said. 'People have summer holidays. It's literally called "the summer holidays".'

I was having daily WhatsApp conversations with Natasha now. She had drawn me out of myself, and I could say anything I wanted to her. She made me feel different. Better. A bit more confident. That was why I was being sassy.

'All right, Mrs Smart-Arse,' he said, looking a bit surprised because *sassy* wasn't the usual Libby way. 'I mean, properly away. Not ten days in Alicante. Not dashing off to find meaning in an Indian temple, even though your mother would do that at the drop of a hat. More like . . . six weeks? How long are your college holidays?

Fancy spending them somewhere hot? Everyone else is going mad this summer. Why shouldn't we?'

I fished the tomatoes out of the hot water with a big metal spoon, and put them into the bowl of iced water next to it.

'Say more,' I said. I thought: *Natasha would like this.*

'Oh good! I was testing the water.'

I tested my own water. It was cold but bearable, and I reached in and started pulling the skins off the tomatoes.

'I just asked for more info.'

'You're sixteen, Libs. Seventeen next month. You might have hated the idea of going away for the whole summer. You know? You'd maybe want to spend the time with friends. I wasn't sure if there might be another play? And your dad will want to see you, and there are the little kiddies. You know. You're old enough to want to do your own thing. Oh shit. I'm talking you out of it already.'

'Somewhere hot, though,' I said. 'And if there's going to be a play, it'll be in September. The college is doing an end-times festival.'

'So,' he said. 'You might be up for it?'

'I might.'

'Your mother would mainly be doing yoga or praying, or whatever, in the sunshine.'

I grinned. 'Yeah, I can live with that.'

'Great! If you're on board, I'll do a bit of research. I know we could probably let the house out for the summer. But really who cares about that? You know, I'm inclined to say fuck it. Let's just go. Because I'm desperate to get away from here, and so is your mother, but neither of us wants to go without you.'

I looked at his face. 'You don't want to come back.' I could see that I was right. 'You want to go somewhere hot, and stay there till the seventeenth of September. Don't you? Even though you officially think it's all a hoax.'

He shrugged. 'I do think that. It's the only way I can do this, but it's hard not to get swept up in the excitement. The unusual excitement of imminent extinction. You're right, I'd like to go away and stay away, but I know life doesn't work like that. We'll come home for the end. We'd never make you choose between being with your mum or your dad and the kids.'

I nodded. I tried to recalibrate the summer in my head. A hot place, with books and nice food, sounded better than mooching around the park fighting the panic, watching everyone else heading off for their wild adventures. Hiding away somewhere idyllic would be the best way of passing my last summer. Maybe we could get trains all the way to Asia.

I would be happy to go away with Mum and Sean for the entire summer, no matter what was going to happen in September. It would save me from spending every day staring at the outside of Zoe's house, and from being used as free childcare by Dad and Anneka while they quietly did some mild things from their 'bucket list' (the phrase 'bucket list' was one of my least favourite things about this whole situation).

'What about your work?' I tasted the sauce and added a lot more salt and pepper, then picked some basil from the little plant and started chopping it.

'Well, Amy can just move her office elsewhere, as long as we have Wi-Fi and a phone reception. And if we're in a close time zone, I can work from home too. We're portable. And also, who really cares about work any more? Not me.'

'Nice.' I carried on cooking. 'Not Asia then?'

'We were thinking southern Europe? Spain? Good to keep your Spanish up, isn't it? You might need it. In fact, you'll definitely need it. You know: in the future.'

When Mum came back from yoga my head was full of Spanish sun. Sean handed her a glass of wine and I served up the pasta. The tomato sauce had taken ages and it did actually taste better than one from a jar, just.

I was about to turn seventeen, and here I was: pleased with myself for cooking pasta for my parents. Eight weeks ago I'd managed to stand up and act in a Shakespeare play, but now I was like an eleven-year-old who has just done food tech at school for the first time, presenting my offering to the family. I was racked by insecurity and self-loathing. It broke over me like a wave. I would be a loser from now until the end of the world.

My breathing went weird. I gasped and shook. I sat down. I closed my eyes and tried to hide it. It hadn't happened yet. The air was still there. I could breathe it. I took a deep breath in, and then forced it out again. I stayed very, very still.

I told myself to get a grip. We are privileged to witness the biggest thing that any human has ever seen. There might be life beyond death; Natasha had opened my eyes to that possibility. I had no idea what would happen after September the seventeenth.

I need to live while I still can.

It was Thursday night, and I knew that half of my year were at a house party, because even the sensible people had been subscribing to Sean's 'who cares?' attitude. It was impossible to care about getting enough sleep on a school night as the weeks went relentlessly on.

I should have been there too. I knew that Zoe was going. Perhaps I ought to try it. Because if I spent all my time with my parents, making dinner, being domestic and helpful, going away for the whole summer, then that would be my life.

I managed to take a deep breath. I forced a smile. Natasha had pretended she wasn't shy until it became her truth.

When I looked up Mum was staring at me.

'OK, darling?' she said.

I nodded. 'Fine.'

'She's up for the idea,' Sean said as we all started to eat. The fact that Mum knew what he was talking about made me see that they'd been working on this potential plan without me, and I was surprised that I hadn't picked up on it before. Perhaps I had, though: maybe this was the thing Mum did in secret on her laptop.

'Oh, wonderful!' said Mum. 'Well, let's get to work sorting something out in that case. How fabulous!'

'Are we going to Spain?'

'France or Spain,' Mum said. 'But yeah. Spain would be good, wouldn't it, for you? Also, as long as you're not by the coast there are amazing places to rent cheaply. So many people are taking their big trips now. There are thousands of houses available. This summer is going to be crazy. I mean, it's going to be hot, particularly somewhere like Spain, but I can live with that.'

'Right. I mean, yes. That sounds good. *Not* by the coast?'

I wasn't really concentrating. Mainly I was swamped by the fact that I needed to live while I still could. I needed to be more like Natasha, because I had nothing to lose.

I was going to die in September.

I was going to *die*.

In *September*.

I left them having another glass of wine and picking at the leftovers, and went upstairs, where I punched the wall so hard that it hurt my knuckles. I was going to die in September. There would be nothing of me left. It would be as if I had never existed. Normally you could say people lived on in other people's memories of them, but this time we would all be completely dead because none of us would be here to remember anyone at all.

I sat at my computer and opened the WhatsApp web page.

Hey Natasha.

How are you? Here's my news for today: I HATE MYSELF. I am useless and stupid. What's the point? What is even the POINT in being here when I can't speak to anyone, can't hang out with friends, don't even have any friends except Max, and we're only friends by default because we're both weird?

I mean, I have YOU, but you live in my computer and my phone. I can talk to you because I can't see you. You're the best.

Everyone from school is at Vikram's party right now. I could be there too but I'm not because I'm at home. I want to go, but I can't. I have this huge barrier inside me and I just can't get past it.

We're going to run out of air in a few months, and I can't get out to a stupid party.

On the other hand, Mum and Sean want us to go to Spain for the summer, so I do have the option of hanging out with my family and

pretending to be five again. So that's
something (something pathetic). At
least I'll get to see a different part of
the world.

What can I do? How can I be more
like you? Why am I so useless? Why,
why, why???

Anyway, I hope you're having a nice
Thursday.

Libby xxx

I regretted it as soon as I pressed send, but she replied straight away. So fast that it was almost instant.

Libs! Intervention! You sure you don't want
to video call? No, of course you don't.

OK then. Here goes: GO TO THE
FREAKING PARTY. You can do it. You're
going to do it. You're going to do it
because I'm telling you to do it. This is
your cousin speaking. My dad is dead
and you have to do this to make me
happy. You can do it thusly: find
something shimmery from your wardrobe.
You'll have something. Put on a bit of
make-up. Brush your fabulous hair and
leave it loose, maybe with a clip at the

front – I think that would look nice. And
go out and have a great time. You don't
even have to speak to anyone. Go with
your weird Max!

Do it. Send photos. This is a direct
instruction from your bereaved cousin.
This is how you can make me happy.

Love you!

N xoxoxox

I laughed out loud.

Seriously?

I sent it, just that word. A minute later she replied:

TASK ONE: go to a party. Send a photo
of yourself there. There must be party
people in the background, and you must
have a drink in your hand. Any drink you
want (doesn't have to be alcohol). Stay
for at least half an hour.

Photo proof required. Time-stamped.

Without stopping to think any more about it, I took one
of Anneka's dresses from my wardrobe. I hadn't tried it on
before, but I had at least hung it up. Some part of me had
decided not to take it to the charity shop.

Natasha had tapped straight into the part of me that wanted to do things. I would do it. I would do it because I couldn't bear to disappoint her. I could not fail my first task. I knew that I wanted to report back with the photos more than I didn't want to go.

I felt like I knew my cousin as well as I knew anyone. These were the things I knew about her now: she made money performing in some way. I wasn't quite sure what it was except that she'd assured me she kept her clothes on; it wouldn't have occurred to me that she didn't until she said that. I had tried to press her on what it was that she did. Singing? Dancing? Was she a concert pianist? A tap dancer? But she always evaded my questions, and I supposed that was one of the features of our WhatsApp relationship. It was possible to ignore a question you didn't want to answer.

It was possible for her to ignore my questions at least. It was, somehow, impossible for me to ignore hers.

Natasha had been shy, but now she wasn't. She travelled around the States working wherever she fancied. Her mum was called Peggy and was a fortune teller (I could not begin to believe that my dad's brother had been married to a fortune teller), and Peggy had gone 'a bit off the rails' since Andy died, and, I thought, was in a psychiatric hospital; I knew that Natasha popped back to Princeton to visit her regularly. Natasha lived impulsively and felt that, since we were all going to die anyway, she needed to be what she always called her 'best self' living her 'best life', and she followed her instincts as to what that involved. In other words: she was the opposite of me.

I held the dress up in front of me. It was a classic little black dress, short and covered in sequins that I was sure could be counted as 'shimmery'. This was so different from my usual skinny jeans and hoody that it felt like a costume, and that meant that when I was wearing it I might be able to play a character, a sassy Juliet. That was a start.

I brushed my hair and clipped it back from my face with three hair grips, as Natasha had said. It didn't look so awful. I'd had my hair as long as I could grow it for years, but I rarely wore it loose.

I owned a lot of make-up because I bought it compulsively: when I was twelve I had gone through a phase of stealing it from Boots and Superdrug and supermarkets. I was never caught, and now when I thought about the risks I'd taken it made my heart pound and my legs tremble. I had felt so bad about it ever since that I bought it legitimately all the time, almost ritualistically to make amends, even though I only ever wore it for plays. I would stand in Boots and put little lines of lipstick on the back of my hand, like other people did, and I'd pretend to assess which I liked best, and then I'd buy them all.

Now I drew a black line across the tops of my eyelids, and put on some glimmery silver eyeshadow above that. I found a dark red lipstick that I thought would do, and applied it carefully. I pulled on a pair of thick black tights but they looked awful so I went down to Mum and Sean's room and took some of her invisible ones instead. While I was there I nicked a pair of her shoes (her feet were half a size smaller than mine, but I could live with that). They were her tango shoes, bought a few weeks ago when she and Sean thought it would be funny to go to a Latin dancing class. I liked them: they were black, with a buckle and a low heel, and they looked like going-out shoes without being ridiculous. (They'd only gone to tango twice. Apparently it was much harder than it looked and they'd felt silly.)

I checked myself in Mum's full-length mirror and felt sick. I was all dressed up for the end of the world, and the fact that everything I was wearing had originally been my mother's or stepmother's made me feel like the most pathetic human on Earth. People at college had their own clothes. They could rustle up outfits for going out. Juliet Capulet wouldn't have borrowed clothes from her mother.

Still. I would go anyway so I could send Natasha the photos and pass the test.

I texted Max.

> You going to Vikram's party?

Obvs that's a NO. Not fucking invited. Also, can't imagine much worse.

> The whole year is invited? We cd go.

67

Y tho?

Proving a point to myself. Am
dressed up but can't go alone.

There was a pause, and then he replied.

Shit. OK. Just for you. Give me
30 and I'll come and pick you
up. 'Twill be like a prom date
from a US movie.

You bringing me a corsage?

If we hate it, we'll leave.

Yes. I just want to make myself
walk through the door. If we
stay 10 mins, that'll be a win.
I need a photo of myself there.
That's all.

OK. Deal.

Mum had asked me a few times whether I would like to
see a counsellor about my 'social problems', and I had said
it was the very last thing in the entire world that I would
ever like to do, thank you. The last time she asked I had
told her that I would prefer to give a TED talk that was

beamed live to every computer in the world about economic theory than speak to a counsellor about my shyness. She hadn't asked again.

I *did* want to get better, of course. I longed to be someone who could speak without giving it a second thought. But I had always shrunk back from doing the things I'd need to do to get to that point. It was like saying to someone who was terrified of spiders: 'Here – just hold this tarantula for ten minutes and you'll be better. Look at its cute hairy legs!' I wanted to be blasé about spiders, but not if I had to hold the tarantula to get to that point.

Now, though, things felt different. Natasha had been where I was now, and she was going to guide me through it, to hold my hand while I held the spider. I felt safer.

'I'm going to a house party,' I said, stepping back into the kitchen. They both looked at me as if I had said I was going to time travel to 1890 and kill baby Hitler. A mixture of *I don't think you actually are* and *Are you sure that's a good idea?*

'Oh,' said Mum.

'Are you sure?' said Sean.

'Is it a good idea?' Mum said. 'I mean, it's Thursday night and . . .'

'New dress?' said Sean. Mum stood up, knocked back the last bit of her wine, and went to look for her handbag. When she'd found it she took out some magic bits and pieces, wiped away my eye make-up and did it properly.

'What if I liked it that way?' I said.

'You're not going on stage,' said Mum. 'Trust me, that was not Thursday-night house party make-up. It was taking the lead at the Old Vic. Are you sure about the dress? I mean, it looks lovely. But it's quite formal and it depends whether . . .'

'It's fine,' I said. 'Anneka gave it to me.' There were tears pricking at the back of my eyes. 'Actually, forget it. I won't go. I can't do this, can I? You're right. I'm not a going-out kind of person. I'm useless.'

They performed an instant U-turn.

'Of course you should go,' said Sean. 'I'd offer you a lift but I'm probably over the limit. We'll shout you a taxi, though.'

'It's OK,' I said. 'Max is coming to pick me up.'

'Oh,' said Mum. 'Max, hey? Great.'

'Stop it!'

'Take a bottle with you,' said Mum. 'If it's a house party you should take a bottle. That's OK, isn't it? In sixth form? Don't get drunk. We've got some cheap red, haven't we, Sean?'

'Châteauneuf du Crap,' said Sean, and he went and looked through the cupboard, emerging with a bottle of red wine, which he handed to me.

I hated red wine, but I took it. This felt like the worst idea Natasha had ever had. I decided that I would just go upstairs and put my pyjamas on and text Max to cancel. I'd mock up a photo for Natasha. Max would be as relieved as I was for sure, and Natasha was thousands of miles away.

I was halfway up the stairs when the doorbell rang.

And Max was standing there in a jacket, holding out a daffodil that he had plainly grabbed from someone's garden on the way.

They were all looking at me. I walked slowly back down the stairs.

8. Gatecrash a party and
drink red wine from a mug

Vikram was surprised to see us. He stared for a moment, and then shrugged and took the bottle I was holding out as if it were an entry ticket.

'Sure,' he said. 'Come on in. Come in. I did say everyone was invited. I'm honoured. Libby – they say you were good in the play. I didn't watch it. I don't do Shakespeare. The immortal bard. Immortal bastard more like. Come on then.' He giggled. 'You look like my mum.'

Max and I looked at each other. Vikram was very drunk.

I hadn't met Vik's mum, but I knew what he meant. I looked like any middle-class mum, like someone who had gone to a Christmas book group to drink Prosecco.

I did not look like a teenager at a house party, and everyone else did.

We followed him, only because it would have been even weirder to turn round and walk away at this point, and I had to get my photographic evidence.

The house was full of people. There were people on the stairs, people in all the rooms, people in the back garden. Every one of them laughed as I walked past.

Coming here had been a massive mistake; I could feel, from the static in the air around him, that Max knew that too. The music was so loud the neighbours would definitely call the police, and everyone seemed drunk, drugged, different.

The worst thing was that people really were laughing as I walked past. I knew it was happening. I wasn't imagining it: I cringed with every step I took. This was exactly the same feeling I had in the terrible dreams in which I found myself on a stage accidentally naked. I tried everything I could to wake up, but I couldn't because this was real.

'Nice dress,' said someone who was sitting on the stairs. I looked round but all I saw were smirking people. I looked ahead again and there was a small explosion of laughter.

'Fuck,' I whispered. Even Max couldn't say anything to that. He reached out and squeezed my hand, which was an unprecedented thing for us and that made it worse.

We stepped over a little group of people sitting on the ground and as we passed they all laughed. Actually burst out laughing, at us. They were cool in their jeans with their drinks and their cloud of smoke, and they laughed in our faces. Ninety-one per cent of me was so mortified that I wanted to die immediately, and the other nine per cent was furious.

Natasha would have turned to them and had it out. I just put my head down and shuffled on.

I was dressed for a cocktail party and Max wasn't much better: he was wearing black trousers that were suspiciously like his old school uniform, and a smart shirt. I curled up into myself as I walked and tried to become as small as I could.

We followed Vik into the kitchen, and he turned round, looked surprised to still see us there, put our bottle down and gestured to it and the other bottles of booze on the side, then went into the garden.

I looked at Max. He made a face, and I forced a smile even though I wanted to cry. There were no glasses, so he opened cupboards until he found mugs, and poured our wine, and we clinked cups. His mug said WORLD'S BEST MUM on it. Mine said PARIS, JE T'AIME.

'Cheers for this, you evil witch,' he said. 'What could be more fun, and less awkward?'

'You're welcome.' I tried to laugh. It didn't work, so I tried smiling, which also didn't work. 'Can we take a selfie? I have to prove I was here.'

'Who to? The Gods?'

We did it. I got my photo and I was free to leave. We stood in the kitchen and drank quickly. I could feel the bassline of the music pounding through me. After a while a boy came past and stopped to chat to Max. I didn't know him, but all of a sudden they were talking about computer games. Max changed. He relaxed and looked happy. He refilled my mug without really looking at me. I edged away from their conversation and he didn't notice.

74

'It has an excellent tie-in to the first story,' the other boy said.

'But the tutorial!' Max was animated now. 'So long! I mean, please . . .'

I decided to leave. I was supposed to stay here for another twenty minutes or so, but I didn't care. I had my photo. She'd never know.

I held the cup between my hands as if it were a cup of tea. My head was spinning because I didn't usually drink alcohol, let alone red wine, which I actively disliked. It made my tongue feel strange. As I edged back through the party towards the door I wondered how different it would be if I were walking through an enchanted wood in a story. I felt there were dangers on all sides. I thought wild animals were snapping at me, creatures dropping out of branches, thorn bushes reaching out to grab me. I did not feel safe. I knew where the door was, and I crept past the hyenas towards it, and home, and safety.

I took a few photos of the scene around me as I went, just to show Natasha.

Then I opened the front door and walked back out through it, still cradling my cup of wine. I smiled as I found myself outside, breathing the air that was still fresh. There was a low wall at the front of the house so I sat on it and sent the photos to Natasha with the words 'Did it!' attached, and sipped my drink. I was still wearing my denim jacket, but I was shivering. It didn't matter.

I heard the clip-clopping of heels, and a woman walked down the street. She was about Mum's age and she looked completely together; she was talking through headphones, laughing. I wondered whether I would ever be at ease in the world like that.

The music was pounding out of the house. It must have been horrible for all the neighbours. This was a nice street. Curtains were twitching. I saw someone on the other side of the road in a front garden and wondered whether it was a neighbour who was coming over to complain, but whoever it was must have gone back inside.

I looked up at the stars and thought how insignificant human life on Earth had been. I looked down at some chewing gum on the pavement. I took deep breaths of the precious atmosphere and smelled all the night-time spring smells: things were growing and budding and unfurling, and it smelled of life.

I yawned. It was close enough to being time to go home now. I had been at the party for a total of half an hour, and so my contractual obligation to Natasha was fulfilled. I needed to take one more photo for the time stamp, and that would do it.

'See how she leans her cheek upon her hand,' said a voice. 'O that I were a glove upon that hand, that I might touch that cheek!'

Only one person had ever said those words to me. Only one, and she had said them exactly like that.

'Ay me!' I said, partly because that was the next line in the play, but also because it felt like the right thing for this moment. Perhaps the wine had made me brave.

Zoe came and sat next to me, so close that our thighs

were touching, and every part of me melted and fell apart. I didn't want to leave. I wanted to stay here forever.

'I miss it, Libs,' she said. 'Don't you? I know it's been ages, but everything feels a bit . . . nothingy.' She took a deep breath in, and then exhaled slowly. I did too.

'I miss it so much.' I could smell Zoe's perfume, her shampoo, and the essence of Zoe that had been everything to me during the play. 'Every day,' I said, somehow hurdling my usual barrier. 'I hate being my normal self again. At least you have friends.'

I felt her looking at me, and I couldn't look back. I knew my cheeks were burning, but luckily it was dark. My self-pity hung in the air between us for a while, and then she put a hand on my back and I leaned towards her.

Her hair had grown out a bit since the play. It was springy on my cheek.

'Hey,' she said. 'I know you're quiet. But you always seem so cool. Like you're not talking to us because you're too busy with more important things. The meaning of life, you know?'

I laughed a bit, or at least made a snorting sort of sound.

'I'm really not. I'd love to join in, you know. I just . . . I suppose I'm really bad at it. I'm trying to get better.'

'So, look at you here. What I'm seeing is someone who aced the lead in a Shakespeare play, and who is right now at a party on a school night, wearing a blingy dress that puts her friend Romeo here to shame.'

I thought of the one last photo. 'Can we take a selfie?'

'Sure,' she said, and we leaned our heads together and did it. Zoe didn't make a stupid pouty face like most people did. Neither did I, because I would have looked ridiculous.

'Send it to me,' she said.

I did, and then I put my phone away and looked at her. That selfie would be the most precious thing I owned. Zoe looked back at me. I leaned my head on her shoulder. It felt a bit weird but I left it there because it was my head. On Zoe's shoulder.

'Thank you,' I said. 'I am just so . . .' My words dried up for a moment but I forced myself to carry on. A motorbike went past, fast. 'Awkward,' I said eventually.

'Oh, Libby,' she said. 'I didn't know you felt like that. I think everyone's struggling right now. It's too awful to think about, isn't it?'

'I was reading somewhere,' I said, thanking Natasha, 'that part of being human is that we can't think about our own deaths. It's like the poles of magnets. You try to imagine yourself dying, and your mind just swerves away from it.'

'That's so true.' She shifted closer to me. 'I'm in total denial about the reality. Complete.'

'Same.'

Zoe's girlfriend Elisha was cheerful and sunny all the time. I longed for Zoe with every atom in my body and I wondered whether she knew that. She had no idea that I wrote to her most days. I had never had a girlfriend, never had a relationship, never even kissed anyone. I had far too many hang-ups to be able to do a thing like that.

But I wanted to. I longed to. It would be a girl – I'd always known that – and that girl would be Zoe. The woman who was beside me right now.

I wanted the moment to last forever.

I couldn't help myself. I turned my face towards her. I wanted to kiss her and, in spite of everything, this felt like the moment. I had wanted to do this so many times while we were doing the play, and now we were sitting next to each other on a wall in the starlight while somewhere, in the permafrost, a chemical reaction was already underway. The world was heating and the air was changing and we had both just said we were in denial.

She pulled away a bit, and then she noticed what I was doing, and she didn't look as if she hated me. She opened her mouth and I didn't know if she was going to speak or to kiss me.

'Woo! Romeo and Juliet!'

It was Elisha.

It was the person I wanted to see less than anyone in the world. The two of them had been together since Year Ten, and the worst of it was that Elisha was lovely. She was always friendly to me. Even now, finding me sitting on a wall looking into her girlfriend's eyes and about to try to kiss her, she clearly didn't consider me to be the tiniest bit of a threat. She came and sat on Zoe's other side.

'Hey there, Libby!' Elisha had bouncy curly hair and she always seemed happy. If there wasn't a conversation going on, she would have one by herself. She was the very opposite of me. 'How are you? Haven't seen you for ages. I like your dress. It's all shimmery.'

Shimmery. Natasha had told me to wear something *shimmery*. Job done, I supposed. Task officially complete. It no longer felt like such a triumph.

'Thanks,' I said, and I looked away from both of them, and anyway Zoe was turning towards her girlfriend and our moment was over. Elisha had said she hadn't seen me for ages, but I was in three of her classes. She saw me all the time; she just didn't notice me.

They also didn't notice when I shifted myself apart from them, put my empty mug on the wall and sidled away. Perhaps Zoe sensed me leaving, but she didn't do anything to stop me, or say goodbye, or do anything other than completely ignore me because she was with her girlfriend.

I walked home. I kept hearing footsteps behind me, but every time I turned round no one was there. In the end I half ran, tripping in my tango shoes, feeling like the most ungainly, friendless person there had ever been. Whoever was following me (if they existed) melted away long before I got home.

I left a note for Mum and Sean.

YES PLEASE. I WANT TO SPEND THE WHOLE
SUMMER IN SPAIN.
How soon can we go?
Let's go now.

I woke at three in the morning to a text from Max.

Thanks fr prty lib. BEST. U still
hr? bit pssed

Then, at six o'clock, Natasha replied to my photos. I
had sent her my proof, but hadn't told her about Elisha
appearing at the crucial moment.

YOU DID IT! Also, Zoe is hot.

Here's your next task. Get a big night's sleep and have a
huge breakfast tomorrow, then send her a text saying:
'Lovely to see you last night x'.

PART TWO

SPAIN

9. Hide

July

Dear Zoe,

I have tried to stop writing these stupid messages and not sending them. But here we are. I'm doing it again. It doesn't matter much, does it? I hope you liked the one I did actually send. The very short and breezy one.

I also hope you're having a nice summer. Are you still in Winchester? The weather here is very hot, and I'm spending most of my time watering the garden or swimming in the pool. I'm a recluse. I'm not exactly living my best life but it's . . . lovely. It feels safe, although that's a ridiculous thing to say right now. It's hot, and getting hotter, and we're hurtling towards destruction, but apart from that my summer is going fine.

It is totally beautiful here. We've rented a house that has a high wall all round it, with a garden that's overflowing with flowers and fruit and vegetables and trees. And a swimming pool: it's a tiny one but it's just right for me. Sometimes it hits forty-three degrees, but I just jump in the pool.

Oh my God, I wish you were with me. This would be the very best place in the world to wait it out with the love of your life. To hide away and look at the flowers and swim in the water and feel the air on your skin and savour every moment while you can.

And that, I suppose, is what Mum and Sean are doing. Ick.

They would be fine with the idea of me going away and having adventures – I know that, because Mum says it all the time. She went travelling when she was young, and she wants me to do it quick while I can.

I could get a bus into Madrid and a train to anywhere, but I won't. I don't even like going to the shops on my own. I thought that playing Juliet would be the start of my new self, and I couldn't believe it when you were cast as Romeo. I know you know this (or you would if you read my drafts folder).

But now I might never see you again.

Let me know if you want to do something mad. There are trains running all over Europe. I could meet you in . . . Paris?

Borrow Cupid's wings, and soar with them above a common bound.

Libby xxx

I saved it into my drafts along with all the others and looked around the house. I was sitting on the little sofa, my legs curled up under me, hiding from the midday heat.

I was brilliantly relaxed here. The walls were thick stone, and the inside of the house felt like a bunker, a place to hide from everything out there.

I was back to treating my unsent messages to Zoe as a diary, and every now and then I would send her a real message too. I'd sent one a couple of days ago, just asking how she was, and telling her a more condensed version of my life in Spain than the diary messages had said. She'd replied with a couple of lines. Everything was casual and breezy; we'd never mentioned the thing that hadn't quite happened between us at the party. All I wanted to do was to keep up enough of a friendship to allow me to suggest we meet up when I was home at the very end of August.

I was writing to Max too. He had travelled overland to Singapore. I'm currently trying to work out how to upload myself digitally so I don't need air, he'd written earlier today.

Everyone's doing that, so why not me? For what that's worth. I'm also having my cheeks pinched by aunts trying to fatten me up, and I'm eating so much that I'm now twenty stone, but I'll soon be casting off this meat suit, so whatever.

My messages with Natasha, on the other hand, had dropped right off. I was relieved she'd stopped giving me homework. I was happy hiding away here. It was a good place to be and I did not, right now, feel that I needed to be challenged with numbered tasks at random moments.

I decided to write to my dad.

How are the babies? I wrote, smiling, as I knew how Sofie would react if she heard me saying that. It would be an indignant '*I aren't a baby!*' Please send photos. I miss them.

I wandered over to the kitchen and poured myself a glass of water. As I was about to put some ice into it I heard the sound of a new email landing and rushed back to my phone just in case it was Zoe. But it wasn't.

LIBBY, GUESS WHAT?

I'm coming to Europe. I'm on my way. I am writing this ON THE FREAKING SHIP!!!

Natasha xxxx

I sat and stared at it. I had a feeling that my quiet summer was about to change.

10. Look after the tomatoes

On the morning of her arrival I got up early, swam fifty lengths and showered, all before either of the adults stirred. My bedroom was downstairs, a little afterthought of a room off the big kitchen, and I had my own bathroom. That meant I never needed to go upstairs: the first floor was completely Mum and Sean's domain. I padded around, pouring a huge glass of orange juice and checking how much bread was left. I started making a hot chocolate but I couldn't concentrate on anything, so I switched off the hob and dashed out to water the plants. I couldn't neglect my pet tomato, not when Natasha was coming to stay.

'Guess who's coming to visit?' I said. I touched it very gently with the tip of my finger. It was tiny and green. A week ago it had been a yellow flower, and now it was a fruit. 'Your auntie Natasha. I know! I wish it was Zoe too, but it'll be exciting to meet her. What? Scary? You're worried you won't be a good enough tomato and she won't like you? Me too.'

I had watered this tomato every day, had tied its plant to the wooden stake, and I was doing everything I could to get it to grow up into the biggest, reddest tomato there had ever been. I also seemed to be confiding in it.

'You're a tomato, Harry,' I told it. 'The tomato who lived.' Then I switched to Spanish. '*Eres un tomate, Enrique.*' Henry was the closest Spanish name to Harry I could manage to find, and I called it Harry because I was nurturing it to maturity just to sacrifice it, like Dumbledore had done: I couldn't wait to eat Harry as soon as he was juicy and succulent. I would share him with Natasha. Natasha would like Harry. Wouldn't she? I didn't even know if she liked tomatoes. For all I knew she might be allergic to them.

I didn't want her to come, but I was keeping that a secret. I had liked it how it was before. But she was my cousin, and she was friendly, and she'd lost her dad and, in a different way, her mum. I had to welcome her because to do anything else would have been monstrous.

Mum had offered to cancel her visit several times, because as soon as I'd read the email I'd started worrying, and Mum could always read me like a book.

'You know what?' she'd said a couple of days ago. 'I'm going to tell her not to come. You've been so happy. I hate seeing you like this. Why don't I just message her and explain that it's all a bit much. Put her off? I don't know why she makes you so anxious – at the start you seemed to love her.'

'Mum,' I said. 'We invited her. Kind of. I mean, we didn't exactly, but she's come on a boat from America to meet her family. Of course we can't cancel.'

Mum was unconvinced. 'I expect you'll relax once she gets here. But if you don't, I'm going to ask her to leave. I won't hesitate.'

'Fine!' I said. That made me more nervous. It raised the stakes.

I stood up, watered the lesser tomatoes (the crowd of Seamus Finnigans and Cho Changs), and then the other plants, and finally the roots of the vines, and turned to go back to the house.

Natasha was a strong character. On social media she was always being funny and scathing about the things that were around her. And now we were going to be the things around her. We would be on her Instagram. I imagined her telling her friends about us. Would she say we were boring? Of course she would: she had been giving me tasks to stop me being shy, but I'd been too dull even for that to continue. The last one had been number three (catch a bus at rush hour and strike up a conversation with whoever sat next to me: I had done it, recording it on my phone as instructed, and had actually had an OK conversation with a boy in my year).

And now she was coming to visit. She had lost interest in me, but now she was picking me up again.

The pool was sparkling in the sunlight. I looked across to the house. Mum liked to sit on the roof terrace and do her meditation, but no one was there now. All I could hear was the gentlest possible wind in the treetops. Our little world of house and garden and pool was encircled by hills that were brown with scrubby trees. I took a deep breath. My lungs filled with tomato and flower and the precious oxygen pumped out by all the plants in the garden. The sun beat down on the top of my head. I looked at my arms. I was getting a tan, even though Mum made me wear factor thirty all the time. The air was relentlessly warming all across the planet, and the Spanish sun was more than a match for factor thirty.

'Libby?'

Mum was shouting from somewhere. I blew a kiss to Enrique Tomato, picked my way back to the house, and saw Mum standing just outside the back door, smiling. She nodded to a mug of hot chocolate on the table.

'I saw you'd started making it,' she said. 'So I warmed it up for you. Sean's gone to get the bread. How are you feeling?'

'Fine,' I said. 'What time shall we leave?' My stomach was flipping around.

Mum smiled. 'Midday,' she said. 'As you know. Her train gets in at one fifteen, so midday gives you loads of time. You can get a coffee at the station while you wait. Don't be so nervous, darling. She's only staying a week. That's nothing.'

'I'm not nervous.'

Natasha had docked in Portsmouth and spent the past few days with Dad and Anneka. From what I had heard, from Natasha and from Dad, it had gone well.

If we *did* get on, then there were things I longed to do. I wanted to take her to Madrid, and particularly to the Prado. I wanted to stand in front of the Hieronymus Bosch triptych, *The Garden of Earthly Delights*. It was the weirdest, freakiest painting, with grotesque details that were stranger the longer you looked at it, and I could barely get my head around the fact that it had been painted hundreds and hundreds of years ago. In my head people from five hundred years ago had been sensible and serious. They didn't have Twixes then or television or phones, and they barely had books, so I thought they were probably incredibly sensible all the time. In most paintings they looked dull and bored. But that painting in the Prado literally had someone with a bird head eating people and then pooing them out. It had blown my mind.

And maybe we could explore further than Madrid too. Like Mum said, it was a time to have adventures. Perhaps this was my chance. I tried to imagine it. The rest of Spain. France. Italy. Anywhere that trains would take us.

I sat at the table on the terrace and picked up the mug. The hot chocolate was cool enough to drink straight away, and I sipped it. It was lovely. The full-fat milk here seemed to be extra full fat, and this drink tasted as if it were made from pure cream.

I heard Mum, in the house, answering her phone.

'Hello?' she said, and there was a pause. 'Oh, really? Hang on. I'm just going to take this upstairs. One moment. Yes, very much so. How wonderful.'

It was still only nine, so I stayed out in the sun for a bit and tried to fill the next couple of hours in my head. I would swim, and try to read, and go online to check Zoe's social media. I should message Max in Singapore (I liked his updates about his attempts to make himself digital; I had absolutely no idea whether he was being serious or not), and generally fill my mind with other things.

And then, when Mum went to her meditation class, I would get into the hire car with Sean and we would drive to Madrid and meet Natasha at Atocha station. I had pictured it over and over again. I would stand there and watch the people coming through the barrier, and one of them would be my cousin, and as soon as our eyes met I would know whether I could speak to her in real life or not.

The sun was hot on the back of my neck. I took hold of my hair and twisted it round itself, tying it into a knot. One of the lovely things about being here was the fact that it didn't matter to anyone what I looked like. I had put on make-up when we had gone into Madrid, but we had only done that twice. I remembered to shower every now and then, but I was almost always clean from the pool. I was going to make an enormous effort, though, for the trip to the station. I had planned my outfit, which involved another dress of Anneka's, a pale blue linen shift with a Swedish label in it.

I went into the kitchen. Mum came down the stairs beaming.

'Nice phone call?' I said. 'You sounded happy.'

She looked into my eyes and I could see that, for once, she really was happy. She looked as if she were going to say something, but then she didn't.

'Just a thing about yoga,' she said, and started washing up the wine glasses from last night. She was wearing her meditating clothes, which were cycling shorts and a T-shirt rather than flowing robes. We had come to this particular village because there was a thriving yoga community, as well as this lovely house to rent. Mum went to her class every day for hours, no matter what else was happening. She had learned lots more Spanish and made a new squad of international friends there (one of whom, presumably, had just called her). It was a bit disconcerting.

I heard the squeak of the gate that meant that Sean was back, which meant breakfast. I took three white plates from the cupboard. Mum poured two coffees, looking poised and peaceful with her hair tied on top of her head. She looked younger than me now.

Then Sean was standing in the doorway, grinning. I had to blink to see him properly with the sunlight behind him.

'Would you believe this?' he said. 'Come out here and see. I've a surprise for you both.'

I knew it before I stepped out on to the terrace. I knew it, but I was still surprised, because I looked at her and there she was.

I wanted to say her name, but my voice stuck in my throat so I couldn't. She ran at me and threw her arms round my neck so I didn't even really see what she looked like, because she was so close. She was right there, up against me. She smelled like flowery perfume.

'Oh my God!' she said. 'Libby! Olivia Lewis! In real life! In Spain!'

Mum took the plates out of my hands, sensing that I was about to drop them. I hugged Natasha back tentatively. She was slight and bony in my arms. She was both more and less substantial than me.

'Hey, look,' she said. 'We're exactly the same height!'

'Natasha,' I managed, though it came out as a whisper. While she continued our extended greeting I gave myself the sternest of talkings-to. *Be yourself. It's OK. She knows you. You just have to speak. Do not let your throat close up. Do not put up the barrier. Not now. Not with her. Even if you do, she used to be shy herself. It will be OK.*

She stepped back, and I got to look at her properly. Natasha looked exactly like her photo, except that everything about her was finer, more delicate. Her hair was dark and shiny, longer than it had been in the pictures she'd sent, and she was beautiful like a film star. She was wearing a red sundress. I felt my knotted tangle of hair, my sticky shirt, my lack of make-up, and I wanted to run away.

I made myself stay right there. I remembered that she had made me go to a party where I had nearly kissed Zoe, that she already knew that I was shy, and I smiled.

'Welcome, Natasha,' said Mum, and she kissed her on each cheek. Mum was working hard at being a proper European now that she had friends who were Spanish.

'And I'm so sorry! Libby and Sean were going to meet you at the station. Did we get the train time completely wrong?'

'You did not,' said Natasha, tying her hair up like mine. 'I couldn't wait. I switched my ticket and came out earlier. I managed to get a seat on a night train from Paris last night, and I got into Madrid this morning. A different station. Chamartín? So I found a bus that came this way and here I am.' She yawned. 'Do you by any chance have coffee?'

I nodded. 'Yep,' I said. I made myself say something more. 'My mum makes the best coffee.' It was lame, but they were words.

'Sit right down,' said Mum. 'I'll bring it out. Milk? Sugar? You must be exhausted if you slept on a train last night.'

'Oh, I'm fine,' said Natasha. 'I didn't really sleep, but I'm OK with that. Black, one sugar. Thanks so much, Aunt Amy.'

Natasha took my hand and we went to sit down on the terrace in the sunshine. She pulled her chair up right next to mine. I was dazed and dazzled and I couldn't stop looking at her.

11. Get some exercise

I was sitting next to Natasha. She and I shared a surname, thanks to the patriarchy. We were family, although we didn't look alike. She was brave. She made things happen. I was the hostess here; I needed to speak to her. Mum was inside making fresh coffee and Sean was getting out breakfast stuff, and I looked at her and I had so much to say and my mind was blank.

'Hey!' she said. 'Libby Lewis! So. Favourite colour?'

'Yellow,' I said. I was looking at the golden tinge of the sunlight on everything. 'Sometimes it's red. Or green for growing things. I don't know. It changes. Yellow right now.'

'Good choice.'

'Yours?'

'Oh, any of the bright ones. Yellow, orange, red. The bolder the better. Also, gold and silver. The vulgar, blingy ones. Nothing subtle.'

I knew she was getting me to talk. I could remember nursery teachers trying the same tactics a million years ago. I tried to step up.

'Have you been to Spain before?' I said, and I thought that I sounded like the Queen making conversation.

'Are you kidding? I've never been to Europe. I'm so glad I'm here. I speak Spanish, though. I've spent time in Mexico. I already love being here. I love everything about it.'

'I speak Spanish too,' I said. 'A bit.'

'Yeah, I know. Remember, Libby? We've been speaking to each other for months.'

She laughed, and I did too. I thought that quite soon I might be able to relax.

When Mum and Sean came back, Natasha made a show of leaning back in her chair and looking around, and I saw the garden, the pool, the morning light through her eyes.

'This place,' she said. 'Oh my God. It's like the Garden of Eden. The most perfect place. So, are you going to stay here through September? Does it have a bunker?'

'No,' said Mum. 'We'll go back. Libby's dad's in Winchester, as you know, and it would be harsh for her not to –'

'Bunker?' Sean interrupted, echoing my thoughts. 'Is that a thing people are actually doing?'

'Sure,' said Natasha. 'You get a compressed air supply and kit it out. People have it worked out so they can live underground for years and years. Or not underground necessarily, but in an air-tight bunker where you just breathe from your own supply.'

'Oh God.' It made me feel faint.

'We're not into anything like that,' said Sean. 'Absolutely not. And we're avoiding the news exactly so we don't have to hear about that kind of thing.' He and Mum both glanced at me. I took a sip of juice and avoided their eyes. I would not think about bunkers. I wouldn't.

'Right?' said Natasha. 'Me too. Can you *imagine* those years? Knowing that everything was dead outside. And then you die anyway, as your air slowly runs out. I mean, why would you do that? Just waiting it out in some kind of apocalyptic hellscape? No thanks.'

'Natasha,' said Mum. 'Please don't.' Her voice was sharp.

I *could* imagine all that. I knew that dwelling on this was not good for me, that I needed to divert my thoughts elsewhere. I took deep breaths and focused on what was in front of me.

Natasha was in front of me.

I could feel Mum looking at me. I needed to change the subject.

'How did you find our house?' I said. I knew I hadn't given her the address.

Natasha paused, a crust of bread in her hand.

'Good question. It's weird of me to walk round the corner when all I knew was that you were somewhere near Madrid and you would kindly meet me at the rail station.'

'Yes,' said Mum. 'How *did* you do that?'

Natasha looked at each of us in turn with a witchy smile on her face. I looked at the curve of her neckline, where she had put her hair up. She was like a ballerina.

'Right. Bear with me on this. The first thing I did was I emptied my mind and looked at a map. Then I put a picture of Libby into my head. Just that. Nothing else. And I closed my eyes and let my finger land on the map. My finger actually came down right here. Moralzarzal.' She said the word with a perfect Spanish intonation. 'Or close enough. Pretty much the right place. That was cool.'

I looked at Mum, who looked confused, her eyes darting around. Sean laughed.

Natasha laughed too. 'However,' she said, 'remember that I was also staying with Uncle Ben and Anneka at the time, and they had your exact address, so that might have helped a bit too. It was easy to find a bus that came out here, and then I saw Sean coming out of the shop. I recognized him from Libby's social media. Job done.'

'How was my dad?' I said. Even though I knew that she had visited them first because her ship went into Southampton, and they were just up the road, I was suddenly jealous. I imagined her chatting away to him, asking his favourite colour, getting him to open up to her in a way he couldn't with me. 'It must be a bit weird. I mean, he's not the easiest, is he, and . . .' *He looks like* your *dad*, I wanted to say. I wanted to say it, but I didn't.

Natasha turned her smile on me and it was like the sun.

'Bit of an oddball, right?' she said. 'And so very like his brother in looks. Entirely different in character. I mean, I think he was pleased to see me under all the awkward. Anneka was lovely – and those babies! *How* adorable? I've got so many photos of them. I wanted to put them *all over* my stories, but Anneka asked me not to.'

I tried not to bristle. Sofie and Hans-Erik were mine.

'They kept asking for you, Libby,' she said, reading my mind again. 'I think they knew I was something to do with you. Sofie said that she had a secret to tell me, and it turned out to be that you'd shared your chocolates with them so they had to brush their teeth again and that you'd let them watch TV after bedtime. That's quite some secret! I was just a curiosity who spoke in a strange accent and threw them in the air.'

Mum reached across and touched Natasha's hand.

'I'm pleased you're here,' she said, but there was something guarded in her tone. She hadn't liked Natasha's thing about emptying her mind. 'I know what went on between your father and Libby's father was difficult, and it feels like the right time for you two to heal things. I know you've already got to know each other by email, and I'm glad we're able to have you here with us for this week.'

Natasha squeezed her hand back. 'It's the best thing in the world for me,' she said. 'You are all amazing. Thank you *so* much for the invitation. I swear I wouldn't have got on that ship without it. You brought me here!'

'Your mother,' Natasha said later. 'She's OK with me being here, isn't she?'

'Yes.' I reached the end of the pool and stopped to talk. I had been trying to do fifty lengths of this little pool three times a day. I liked the way it made me feel. 'Of course. She told me to invite you as soon as we found out about you.'

'Yeah, before she met me. I was wondering. Is she ... spiritual? I mean, you said she started going to church, right?'

'Right,' I said. 'She's very spiritual now. She wasn't before. It's one of those Creep things. I think she freaked out, but she couldn't properly freak out because, you know, she's in her forties and she's a mother. She focused it all on looking for a solution instead. She can't solve the science, so she started going to church. And then she scrolled through a lot of churches. Tried a bit of everything. Synagogue. Mosque. Hindu temple. But she was worried about cultural appropriation, and patriarchy, and things like that.' A part of my brain was listening to me, talking and talking and talking to someone I had only just met, and marvelling at it. Congratulating myself. 'She's ended up with meditation and yoga. She goes to a class in this village every day. They're part of some bigger movement. I don't know.'

We started swimming again, side by side. Natasha, in her swimsuit, was more toned than me, and generally, I thought, better than me. We were, as she had said, exactly the same height: in every other way she was better. We swam, though, in the same way, at the same speed.

I had calculated that one hundred and fifty lengths a day was about a mile, and a mile of swimming every day had to offset the bread and cakes and general lounging that filled my life the rest of the time.

We swam another length: number eighteen.

'So she's interested in the afterlife?' Natasha said when we reached the other end. 'That's her solution? If the scientists don't come through, reset what you thought death was, right?'

'I guess. Pretty much. Like you?'

'OK,' she said. 'You might hate this. She might hate it. I don't know. I'm not sure whether she'd be receptive.'

'Go on,' I said.

She took a deep breath, looked at me and looked away.

'You know I believe in spirits. You know I know there's another realm after we die. Well, my dad is in it. I have conversations with him. I hear his voice in my head. I tell him everything. I listen to him.'

'OK.' I started swimming again, but Natasha stayed where she was, at the shallow end, and I went all the way up and down the pool and then stopped again, feeling a bit silly (twenty lengths). 'Do you . . .? I mean, do you feel like you hear his . . . real voice from the afterlife? Or is it, like, a way you comfort yourself?'

That didn't make sense, but she knew what I meant.

'It's him,' she said. 'Real him. He's talking to me from . . . whatever you want to call it. The other side.'

'Heaven?'

Natasha looked up at the deep blue sky and waved. 'Yeah. He's not up there perched on a cloud. If there were any clouds. He's not down there either, in the flames, though he should be in some ways. He's all around, like the air. But I'm not sure whether I can say this in front of your parents. That's why I was wondering. I'm sensing that Aunt Amy believes in a different kind of spirituality from mine, but I'm hoping we can find common ground. We're looking at the same thing after all.'

'Are you psychic? Like . . . like your mother?'

'Always have been. I didn't spell it out in my emails because people can have odd reactions. I've been listening to Dad ever since the day he died. In fact, I knew he had died because I heard his voice screaming in my head.

'He told me to come to Europe. Straight after that, you and your dad both kind of invited me to visit. I knew I was meant to do it. I was like, but, Dad, there's no planes! And he was all, *Hey, you can get the ship, honey.* What an adventure! Before Dad – I mean, before he was in that realm, I had my normal spirit guide. Walter. He's been with me for years.'

'Wow.' That was all I could manage. *Wow.* How pathetic. Part of me wanted to say: 'You have a *normal* spirit guide called *Walter?*' But I pretended it was a perfectly usual thing for someone to say.

We swam beside each other, turned at the end of the pool, and started swimming back, and I knew I had to say something to show that I wasn't having an odd reaction, even though I wasn't sure what I thought. 'So . . . how do you talk to him?' I said. 'Your dad. Or . . . Walter. How does it work?'

When we reached the shallow end again (twenty-two) she stood up, slicked the hair back from her face, looked at me with clear blue eyes. 'It's a hard thing to talk about because everyone thinks you're deluded. You secretly do, but you won't say so.' I tried to arrange my face to look more open-minded. 'Only my mother understands, and she's a bit . . . unavailable right now.'

'Have you always been psychic?'

'I knew you were going to say that!' She grinned. 'Not really. It took me a while to tune in, but there were things I thought everyone could do. I would dream something and then it would happen, that kind of thing. I told Mom, and she explained that she did that too but that we were unusual. I had to work on it and then I found I could channel the gift. I found my spirit guide, or rather opened my mind so he would find me, and there was Walter. He's a bit put out because my father's taken over his spot. And you know what? Right now talking to my dad is the thing that keeps me strong. He wishes he'd met you. I do too. He says, *Hello, little niece. Believe in yourself.*'

'Believe in myself?'

'Yes.'

'Oh. Thanks. You too.' Oh my God, that sounded stupid, but I managed to keep talking. 'Does he . . .?' I started swimming again, because it was easier not looking at her. 'Does he have any thoughts about, you know? The future?'

She sighed and plunged into the water next to me. 'I wish! But no. He doesn't see the future any more than we do. Everyone asks that. When I'm doing readings. They think I'm seeing the future when I'm not. But I don't like to say that none of the spirits know either, so I just say it won't happen. It's not healthy to be waiting for civilization to suffocate. Much better to say, no, as long as we start to behave better, it'll be OK. Our scientists have got this. We'll carry on with a new appreciation of the majesty of life. I tell everyone that. I almost believe it myself, because you might as well. It's just better to believe in life, isn't it? To swerve away from looking at death. What I believe isn't going to change anything, so it's better to be cheerful.'

I imagined how incredible it would feel to wait for the air to go, but to carry on breathing anyway. It would be a portal into a new universe.

'Do you hear his voice?' I said. 'Like his real voice, or is it like you have thoughts and you know it's from him?'

'Oh, his voice,' she said. 'One hundred per cent, his voice. I hear him, but not with my ears. It's the oddest thing. I hear it with my brain. You know how our ears pass the info to our brain, about what we hear, and it's our brains that interpret it into words and noises and music? Well, my brain interprets these signals into words in my dad's voice, but they don't come from my ears. They come from somewhere else. The signals are all around us, and not all of us can decode them.'

I swam slowly, battling scepticism, an urge to laugh and a desperate desire for this to be true. I knew Natasha believed it. That was a start.

'I think my mum would get it,' I said. 'Better than me actually. I think it would have an overlap with the meditation stuff she's doing. She's open to things now.'

A year ago my mother would definitely have thought all this talk of afterlives and voices from the other side was rubbish. Now I didn't know what she'd think. I looked across to the house and saw her cross-legged on the shady part of the terrace, with her back against the stone of the house. She was far away, but I knew that her eyes were shut and she would be repeating her secret meditation words under her breath.

'Good,' said Natasha. 'I felt that too, but I don't really know her so I thought I'd check.'

'Sean will be fine with anything.'

'Yeah, he seems that way.'

I reached the end and turned and swam back again.

Later I wrote to Max.

> My cousin Natasha is here. And she's
> psychic. She talks to dead people.
> Like her own dad.

Like fuck she does! What a load of shite.

I laughed. I wouldn't have said it so bluntly myself.

12. Learn some magic

Two days later

Two children were playing some form of hopscotch on the stony ground outside the cafe. I thought it looked quite fun.

'If someone died when they were young,' I said to Natasha, 'would they be able to talk to you, or would they always stay the spirit of a baby?'

Natasha put her drink on the table. She was chic, in a navy blue top, with huge sunglasses and tiny shorts, and wedged sandals that I wouldn't have been able to walk in. I loved to look at her. She was like a person from a magazine.

She seemed to be poised and in control of herself all the time. I knew she must be sad about her dad, and incredibly upset about her mother in hospital thousands of miles away, but she never showed it. Not at all.

I looked around. Apart from the children and their parents, there was a woman on her own, across the square, who was drinking something flamboyant and alcoholic, and there were two men dressed in black with glasses of lager.

'Good question,' said Natasha, pushing her sunglasses up on to her head and smiling. 'Great! So, this I do know because I asked Walter a while ago. I saw a story in the paper back home about a kid dying of one of those terrible diseases, and I wondered the same thing. Turns out that if it's a small child they'll grow into their spirit. They actually have the best of it, which I think is good, since if they're sick, they have the worst time here in the physical world. They become their best selves in the spirit world. I've spoken to a few now. They're the wisest, most gentle people you'll ever encounter.'

I smiled into my drink. 'Thank you,' I said. 'I was thinking of Sofie and Hans-Erik.' For some reason I needed to blink back tears. The very idea of them gasping for breath. It was the ultimate horror.

'Hey,' said Natasha. She took my hand. 'You know, I hadn't even thought of that. I'm so sorry. They're your brother and sister. It's a horrible thing to think about. I know you'll be with them at the end. You know, they might just get to grow up in a world of gas masks until we get things back under control. They might even be the ones who fix it.'

I managed to smile. 'Yes. Though I've never been sure what the gas masks are meant to do. In the war they were to protect from poison gas, weren't they? But now it's not about filtering things out. It's about there actually not being anything to breathe.'

I was so glad I could say things like this to her.

'Yes,' she said. 'I don't know. But it might be OK. It still might.'

The woman walked past us, taking her empty glass back into the bar.

'*Hola*,' she said, giving us a big grin as she went. Up close she was older than I'd thought, with bright orange hair.

'*Hola!*' said Natasha. She turned back to me. 'Not to change the subject, but this place is great, isn't it? I like the way a woman can drink cocktails on her own, and there's children playing, and those guys aren't giving us any hassle.'

'It's nice just to sit here and watch things,' I said.

'It is.' Natasha nodded. 'But you can't just sit and watch things happen. You have to do them too. So. I want to talk about Zoe. Your first task was going to that party, and you looked so cute and so did she. What are you going to do about her?'

I sighed. The children were jumping around and giggling.

'I'll go home at the end of this month,' I said, 'and I'll meet up with her. I don't know. She still won't be single.'

'You need to be more proactive, Libby Lewis.'

'How, though?'

'I'll teach you some things. Also, dump that Max boy. He's no good for you.'

I was stung by that, but decided to ignore it. She didn't know him. I saw Natasha's eyes flick to the children, and then back to me.

'You speak Spanish,' she said.

I nodded. 'I'm doing it for A level.' She looked blank. 'Exams you take at the end of school, if the world doesn't end before then.' I realized that she was about to try to make me talk to the kids, so backtracked. 'I'm not great at the speaking part, though. I have to pretend to be a character called Carmen or I can't talk to anyone. I'm better at reading and writing. Also, it turns out that when you speak to people, they talk back really fast and it's hard to understand. Anyway, you speak it better than me.'

'Oh yeah,' she said, 'but just because I've spent time in Mexico. I mean, my Spanish probably sounds strange to these actual Spanish people, so you must have a more authentic Spanish-Spanish accent than I do. But the upshot is, we both get by. Come on then. Watch this.'

She walked over to the children. They looked receptive as she crouched down and started talking in fast Spanish that I could only just follow.

She got some coins out of her pocket and started doing a magic trick. I stood back a little way and watched her showing that the coins had disappeared. The children squealed with laughter as she pulled one out of the little boy's ear and handed it to him, then took the other out of the girl's wild hair and gave it to her.

The adults were looking over and laughing. I thought children shouldn't be speaking to strangers, but I supposed that, as teenage girls, we looked safe enough.

'*Gracias*,' their mother called over when it was over, and Natasha was back at our table.

I looked at Natasha and she looked at me. 'That was amazing!' I said. 'It was so cool!'

'So,' she said. 'Want to learn some tricks? I'm not saying Zoe will be swayed by you grabbing a coin out of her hair, by the way. Just that this will make you more confident. Let's call mastering this task four.'

I nodded.

The late sunlight was golden, and the shadows were long. The four of us sat on the terrace. There were two bottles of wine on the table, one of each colour, and a bottle of Prosecco. Natasha had a glass of red wine, and so they offered me one too.

'Can I have some of that instead?' I pointed to the Prosecco.

'Sure thing.' Mum popped the cork, poured some into a tumbler and passed it over.

'Thanks,' I said, and sipped it. I liked the bubbles in my nose, but the taste was harsher than I had expected and I put the glass down. I kept expecting Mum to announce that she was teetotal with her new lifestyle, but so far that was very much not the case. Mum and Sean drank wine every night. I didn't think they'd had a day off since we found out about the Creep. If life somehow carried on, they would have to stop, but for now it really didn't seem to matter. Lots of people were drunk, a lot of the time. Mum and Sean's version was mild compared with the things that were going on out there, in the wild, wild world.

I picked the tumbler up again and took a tiny sip. Prosecco was easier to drink than wine, and it didn't stain your lips and teeth, though red wine suited Natasha. She was like someone in an old French film. I thought of myself drinking red wine from a mug not so long ago. Sitting on a wall. Leaning in to kiss Zoe, and then running off home when her girlfriend turned up.

I had done that because of Natasha. I had been humiliated and miserable when I got home, but now I was glad it had happened. She had made me be brave: I felt she held the key to something big.

'Libby has something to show you.' Natasha smiled her witchy smile at me. I knew I couldn't be shy with my actual family, so I nodded. I could do this. I psyched myself up and remembered what she had told me. It was like acting. Almost all the 'magic' was really confidence. And confidence was what I needed.

I took a deep breath and assumed my persona. I was going to be Juliet Capulet, if she hadn't stabbed herself, had got over Romeo and somehow become a street magician in Southern Europe.

'Right,' I said. 'See these coins? Can you check that they're normal?'

I handed them to Mum, who indulged me by taking and scrutinizing them. She passed them to Sean, who pretended to bite one. They gave them back with nods of agreement. These coins were normal.

This was part of the misdirection. Of course they were normal. The trick had nothing to do with the normality or not of the coins. It would not have worked better if the coins had been secretly chocolate, for example.

'So,' I said, 'we're going to make them vanish. Here we go.' I put one coin on the table and held out the other one. 'This is real genuine magic,' I said. 'It's a gift we have in this family: unfortunately it's on the Lewis side, so neither of you can do it. I'm going to make this coin vanish, and who knows where we might find it?' As I spoke I hid the coin in my hand, between the base of my thumb and my little finger. 'Oh, look! It's gone. Where could it be?' I pantomimed looking for it, and then did an exaggerated *oh there it is!* face and pulled it out of Mum's ear (or rather put my hand next to her ear and produced it).

They applauded, even though it was the most basic magic trick there had ever been. I did it with the other coin, finding it in Sean's beard.

'Good work!' said Natasha. 'Let's teach you more. This is fun.'

'Yes,' I said. 'It is.'

'So this is what you did today?' said Sean. 'Magic tricks?'

'Yep,' I said. 'And we swam in the pool and went to the cafe.'

He laughed. 'Are you bored or is it OK?'

'This is great, Sean,' Natasha said. 'Seriously great. It's the most perfect little paradise. I love it.'

'It is,' said Mum, sipping her wine. 'But, you know, if you girls want to go further afield and see more of the world, then you should. Get a bus to Madrid. Or beyond. Don't feel you have to stay here with us. Natasha, you've come thousands of miles to be here. You should see more

115

of Europe. I know you said you were staying a week or so. Well, don't feel that you're tied to us.'

I looked at her hard, but she did seem to mean it.

'OK,' said Natasha. 'I actually want to go to Paris. I've always wanted to. Libby, do you fancy coming with me?'

Mum laughed. 'Natasha! You would fit right in. You're every inch the Parisian.'

'Mum,' I said. Sean was looking at her in the same way I was. 'Are you serious? Would you let me go to Paris with Natasha, without you?'

'With some rules attached,' she said. 'Yes I would. Because these are strange times and you're not a little kid any more. I can remember the way I felt travelling in my youth. There's nothing like it.' She turned a tight smile on Natasha. 'And you're an experienced traveller, and I believe you'd take care of her, though she'll hate me for saying that.'

I did hate her saying it.

'Well,' I said. 'I'd like to go into Madrid to start with. Why don't we go tomorrow?'

'Do it,' said Mum. 'Good idea.' She had lit some incense at the other end of the terrace, and it smelled terrible, as if someone had thrown toilet cleaner on to a bonfire. I had a feeling she had her own reasons for wanting us to go, but I couldn't imagine what they could be.

'Well.' Natasha turned her bright smile on me. 'Let's do it! We can go and look at that painting you like. And see the city. What a contrast to here! We'll have a fabulous day.'

'Perfect,' I said.

'Would you two like to come?' Natasha said in a polite voice.

'Absolutely not,' said Sean. 'You go for it.'

Natasha reached under the table and squeezed my thigh. I patted her leg.

13. Look at great art

I woke up slowly in the middle of the night, knowing that I'd half heard her coming into the bedroom a while ago but that it had taken me ages to come to consciousness. I'd left her sitting on the terrace writing things on her phone, and I had no idea what time it was now.

The room should have been perfectly dark. The walls were thick, the floors all tiled, and the shutter over the window was metal and worked by pushing a button; when it came all the way down it made a complete blackout. I couldn't sleep in the dark, however, and had brought over my fairy lights just in case. They were my flamingo ones, and they were now draped across the top of the mirror because there was a ledge there, so when I opened my eyes a tiny bit I could see Natasha by their pale pink light.

I was about to speak when I noticed what she was doing. Natasha was standing in front of the mirror, staring at herself. She had her weight on one leg and had her chin down, while she twirled a strand of hair round her finger.

I had no idea what she was doing until she whispered 'Hello. I'm Libby' in a British accent. She shifted her posture.

I knew I fiddled with my hair. It was just a thing that I did without wanting to, a form of self-soothing.

Natasha was pretending to be me. I watched her turn this way and that and try out different mannerisms until it was too weird.

'Am I that annoying?' I said, and my voice sounded loud.

She jumped, turned and laughed.

'No, silly,' she said. 'I just think a British accent would be cool, and you're the best person I know who's got one, so I'm modelling it on you. Sorry for waking you.'

'That's OK. But you should keep your own accent. It's lovely.'

She looked at me for a few seconds, then smiled.

'Maybe you're right,' she said. 'I should just learn how to be myself. Anyway, sleep. Sorry, Libs.'

I couldn't get back to sleep after that. It was too unnerving. Did Natasha really not want to be herself? Was she always changing? It made me feel sad for her.

Sad and a little bit wary.

She went to sleep, but I was still wide awake.

I was imagining myself travelling around Europe. I had said to Zoe, only the other day, that we could meet in Paris (admittedly Zoe didn't know I'd said it). Perhaps it might be possible. I could go to Paris with Natasha, and – perhaps – meet Zoe there too, though I would have to send her a real message about that, rather than a pretend one.

I would write to her in the morning and tell her I might be going travelling.

I could do street magic now (a basic trick, but it was a start). I hoped I would be able to do that kind of thing with strangers, because it was *performing*. I was seized by a heady urge to run and travel and live and do everything I could, while it was all still here.

If I spent the summer learning, I could show my new skills to people at home, and I might end up with more friends. Although I knew that, as Natasha had said, my extracting a coin from Zoe's hair wasn't going to make her fall into my arms, I still hoped it kind of might, because it would be a different Libby who did that, and so she might notice me.

I listened to Natasha's sleepy breathing and tried to imagine the rest of my life. Each heartbeat took me closer to the end, but whenever I pictured September the seventeenth my mind swerved away like the pole of a magnet. I could see why people were building bunkers with air in them. Anything. Anything to stop it happening. Anything.

I could see too why they believed in life after death. I looked across at Natasha sleeping with her back to me. I desperately wanted to buy into her happy afterlife, where babies grew into their best selves and no one could die. I concentrated and tried to commit to it, but I couldn't. I wished I could.

I wondered whether this was what Mum had been through with the churches. Had she tried with all her might to believe in what they were saying, but failed? Had she finally found something that worked for her?

Natasha had said the dead were all around us. I imagined the bedroom filled with ghosts. They stood round my bed. They drifted through walls. I pictured my grandparents standing there. They looked at me, and then turned to look at Natasha, their other unknown granddaughter. They both settled down on the floor to watch over us all night.

It was no good. This was a load of absolute rubbish and I couldn't believe it for a single second.

I still couldn't sleep. I used my phone to look at Natasha's social media, because I hadn't done that since she arrived here.

Her Instagram account had been renamed @Eurotash and had thousands of followers: she had, somehow, posted twenty-eight photos since she'd been here. I looked at them. There was only one with any people in, and that was a shot of Natasha and me, arms round each other, smiling on the terrace. Her other pictures were of the still surface of the pool and drinks on the cafe table. There were flowers in the garden and wine glasses on the terrace. There was a photograph of my pet tomato. I saw her hashtags: #family #holiday #love #cousins.

Further back there were pictures of Winchester, and one of her with my dad, which was odd to see (#uncle #love #family), and nothing with the babies in it, as she'd said.

Beyond that I had seen all her pictures many times before, but I looked anyway. I went back beyond the European landscapes, back to the photographs of New York and her father. I looked at her dad and imagined his voice in her head. I wondered whether he had sounded British or American, or a bit of both. I wondered why she had no pictures of her mother, and how Peggy was doing in her psychiatric hospital, and whether they were in touch. When I tried to ask she just looked away and managed never to answer.

I found a blog that I'd never seen before, from a link on her Twitter account that I'd missed, and read a flurry of posts from a few months ago. I read her excitement at being contacted by her British cousin, Olivia, and, before that, I read about her father dying. I looked at photographs of the funeral. I read the post in which she said she was setting off for Europe because her father's spirit had told her to go, and anyway this summer was a time to live. I read the comments from her friends wishing her an amazing time. I felt jealous of her friends, of everyone else who had ever met her, because I liked having Natasha to myself.

I comprehensively cyberstalked the girl who was sleeping a couple of metres away from me. By the time I returned the phone to the bedside table I was feeling really quite shabby.

I stared at the pinkly glowing ceiling. I definitely wasn't going back to sleep tonight.

*

'Libby!'

Someone was shaking me. The room was half light. I wanted to stay asleep. I was in the middle of a lovely dream that melted away as I came to consciousness until it had vanished so completely that I didn't know anything about it at all. I just felt an unfocused longing.

I was tangled in my sheet. It was hot. I was asleep, and comfortable. I did not want to get up.

'What?' I managed to say.

It was Mum. If I needed to be woken up, it was always Mum.

Then I remembered we were going to Madrid. I opened my eyes and looked at the empty bed and yawned.

'Darling,' said Mum. 'Sorry! It's eleven o'clock. You've slept in. Do you still want to go to Madrid today?'

I tried to concentrate my mind, but it took a while to shake off the sleep.

'Does Natasha still want to?' I said.

'Very much so, but she says if you want to sleep she can wait for tomorrow.'

I yawned again.

Mum laughed. 'OK?' she said. 'I'll come back in five minutes.'

That was what she did on school mornings too. She would wake me up, open the curtains, and come back every five minutes until I was actually out of bed.

I rolled out of bed. I had been lazing around like a slug, comfy and snoozy, and all along Natasha was waiting for me, probably swimming up and down my pool, watering my tomato, drinking coffee with my parents, smiling at my long sleep, and narrating it to her dad in her head.

I pulled on some denim shorts and a baggy T-shirt and saw that the shutter was a little bit open. Mum must have done that when I was fast asleep, to try to coax me into consciousness.

I looked a mess, obviously, and did my best with a hairbrush and some moisturizer, though there was nothing I could do about the pillow crease that ran down the side of my face. I took a deep breath and walked down the little corridor and out on to the terrace.

'Hey, Rip Van Winkle!' That was Sean, being Seanish.

I walked out there and took the cup of coffee that Natasha was holding out, and I sat down. 'Sorry,' I said. 'I didn't sleep well. And then I did, I guess. Sorry, Natasha! We should be in Madrid by now!'

'You're on vacation!' said Natasha. 'You need to sleep. There's nothing to be sorry about. You looked so peaceful and pretty. We can go any day.'

The sun was already burning hot in the sky. I had missed the best part of the day, the bit I loved, when I watered Harry Tomato and his friends, and when I swam, and when I enjoyed the paler heat.

I sipped the coffee and started to wake up properly.

'Right,' said Mum. 'So, if you want to go, there are buses every half hour.'

'I do want to!' I said.

Natasha sat down next to me. I was acutely aware of the fact that she was wearing a green bikini and nothing else.

She had a scar on her stomach from when she had had her appendix out, and I thought it looked nice. It was a mark of her life being saved. She shook her hair out and pushed her big sunglasses up on top of her head.

'I took the bus here,' she said. 'It was so clean and air-conditioned and smooth. Let's do it. Let's get the next bus. Drink your coffee, Libs, and eat something, and then we'll go.'

I was starving. I found some half-stale bread in the kitchen, and covered it with Nutella, and then I had a quick shower and we set off for the bus stop.

This was my third time in Madrid, but it was completely different being here with Natasha. The sun was bright, the sky deep blue, and the air was hot like a furnace. I felt it coming off the pavements, off the buildings, as if the city were a huge radiator. I listened to my flip-flops slapping on the pavement. My skin was itchy with heat. My hair, which I'd used as a comfort in the British winter, was a burden now. I felt as if the sun knew it might not be able to sustain us all for much longer, and so it was giving it everything it could.

In fact, of course, the ever-increasing heat was part of the Creep. It was part of the greenhouse effect, and Madrid, today, was hardly bearable at all.

'It's hot,' I said stupidly as we walked from the Metro towards the Prado.

It was more than hot. It was a dry heat that made every movement such an effort that it didn't feel worth it. I dragged my feet, felt a bit dizzy.

'It sure is,' said Natasha, looking down a road. Mostly the streets were empty, but as we got closer to the gallery there were more people around. Most of them looked as if they were here to see Madrid while they still could, but down some streets there were people sitting in the road, and there was shouting and singing, with banners and sudden bursts of laughter. It was a bit too far away for me to work out what was going on (a riot? a party?) but I was seized unexpectedly by an urge to join it. I imagined myself running down the street and joining in. For a moment I wanted to do things while I still could. I wanted to become part of the wild panic of the end times.

'There's lots going on in the world,' I said. 'Don't you want to be a part of it? All the extinction festivals? Why do you want to be tucked away with us?'

Three cars raced past, speeding as if they were on a Formula One track. Natasha took my hand, and even though our hands were slick with sweat I didn't take mine away, and neither did she.

'It's a bit exciting, isn't it?' she said. 'Being in a city. You should see New York right now! But I'd rather be in your Garden of Eden. At least for long enough to catch my breath.'

'You really want to go to Paris,' I said.

'You should come too.'

The queue wound round the side of the building. Even though Madrid felt empty, everyone who wasn't rioting wanted to go and see the great art, just in case. The end of the line felt a long way from the museum door, but it did

126

move fast and, after waiting in silence for about twenty minutes (it was too hot to speak), we were inside.

'Oh my God,' said Natasha, standing under an air-conditioning unit and holding her face up to it. Even her hair was stuck to her face with sweat. 'Maybe we have died, you know. Because this does feel a lot like heaven.'

The Prado was a place in which you could lose yourself and find yourself. The walls were thick stone, and even without the air con it would have been bearable in there. I saw posters in the atrium advertising free entry for the whole week of September the seventeenth, and I thought it would be a wonderful place to wait for the change.

I had no idea why anyone would want to do anything other than walk straight to *The Garden of Earthly Delights* and stare at it. Unfortunately everyone else did want to do exactly that, and the room was rammed. As we edged through the crowd Natasha said, 'You know, I'm not sure your mother really likes me as much as she says.'

'She does!' I said, and only after saying that did I stop to wonder whether Natasha was right. I thought Mum did like her. She wouldn't have been encouraging me to go off adventuring with her otherwise. 'What makes you say that?' I added.

'Just thinking about it,' said Natasha. 'This morning, when you were sleeping, I tried to talk about the afterlife but she wasn't having it. She got quite annoyed with me, so I stopped. I thought she'd be receptive.'

'She wants you to take me travelling, so she must like you.'

'Yeah. She doesn't hate me. But, although she likes the meditation and the yoga and whatever it is she does, she doesn't believe in psychics. Scratch the surface and she'd say we're all charlatans trying to part fools from their money. She likes me because you like me, and because she feels sorry for me. There's something else, though.'

I didn't reply, because I had no clue what the 'something else' thing would be. We got to the front of the crowd and then we were in front of the painting.

'Oh my fucking God,' said Natasha. An older woman looked over at her and laughed.

'I know,' she said in accented English. 'Exactly!'

It was a triptych showing what I thought was the Garden of Eden on the left, a kind of weird earthly paradise in the middle, and Hell on the right. All of them were amazing, but I found it hard to look away from the right-hand panel.

'Look at them,' Natasha said, pointing to the people in the middle piece, who were naked, doing all sorts of things. 'They look like people who think a change in the atmosphere might just happen any moment to spoil their fun.'

'They do,' I said. These people were certainly living each day as if it might be their last. They were riding strange animals, cavorting, eating a giant strawberry, and doing all kinds of rude things to each other in public.

'I like it that it's not just the chicks who are naked,' said Natasha, pointing. 'Look. It's everyone. That's much cooler than on most of the paintings in galleries like this. You know, it's always paintings by men of women who just happen to have forgotten to put on their clothes. The history of art should be called the personification of the patriarchy, if you ask me. More dicks in art, that's what we need.'

The same woman looked over and gave a nod of agreement.

'Mmm.' I agreed with her sentiments, but I wouldn't have said it out loud in a crowded room. I tried not to show that I was embarrassed, but she noticed, of course.

'Oh, Libby!' she said. 'Sorry. I said "dicks" in public, didn't I? That made you embarrassed.' She raised her voice. 'Stop saying "dicks", Natasha!'

Lots of people looked round at that. I didn't know whether to laugh or to try to disappear. I felt my cheeks flaming.

'Have you looked at this panel over here?' I said quickly. 'There's so much to see. Look at this side of it.'

The right-hand panel showed a man whose body was a broken eggshell. There was that bird eating the people and pooing them out. A naked man was being kissed against his will by a pig in a nun's habit. Everywhere you looked there was a weird, horrifying thing. I could stare and stare and stare at it, and so, it turned out, could my cousin. We stood there in silence for five minutes. Ten minutes. Probably more.

'This is my favourite piece of art in the world,' she said in the end. 'Before this it was a sculpture by Niki de Saint Phalle, but now it's this.'

Natasha whipped out her phone and took a photo, and was immediately told off by a security woman. She apologized and we edged back into the crowd a bit. 'Still got the photo,' she whispered. 'I knew they wouldn't make me delete it.'

I could smell everyone's deodorants and perfumes, and the sweat that had dried on to them, and the very humanity of it all, and it didn't feel so different from that right-hand panel of the painting.

It felt the same. All these people crowded together, and the people outside, and the heat that made it hard to breathe, and the fact that time was running out.

The people around me were the people from the painting and I was scared. They were running around doing mad things to each other, and I didn't want the bird man to get me. I didn't want anyone to slice my ear with a blade, or to crucify me on a harp.

I felt the world pressing down. My head started to spin, but there was nowhere to go without the people getting me. My ears were ringing, and there were blotches across my vision. I felt myself wobbling, and then Natasha had my elbow and someone else had my other arm, and I was pushed down and I was sitting in a chair. I felt a hand push my head down, and I sat there, my head between my knees, touching the floor with a hand, until it began to clear.

I was not inside the painting. I was here, in the world, but it almost felt like the same thing.

'Sorry,' I muttered. The security lady was on the other side of me, but I could only speak to Natasha.

'What are you even talking about?' she said. 'You don't say sorry for keeling over. Stay there until you feel better.

Don't you dare go anywhere. I'll find you a cookie or something.'

I heard her talking to the security guard, and I understood their Spanish. The security woman said everyone wanted to come and look at this painting because of the end of days, and that she could see why. She said she liked to stand and look at it herself before they opened in the morning. She told Natasha that it was more popular than everything else in the museum combined.

I had thought I was being very cultured and clever, linking the current time to the Bosch painting. It turned out I was completely unremarkable and predictable.

The guard said she didn't have anything sugary but that someone would, and she clapped her hands, and Natasha shouted out in Spanish to ask everyone in the room, and then chatted quietly to an American woman behind me, and handed me a chocolate-chip biscuit, and it did actually make me feel better. I managed to thank the room at large in Spanish, and the guard said I was very welcome. I looked round for the American cookie woman to thank her, but she had gone.

Natasha and I wandered through some of the rest of the gallery arm in arm. It was, indeed, hardly busy at all. I was still trembling, but I calmed down.

'I'm sorry,' I said again. 'I just freak out sometimes.'

'Hey,' said Natasha, 'don't we all?'

I stopped and turned to her. We were in front of another famous painting, *Las Meninas*. It was a strange one: a painting of a painting that was being painted, with a million brilliant details.

'You don't, though,' I said. 'Natasha, you never freak out. You've been through so much. You're *going* through so much. With your dad. And your mum. You're so brave, and so strong, and you never show any weakness at all.'

She smiled. 'I've got my coping mechanisms,' she said. 'Believe me. I've freaked out in my time. But I'm OK now. I know how to get through.'

14. Climb over a locked gate

We got back to the house early in the evening, when the light was golden and the shadows were long. Mum and Sean were waiting for us with a home-made tortilla that they were very proud of.

'Maybe Libby and I could head out for a drink tonight?' Natasha said over dinner, a glass of rosé in her hand. 'We had such a great time in Madrid, but it was so hot. It would be lovely to sit in that square in the cool evening, you know? I love that cafe. I mean, you guys could come out with us, if you like?'

'Oh God,' said Mum. 'That's so sweet of you, Natasha, but I can't face going out tonight. Finding something presentable to wear, and so on. I'm ready to crawl into bed tonight. I've been busy with work and meditation all day.'

'Sure! We'll go then.'

I watched my mother hesitate. She knew she ought to say yes, but she didn't want to. She froze, staring down at her plate. Then she said, 'Please, not tonight, Natasha.

I know it's hypocritical, when last night I was telling you to have adventures. But I've been worrying about you all day and then you came home. Now I just want to go to bed. I can't wait up. There's plenty of drink in the house; we'll be upstairs asleep and you two can sit up drinking wine as late as you like. Go out another night, but I couldn't rest until I knew you were home.'

I saw Sean looking at her. 'I'll wait up,' he offered.

'I'd have to too,' she muttered. 'I've spent the whole day worrying.'

'Sure,' Natasha said lightly. 'We understand. No problem. I guess worrying about your daughter is part of being a parent. It must be hard work. Another night, and maybe the four of us could go.'

'Tomorrow might be good?' said Sean.

'It sure would!' said Natasha.

Going out drinking was not a thing I ever did – was not a thing I had ever, actually, done, unless you counted that house party – and I was pleasingly tired after our day out. I was glad when Mum vetoed it and gave her a grateful smile, which she didn't notice because she was looking at Natasha with an odd expression on her face.

As soon as we'd finished eating, Mum said, 'Right. I'm done in. I'm off to bed in a minute. See you in the morning. Girls, help yourselves to anything.'

I had planned to have a late-night swim, but when it came to it I couldn't even be bothered to do that. I changed into my big T-shirt and brushed my teeth.

'Night!' I said to Mum, who was still clearing things up in the kitchen. She kissed my cheek.

'Night, darling,' she said. 'Love you.'

I tried to reach for the words I needed.

'Mum,' I said. I lowered my voice to a whisper. 'Are you . . . OK? Is something wrong?'

She looked at me for a few seconds. In a sense she looked more healthy than I'd ever seen her (her skin was glowing, and her hair was amazing) but her eyes were lit up with something wild.

'Libby,' she whispered. 'How much have you wished for a sibling all your life?'

She said it as if it were the most urgent question there could be.

'You're not pregnant.' I was horrified.

'Oh God no! I mean, of your own age.'

'Thank God. Yeah, I used to wish that every day. I wished for a big brother or sister. I'm sure I wouldn't have been shy like this if I'd had someone looking out for me.'

I thought of the babies again. Sofie would look out for her shy little brother as they grew up. If they grew up.

Mum nodded. 'Yes,' she said. 'I sensed that. Does Natasha being here make you feel a bit better in that respect?'

'Yes. I know she's not my sister,' I whispered carefully, 'but it's the first time I've had that feeling in real life.'

Mum nodded and hugged me very tightly for a long time.

135

When she and Sean went upstairs I switched on my fairy lights and got into bed. I listened to them walking around up there.

As soon as their footsteps stopped Natasha came in, switched our light on and clapped her hands (quietly). 'At last!' she said. 'I thought they'd never go. Come on, Libby! Get your shorts back on. We're going out, but I'm not having anyone waiting up for us. That was a masterstroke actually getting into bed. You're better at this than I expected.'

I was already half asleep and didn't really follow.

'But we're staying in?'

'Like hell we are! We'll have to climb over the wall because we might wake them if we open that clanking gate.'

'Oh.' I rubbed my eyes and tried to compute this. I didn't want to go out. And yet it was impossible to say no to my cousin. I found myself doing the exact things she told me to do. I climbed back into my shorts. I changed into a nice top (I was no longer even self-conscious about my body in front of her) and let her sort out my face, which took much longer than I would have thought.

When she finished I looked at myself in the mirror and giggled. Natasha giggled too, but then shushed me. I had sleepy hair that had already been mussed up by the bed, so it was hanging down my back like Barbie's hair when it gets matted, but my face was made up like a Hollywood starlet's from the forties. I had smoky eyes smudged with black, and my cheeks were so delicately rouged that it looked like a natural healthy glow. My lips were amazing. They were bright red and magnificently shaped. I cringed to remember my own attempt at make-up for Vikram's party.

'*Voilà*,' Natasha whispered. 'You look spectacular, Ms Olivia Lewis.'

'What about you?' I whispered back. 'Aren't you doing your own make-up?'

'Nah. I'm OK. I just wanted to have a go at painting your face. You're so pretty.' She paused, thoughtful, and then said: 'Actually, maybe I *will* do mine. You're right. Let's see what we're like, matching.'

I sat on the bed and watched her do the same to her own face as she had to mine. The end result was strange. We looked as if we had faces painted by the same dollmaker (I imagined a spooky man from a Victorian story), but apart from that we were different. My hair was blondish and messy and long, and hers was sleek and dark. My body was curvy, and hers was muscular and strong. I was in shorts and a flouncy top, and she had pulled on a tight dress.

'There you go,' she said. 'Something for everyone.'

I smiled. 'You do know we're in a little village? We could go, I don't know, to a nightclub in New York or something dressed like this, couldn't we?'

She laughed. 'An underground jazz club in Paris! Yeah. I'm just having fun. The bar's our backdrop. Whatever, you know? It's for us. Not them. I would love to go to a Parisian jazz club. Can we do that one day?'

'Maybe.'

We crept out of the house, leaving our bedroom shutter open with the window slightly ajar, and then scaled the wall beside the metal gate. That part was very difficult for me. I had to stand on the hinge at the side of the gate, and kind of launch myself up the wall next to it, then dangle down, hanging on by my fingers, and drop to the street. It took ages, and I scraped my leg and I felt ridiculous and exposed, like an inept burglar. When I had done it, Natasha somehow hopped over elegantly with one bound in her dress.

'How did you do that?' I was still whispering, just in case.

She shrugged. 'I've escaped from places in my time.'

We set off down the street. The sky was filled with billions of stars, and the air was sweet and glorious with everything that was growing. Occasionally a dog barked as we walked past a house, but mainly it was silent except for our footsteps.

'Are you sure people go out at midnight?' I had been in bed long before midnight every night I'd been here. I had never seen a Spanish midnight sky.

'No bar in Spain will be closed at midnight. Not one. I mean, this is my first time in Spain, but I've done my research.'

In five minutes we had reached the bar we'd been to for Coca-Cola and street magic the day before. It was, of course, open. There was music coming out of the door, and a few people were sitting at the outside tables. The night was warm and lovely, and Natasha took my hand and led me to a table as if I were three years old.

I didn't mind. I sat where she told me to sit.

'Right. You stay there,' she said. 'I'll go in and get drinks. Back in a minute.'

She hadn't asked what I wanted. I leaned back and smiled. There weren't many people here (it was Thursday night, in a small town, after all) but a group of three men at a nearby table looked over at me and talked among themselves. I fiddled with my hair, wishing I had something to do with my hands; I almost wanted to take up smoking. I was uncomfortable, feeling those men staring, and the more I tried to look casual, and to pretend I hadn't seen them, the worse it became. I looked at the door of the bar, willing Natasha to come out before the men started speaking to me. I could, of course, have got up and gone in there after her, but for some reason it didn't occur to me.

When one of them shouted something in my direction I ignored him. I kept my eyes on the door of the bar.

Another one said something, and then the third said, 'English?'

I looked round.

'Oh, English!' said the first one, and he seemed to take this as an invitation to come over and sit at the table.

'Sorry,' I managed. I frantically tried to channel Carmen and switched to Spanish. 'My friend's sitting there.'

I hated myself. I should have sworn at him to go away. Instead I had apologized.

He sat down anyway. 'What's your name?' he said in English, and I shook my head and looked away. 'Come on! I said, what's your name? It's not very polite to not tell me. Why would you come to Spain if you don't want to talk to Spanish people?'

'I'm just waiting for my friend.' I looked at him and looked away.

'My name's Miguel.'

He looked at me expectantly, and back then I was so cowed and silly that I muttered, 'Olivia.' I didn't even make up a name, let alone tell him to fuck off.

'Olivia.' He smiled at me. 'On vacation?' I didn't reply. 'Here? Airbnb, right? Vacation for the end of the world? It's true, everyone should see Moralzarzal before the world ends. This is what they say.'

I wasn't going to tell a strange man exactly where I was staying. I nodded and looked away. When I realized that Natasha was coming towards the table with a huge glass of beer in each hand I wanted to leap up and kiss her. She put the glasses down on the table and said some things in very fast Spanish to the man, who shrugged and argued back. I should have been able to follow their conversation, but all I could make out was that he was saying I'd invited him over and Natasha was loudly not believing him. It didn't take long. He called us both some rude words in English and in Spanish and went back to his own table.

'Oh, Libby – you *didn't* call him over, did you?' she said, a hand to her mouth. 'Have I just massively messed things up for you?'

I laughed. I laughed a bit too much, because I had been so anxious.

'Of course I didn't!'

'I thought not. I should have checked, though.'

'I wouldn't.'

'I know,' she said. 'I do know that.' She held up her glass and we clinked beers. I didn't even like beer, but I was going to drink it now. For Natasha, for the hot Spanish night, for the fact that we still had air to breathe.

'You know, you're different in real life, Libby. You're very interesting. When you were writing, you were so open. And, like you said, you're much more nervous in the flesh. I don't know why, though. If I looked like you I'd be parading around, getting everyone to be my slaves and bring me peeled grapes.'

I looked away, unsure if she was taking the piss. 'I don't believe you. If I looked like you . . .' I tailed off, shy.

'Are you kidding me? You're completely gorgeous. Look at your hair! And your lovely face. You're perfectly perfect, Libby Lewis. We need to teach you a bit of serious assertiveness and confidence. Because here's the thing: it doesn't matter if some people don't like you. Fact. That jerk was rude to you, and you need to get rid of creeps like that. He called us bad names – who cares? We can call him bad names right back, but more so because he started it. So, in your emails you talked about the cute girl. How are we going to get her for you?'

I was excruciated inside. 'Zoe?'

'Yes. Zoe.'

'We're not. Not now.'

'We will. I mean, we're not going to head to England and throw stones at her window tonight. But it starts here. Focus only on Zoe. Have you got rid of that Max yet?'

'No.'

'Well, it's up to you, but he sounds like someone who drags you down. It's time to take charge. So here is your task five: stop being polite to creeps. Start to open up to the person you do like. Two sides of the same coin. Before we leave this bar, we will have taught that guy a lesson, and you'll have told him to fuck off. Right? We will get you confident by the end of the summer, and you'll head back home ready to turn her head right away from that girlfriend. No matter what else happens. Maybe you'll have a week of bliss before we all die. Maybe you'll get married and have a huge family.'

I sipped my beer. 'And I'm going to do that with street magic and swearing at aggressive men?'

'If that's where it starts, that seems fine to me. That and your Parisian jazz club look, which is pretty damn hot.'

I smiled and sipped my beer. I still didn't like it, but I would drink it.

'How about you?' I said. 'I mean, you've never mentioned a partner or anything. Boyfriend? Girlfriend?'

'Me?' She smiled. 'Oh, I'm not fussy.'

'What do you mean?'

'Boys. Girls. Whoever takes my fancy. I've had some adventures, but it will not surprise you to know that I'm terrible at relationships. I can't do that give-and-take business.'

She was laughing, and I found that I wanted to hear all her stories.

'Who was your last . . .' I searched for the word. Partner sounded too bland. 'Conquest.'

She looked to the side, smiling at a memory.

'It was a girl I met in London when I was there. Her name was Violet. She was very cool.'

She looked me in the eye, and I nodded, waiting for more.

Natasha shrugged. 'She was passing through too. She was from . . . I can't remember. Maybe Argentina? Actually she was Violeta. We spent a couple of days together and didn't even swap details. That's the way I do things.'

'I didn't know you even went to London,' I said. 'I thought you came on the ship to Southampton, and then stayed in Winchester, and then came here.'

'Straight here,' she said, 'via a couple of steamy days in London. I had to go there anyway for the Eurostar, so who's not going to take in the city on the way? I mean, it's fucking *London*!'

The dates didn't add up, but I couldn't quite focus on that. The beer was cold and the night was hot. I would never have thought myself capable of drinking a huge beer like that one. It had to be bigger than a pint. The glass was enormous, yet that particular evening it slipped down. My head started to spin, and I relaxed, and Natasha spent ages telling me I looked adorable, that I was adorable, that she would like to spend the rest of the summer with me, and that we could go on trips all over Europe and come back here in between.

'Do you have enough money to do that?' I said, though I knew too that I had enough money. Dad had given me all the money my grandparents had saved for me, and those had been Natasha's grandparents too, so if she needed me to, I would share it with her. I didn't say that, though.

'I know how to *make* enough money,' she said. 'How about you?'

'I don't know how to make money,' I said. I spoke carefully because my head was spinning. 'But I do have access to some. I'll be fine.'

'You shouldn't use savings,' she said. 'That's being negative, and assuming you won't need anything in the future. We'll make our own money. It'll be easy this summer. Everyone's spending. Everyone is going absolutely wild. Oh, Libby. I know it's gorgeous here. But let's get out there and scream along with the rest of the human race.'

'Yes!' I said. 'You know when you said we're privileged to be here now? You wrote that in an email.' She nodded. 'Well, that changed things for me. It made me look at this time differently. It gave me a chink of . . . hope.'

I was happy.

We talked about her travels, and about magic tricks, and about Hieronymus Bosch. I found I could say anything: the words just came. I opened up, properly, and it felt like the universe was opening right up with me.

'Right,' she said after a while. 'Come on. Let's have a little fun. Time for you to complete your fifth task.'

Against my better judgement, I followed my cousin – my favourite cousin, my perfect cousin – over to the table of annoying men. I had no idea whether they'd been looking at us while we talked because I'd only been interested in Natasha, but I could see that the moment they saw us coming they sat up and got ready for . . . something.

'*Hola*,' said Natasha in a cheery voice, putting our glasses on their table and pulling two chairs over. 'Sit down,' she said to me.

The men looked wary but she started talking in fast Spanish, immediately making them laugh. Again I should have been able to follow, but my head was spinning and so I just sat back and watched. I pretended not to notice the guys looking me over. After a while Natasha got out a pack of cards.

I was suddenly very tired. I didn't want to be playing cards with horrible men. I didn't want to be drinking beer in the middle of the night. I wanted to be asleep. I yawned and leaned back in my chair. There was a skinny cat under the next table. I watched it prowling, wondering where it lived and whether it was feral.

'Don't worry,' Natasha said quietly. 'Watch. This is just to teach them a lesson.'

And she did. I didn't see the details of how she did it, but she dazzled them with card tricks, bought everyone another drink, then got them to start to bet. It took about an hour from beginning to end, but then everyone's money was on the table, and she did her trick, and they all shouted because she had won. She scooped up the money.

'*Hasta la vista*,' she said, and she nudged me.

'Fuck off,' I said to the men, completing my task. I looked at Natasha and laughed. Then we set off. Two of them got up to come after us, and we held hands and ran as fast as we could, the coins jangling in Natasha's handbag.

'Lesbians!' Miguel shouted, and we laughed and laughed. We ran randomly around the village streets, and then stopped when we had shaken them off, and leaned on a wall and laughed some more.

'Justice,' she said. 'Take that, Miguel. Thanks for giving us all your cash.'

I linked my arm through hers. 'Revenge.'

'Sorry you were so bored. Let's get your Spanish woman – what's her name?'

'Carmen.'

'Yes. Let's get Carmen to help you out and then we can work as a double act.'

I laughed. I was feeling a bit drunk, and I wondered what it would be like to be Natasha's partner in crime, powered by an imaginary Spanish woman I'd made up to help me through exams. As we walked home I decided I was excited about the future. I hadn't felt that way for a long time, but even if the future was only going to last a matter of weeks, I knew there was a lot out there. There were still infinite possibilities.

We couldn't climb back over the wall because there wasn't a hinge on the outside. We ended up running through a neighbour's garden and scaling a tree, then dropping down next to the pool.

'Shall we?' said Natasha, indicating it with her head, stripping off her dress. I pulled off all my clothes, and jumped in. The water was like velvet against my skin.

15. Go to the bar

We got up late and spent the day by the pool, swimming and talking and laughing and doing magic. Mum and Sean were happily oblivious to our late-night excursion, and I had a new feeling: it was me and Natasha against the world, and my mother, for the first time, was on the outside.

I learned two new tricks: one was a card trick that involved a corner of a queen of hearts that was taped on to a seven of spades, and the other, the one I liked best, just needed what Natasha called her 'Svengali notebook'.

She demonstrated it to me first: 'OK,' she said, holding out a flippy book. She flicked through and showed me that on each page there was the name of a city. I watched New York, Madrid, London, Bogotá, Reykjavík all flick past. 'See? There are different cities written on each page of this book. You're going to pick one by sticking your finger in wherever you like, but first I'm going to write down what I think you're going to pick. Now I've got to know you, I have a pretty good idea of where your subconscious will lead you.'

She took a piece of paper, gave it to me to check that it was blank, then turned away to write on it. She folded it up and handed it to me.

'Don't look at it. Just look after it so you know there's no trickery.' I put it in the back pocket of my shorts. 'OK. I'm going to flick through the pages and I want you to stick your finger in at a random page. Don't even look at the pages. Just stick your finger in.'

She flicked through the pages of the book and I stuck my finger in at random. She opened the book and we both looked at what was written there.

'Paris!' she said. She paused, smiled a bit, raised her eyebrows. 'Who would have thought it?'

I took her piece of paper out of my pocket and unfolded it. She had, of course, written Paris on it, with hearts and kisses around it. I looked at her and laughed. That was brilliant.

Then she showed me how it was done. It was a trick notebook, with pages of slightly different lengths, and when she flicked it one way it had all those different cities on the page. When she did it the other way, every single page said Paris. I practised flipping, and I practised the misdirection of turning the viewer's attention to the fact that I was writing on a blank piece of paper and giving it directly to them to look after, and once I felt happy with it I went to find Sean.

'This notebook,' I said, 'is filled with the names of cities . . .'

And I did it, and it worked. Sean laughed and laughed and told me to try it on Mum when she got back from yoga. Then he went back to work, and I went back to the pool.

Our secret night out had changed things between Natasha and me. It was easy to be in her company and I felt she saw my real self.

By the time the afternoon shadows grew longer, we were lazy and silly, giggling at nothing and full of sunshine and swimming-pool water. We'd barely seen Mum, and had only seen Sean for the magic trick, and I knew they had no idea that we'd been anywhere last night.

Later than usual, the gates clanked open and Mum came in with her yoga mat under her arm. Her hair had grown since we'd been in Spain and she was frowning and muttering to herself.

'Hi, Mum!' I shouted, and I waved at her from the shallow end. She diverted her course and walked down towards us.

'How was yoga?' said Natasha.

Mum stepped out of her sandals and sat on the edge of the pool. She dangled her feet into the water and sighed.

'This pool is bliss,' she said. 'It's not really yoga. It's more meditative. Now that I understand what they're saying, I can see that it's all about September. More than I realized. We work on focusing our energies on making sure we are at peace, and then on keeping the world safe, and then, after that, all the energy will go on healing. No more wars. Stopping climate change. Healing the natural environment. We use our own energy because it's the most powerful force we have.' She looked up, defensive. 'I don't care if it sounds ridiculous. It works for me. It does no harm.'

Her phone made a sound, and she took it out of her bag, looked at it and closed her eyes for a second, then opened them again. She looked pained, as though she was trying to hide it. She inhaled so sharply that it was almost a sob, and pretended she hadn't.

'That's awesome,' said Natasha. 'The power of the mind is an incredible thing.'

I tried to smile and say the right things too, but it was difficult. The idea of my mum attempting to use her mind to stop the thawing permafrost changing the air made me so sad that I wanted to cry. For my whole life I had looked to her for reassurance. Now I felt stronger than she was, and that was weird and wrong. I wanted to hug her and tell her it would all be all right. I felt a sob in my throat, so I dived down and swam a length underwater so no one would see. By the time I resurfaced Mum had gone into the house and I hadn't shown her my trick, or hugged her, or asked who had messaged her and what they had said.

'It's half past five,' Natasha said. My arms were achey, and I could feel my muscles toning up.

I pulled myself out of the pool and tried not to be sad about Mum and her delusions. The sunlight was golden, the shadows long. The garden here was wild, alive. I could smell it all, the scents of tomatoes and flowers and fruit all mingling together. Everything felt possible at that moment. I felt that the air would always be this pure.

'You look gorgeous,' Natasha said. I was suddenly self-conscious in my red and white gingham bikini. I grabbed a towel and wrapped myself up.

'Thanks,' I said.

'I might get my hair bleached. Go blonde, like you,' she said. 'When we go to Madrid next. Shall we do that? We could get an early bus into the city one morning. Have a day of fun. We could even try some street magic?'

'I'd love that,' I said. 'But I think I should go dark, like you. You look like a movie star.' I realized that she looked like Uma Thurman in *Pulp Fiction*, which was an old film that I'd found in our DVD collection and watched in secret a couple of years ago. It was shocking and brilliant. 'Uma Thurman,' I added.

'Are you kidding?' said Natasha. 'Uma Thurman must be, like, fifty or something. Oh, you mean *Pulp Fiction*?' She ran her fingers through her hair. 'Yeah, that was cool. I'll take that. Thanks.'

'Yep, that. Sorry.'

'No, that's great. But you need to stay blonde, Libby. I'm going to change my colour because I think you look gorgeous. You've inspired me.'

'*I've* inspired *you*?'

'How about this?' she said. 'I'll go blonde and you go shorter? We can meet in the middle and end up matching?'

I grinned. I felt warm inside.

'Thank you,' I said. 'That would be amazing. We'd look like sisters.'

'Better than that,' said Natasha. 'Let's be twins.'

By the time we'd showered and dressed and dried our hair, and Natasha had done our make-up the same way as before, it was half past six. We found Mum and Sean drinking wine on the terrace, predictably.

'Hey!' Mum looked a bit unsure. 'Hey, look at you two!'

'Oh my God,' said Sean.

I frowned at him because he looked genuinely astonished at the way Natasha had transformed me.

'It's my doing, I'm afraid,' said Natasha. 'I can't help myself. Libby has such a perfect face, I didn't mean to treat her like a colouring book. Or one of those plastic heads little girls get to practise on. You know. I do know she's not that. She's an amazing human being.'

'Yes,' said Mum. 'Libby – I don't think you realize how stunning you are, darling. You never have.'

They offered us a glass of wine but I said no and went to get some water. Natasha accepted a glass of red and sipped it while looking sophisticated. I was trying to imagine her blonde. I touched the rope of my own hair. I imagined reaching for it and finding nothing there. The two of us matching. As she had said: twins.

'Show your mum that magic trick,' said Sean when I sat back down with my drink. I found the notebook and did the trick. This time I downloaded a photo of the Eiffel Tower, wrote PARIS over it in wobbly phone drawing, and messaged it to her before I started.

'Don't look at your phone,' I said. 'Not until I tell you to.' I showed her the names of all the cities, then flicked through the book the other way and got her to stick her finger in.

'Paris,' she said, and then checked her phone. She was delighted, although I noticed that she pressed a few other things on her phone screen and winced. There was something else going on with her.

Sean asked how we did the trick, and we refused to tell him. It was our secret.

'How do you know all this stuff, Natasha?' said Mum.

She shrugged. 'A bit of street magic can get you out of a tight spot.'

I opened my mouth to ask her for stories, but then closed it. I was scared to ask Natasha too much about herself, because I knew she was grieving and I didn't want to poke at it.

'Do you girls fancy a walk down to the bar?' said Sean. 'We thought it might be a good thing to do, you know? Head out for an aperitif? You made no inroads into our booze supplies last night, after all that, so you're allowed a drink. Not that I'm after pushing the alcohol on you now, you understand. Have an ice cream if you prefer.'

I saw him stroke Mum's arm and give her a questioning look. I saw her mouth, *Later*.

We ended up at the same bar as last night. I asked for a Coke, Natasha for a beer, and Mum said she'd have a glass of white wine. Sean went in to buy them.

'It's nice here, isn't it?' said Mum, looking around. I could see that she was upset about something, and I decided we ought to give her some space to talk it through with Sean. She clearly didn't want to share it with me.

'It's great,' said Natasha. I just nodded.

'So,' said Sean once he'd given us all our drinks and put a bowl of peanuts on the table. 'Drinks for the ladies.'

'Thanks,' I said. He handed Natasha one of those massive beers, and she mimed astonishment.

'Wow,' said Natasha with a big smile. 'I wasn't expecting that. Thanks, Sean.' I watched her pick up a peanut. Her fingernails were short but perfectly shaped and painted the palest of pinks.

'So,' said Mum, transparently making an effort to focus on us. 'Natasha, you didn't know anything about us – about Libby – until Andy died?'

'That's right,' she said. 'I knew he was from Britain, of course. He sounded almost as British as you guys do. More so than you,' she said with a nod to Sean. 'But he said he was an only child, and that his parents were dead. I had no idea he had a brother, and I didn't realize my grandparents had still been alive until recently.'

'That must have been a terrible thing,' said Sean. 'The accident.' I wondered how it was so easy for him to talk about it, and so hard for me. I had been wanting to ask her, but the question had felt too intrusive. I had been scared to say it. But actually it was easy. Sean had just done it.

'Yep,' said Natasha. She closed her eyes for a moment and then forced a smile.

Everyone was silent for a few seconds. I could only hear the crunch of some footsteps across the stony ground.

'I can't even imagine,' I said after a bit.

'I know.' She was looking at the table, blinking. For a minute or two all her bravado was gone. 'No time to prepare. No time for anything. He was there, and then he wasn't. It's the worst thing. Your life is one thing, and then it's another, and no amount of wishing can bring it back and make it happen differently. Mom and I didn't even know he was out in the car, and that's because he was with . . . someone he shouldn't have been with. A woman. I hate her. I hate her more than anyone else in the world. I can't even say her name I hate her so much.'

'Oh God,' said Mum. 'I'm so sorry. No wonder your mother's found it difficult.'

'I know. I feel bad for leaving Mom behind, but honestly she's in the best place, and seeing me doesn't do her any good. It makes her worse. She's on some . . . heavy treatments.' She paused and did some deep breathing. 'But I don't really like to talk about it unless I have to. Libby, you've been very sweet at not asking. I've spoken to Dad about it and he's truly, truly sorry. He wants to make it better with Mom, but she won't let him. She's fighting him in her head all the time and that's why she's ended up . . . where she has. Medicated. So now he just talks to me. That's another of the reasons why I'm here. Staying at home with his voice in my head was going to send me over the edge too.'

I reached for her under the table. She gripped my hand tightly.

'It's a terrible thing, Natasha,' said Sean. 'And you're coping well.'

'Yeah,' said Natasha, and she sighed. 'I look like I am, but I just can't stay still or it'll overwhelm me. I mean, what the hell was he doing? Driving too fast at night under the influence of alcohol and his trashy girlfriend. When someone's there, and then not . . . I'll have to live with that forever. However long that turns out to be. And she just got to get up and walk away.'

We sat in silence for a while. After a bit Natasha put a big smile on her face and said, 'Sorry! Aunt Amy? Did you meet him? Long ago?'

Mum was so nervous that I was alert. There was something else that was strange here. 'No,' she said. 'He was already settled in the States with Peggy by the time I met Ben. It's such a waste of time. You girls could have known each other all your lives.'

'Oh,' said Natasha. 'Yes. Wouldn't that have been incredible? And I would so love for you to have met him. It would have meant I could talk to you about him and you'd have him in your memories too. He's with me all the time anyway.'

'Yes,' said Mum. 'So you said.' Her tone was sharper than it should have been.

'Mum!' I said.

'Aunt Amy?' said Natasha.

'Please don't call me that. It makes me feel so old. You can just call me Amy.'

'Oh, OK. I thought "aunt" was a kind of respectful thing. Well, OK then. Amy?'

Mum forced a smile. 'Yes, Natasha?'

'I'm kind of wishing I hadn't said that I speak to my dad in the spirit world. I can see that you don't believe me and it makes you uncomfortable, even though you're so spiritual yourself. And you, Sean. You don't believe in it at all, do you?'

'I think it's a crock of shit,' said Sean.

'Exactly. Amy, your focus is different. We all believe in our own impossible things. Well, apart from Sean. So. You probably won't like this, which is why I haven't said it before, but there's something I have to ask you.' She took a deep breath. 'After that we don't need to talk about this again.'

A car went past along the road at the top of the square. Everything else was suspended.

'Go on,' said Mum. 'What is it?'

'I *am* psychic. I know I do card tricks and coin tricks and street magic, and that's a different thing. The thing with the notebook, all that. That's entertainment. Obviously it's just tricks. But the psychic thing is a connection in my mind to spirits in a different realm. They're here, on this planet, but in a place we can't see or feel, and if the Creep does happen, every one of us will be crossing over to where they are. Occasionally a door opens between the worlds, and I've got one of them. I can't tell you how that works, but it does.

'So. Since I've been here I've had a barrage of messages that I didn't understand or want, coming from over there.' She paused, sipped her drink. I flicked my eyes over to Mum. She was pale. 'They're from a girl called Violet,' said Natasha. 'She wants to talk to you. She's bothering me non-stop – I wouldn't have mentioned it otherwise. I just . . . feel that I need to pass it on.'

The words hung in the warm evening air. Mum was staring at Natasha, who was meeting her gaze. Sean was looking at the table, his face pained. I'd never heard Mum mention anyone called Violet. Natasha had told me about the woman in London, who was called Violet; that was where I'd heard the name recently. But this was something different.

It was Mum's reaction that was giving this question traction. She could have scoffed and it would have gone away. I was amazed that she hadn't.

'What,' said Mum, 'do you mean? What do you mean by that, Natasha? What the hell are you saying?' Her voice was quiet and deadly.

'Just that.' Natasha held Mum's gaze. 'Violet wants to talk to you. She's coming through in my head really clearly. I've been blocking it out for the past two days. I have no idea who she is, but she is absolutely lovely. Such a gorgeous spirit.'

'I don't know what you think you know,' Mum said, 'but I can see what you're trying to do and it's not going to work. Stop it. You've got it all wrong.'

Natasha nodded. 'I understand.'

'You don't.'

'She was very young.'

'Natasha!'

'She wants me to say –'

'Stop it!' Mum shouted it, and everyone in the dusty square looked over at us.

Mum stood up. Sean stood with her. My eyes met his and I could see that he knew something I didn't.

He put a hand on her arm. 'Hey,' he said. 'Come on. There's no point worrying about this because what Natasha says is, as I said, a crock of shit.' He pushed Mum down gently, and she sat back in her chair. When she picked up her glass her hand was shaking.

'Natasha,' she said without looking up. 'Go. Back to the house. Never say that name again. I know what you're trying to do and it won't work.'

'Sure.' Natasha stood up and looked at me, a question on her face.

'Who's Violet, though?' I said to Mum.

'It doesn't matter!' Mum hardly ever raised her voice, but she did now. She was furious and there were tears in her eyes. 'Go on. Give me some space. Both of you!'

'Oh, Amy,' said Natasha. 'I am so sorry. Of course. I apologize. I apologize for striking a nerve. I hadn't realized it was a bad thing to say. I'll tell her to leave us alone.'

'You know exactly what you're doing.' She looked away. Mum never cried but she was crying now.

'Sorry,' said Natasha, and she stood up to leave. I stood too. Mum put her arms on the table and her head on her arms. I put a hand on Mum's back but she shrugged me away.

Natasha and I walked away from the table. Sean ran after us and gave me the key to the house and the fob for the gate.

'Give your mother some time,' he said. 'She'll be OK. Natasha, your stay here is over. Time to move on, I think.'

We walked back side by side. I didn't know what to say, and so I didn't say anything.

16. Run away

I followed Natasha into the house and straight into our bedroom, where she started to pack her things.

'Right,' she said. 'You heard the man. I'm off. Come with me, Libby. Pack some things in a bag and come to Madrid. It works for everyone. Aunt Amy gets some space, you get your adventure, and I get my twin. You know I messed that up. I feel terrible about it. Let's let her calm down while we go off and have a look at the rest of the world.'

I shook my head. 'I'd like to,' I said. 'But I can't just run away.'

'Why not?'

'She needs me.'

'Why? She needs Sean, and she has him. What does she want for you most of all?'

'She wants me to be happy.'

'By . . .?'

I sighed. I knew what she meant.

'She wants me to have adventures while we still can.'

'So? Are you sending me to Madrid on my own?'

I had no idea what I ought to do, or what I wanted, but Natasha kept firing questions and I started to see that she was right. My going to Madrid with her might work for everyone.

Still, I called Sean before we left.

'If I go to Madrid with Natasha,' I said, 'do you think that would be OK? Will Mum be all right?'

He spoke quietly. I could hear from the background sounds – the birds, the odd car – that they were still outside.

'Actually, Libby,' he said, 'I think it would be a good idea. Enjoy yourself. Have fun and don't worry. I'll take care of her.'

I picked up my suitcase. I put it on my bed and opened it.

Madrid was a half-hour bus ride away, so I was hardly getting on a boat to New York. I wasn't running away forever. I was just going with Natasha – who had lost her dad, who had said she couldn't stay still or the grief overwhelmed her – and in a day or two I would come back.

And then we would all suffocate when the air ran out, and in millions of years, when the planet had recovered and people had evolved again, a future civilization would dig out our bones and put us in a museum and marvel at the weirdness of a society that knew it was destroying its own habitat but carried on anyway. Except that even that wouldn't happen, because the sun would be running out of power by then.

Nothing mattered. I felt it seep through my body until every cell was energized. I needed to go. I was reckless and ready for it. Why not? I had nothing to lose. Nothing at all.

'Where will we sleep tonight?'

'Somewhere good.'

I walked across the room and opened a drawer. I took out all my underwear and put it into my suitcase, and then took most of it out and put it back, because I was only going for a few days. I took a few things from the rest of my drawers and packed them too. I put in my phone charger, my iPad, my book.

I went to the drawer in the sitting room and took out my passport, just in case we did end up going to Paris, like the Svengali notebook had said. I had my purse, and my debit card. There was some money in my current account. I was pretty sure I had enough to stay away for a couple of days, and I also had the card to my big savings account, just in case I needed to dig into that.

I wrote them a note.

> Mum! Take care of yourself. I'll be in Madrid for a couple of days. You wanted me to have adventures, and it was so exciting the other day.
>
> I don't really understand what happened but I'm sorry about it. I know you probably need a break, so we'll give you a bit of time. I feel like this is the right thing to do. I hope it is. Sean said it was.

We'll be fine. I'll come back soon, maybe at the weekend.

Love you, Mum,

Libby xxx

Natasha was watching me. I zipped up the case and looked at her.

'Ready?' she said.

'Ready,' I said.

We walked out on to the terrace, and I looked around. This place had been idyllic enough to distract me for weeks, and now it felt closed in, cloying, with its high walls, metal gate and wild plants.

'It's like leaving the Garden of Eden,' I said, staring around. 'Don't you think?'

'It is. And we're heading to *The Garden of Earthly Delights*,' said Natasha, and, even though I kind of hoped we weren't, I knew what she meant.

I left my suitcase and ran to the tomato plants near the pool. Harry the tomato was huge and red now, and although he would get riper over the next few days I knew this was his moment. I picked him and took a huge bite, as if he were an apple. The tomato pips ran down my chin.

I handed Natasha the tomato, and she took a big bite too.

'And that,' she said, 'means it's time to get the hell out of Eden.'

We opened the metal gates and walked back to the main road. I thought for sure we would see Mum and Sean on their way back to the house. But we didn't. We walked to the bus stop and only passed a couple of people.

It was half past eight, and there were plenty more buses listed this evening. We stood for a while on our own, and then a bus arrived. It was a number 671. The driver flipped a switch when he saw our bags, and the side of the bus hissed and slowly lifted on a hinge so we could put them under it.

Natasha bought tickets and marched me to the back seat, and we sat there, side by side, as the bus left the stop. We were like the cool kids on a school trip. She took my hand and squeezed it.

'Thank you, Libby,' Natasha said. 'This means the world. It really does. I'm not sure why it went so wrong, and I really wish I hadn't said it. You coming with me actually is the most wonderful thing that's happened all year. And Sean's got her. He really has.'

'I know,' I said. 'I'm sorry about . . . whatever that was.'

'Oh God, don't be. I touched a nerve, much more than I realized. I had no idea or I never would have gone there.'

'Who is Violet? I thought she was your girlfriend in London?'

'No. That's completely different, and actually that was Violeta. Your mom's Violet is a voice in my head.'

I wanted to ask a million questions, but I was scared.

Mum will tell me when she wants me to know, I thought. *We're giving her a bit of space*, I thought. *I'll go back in*

*a few days, and then we can talk properly. If Mum has
a secret, I don't want to hear it from Natasha. That would
feel all wrong. It would be a betrayal, like reading
someone's diary.*

'OK,' I said.

It was properly dark by the time we arrived. The city
appeared, sparkling, on the horizon, all its street lights
shimmering, and then the bus was driving through city
streets and stopping at traffic lights, then going down a
ramp and into the underground bus station lit with harsh
lights. Everyone got off, and we took our bags from the
luggage compartment and all the people dispersed.

Madrid was a completely different place at night from
the way it had been during the day. It felt as if everyone
was going somewhere quickly.

We walked towards the Metro. I was wheeling my case
and Natasha had hers on her back. She looked like a proper
backpacker would if they were played by a Hollywood
actor, and I looked like a clueless tourist filling the 'clumsy
best friend' role.

'Where are we going?' I said. My suitcase had a wonky
wheel, and it made a loud sound when I pulled it. I ran a
little bit to keep up, then tried to get my case on to an
escalator.

'How much money do you have?' she said.

'On me? About thirty euros. I've got more in my
current account. And then I've got some in savings. How
about you?'

'I need to make some cash, so let's do that. Let's fund ourselves without dipping into anything. However.' She looked at me and her face lit up in a wicked grin. 'We'll do something good first. Two nights in a great hotel – without touching savings – and then we'll worry about everything else after that. I've got enough for that, and you have too, right?'

I liked that. Two nights in a great hotel. Then we would go back to Mum and Sean, and talk about whatever had happened when Natasha had tried to pass on that message, and be sensible again.

'Right,' I said.

In the Metro hall, with people bustling past us, Natasha stood shamelessly in everyone's way and fiddled around on her phone, while people tutted and walked round her. Eventually she looked up and nodded.

'Come on,' she said. 'You're going to love this. Madrid is so empty and the hotels are mostly still open. I've found a five-star hotel that is cheaper than some of the three stars. One of those weird algorithms. Can you chip in a hundred euros? I'll take care of the rest.'

'Sure. I'll have to go to a cashpoint.'

'Oh, don't worry for now. I've put it on my card. It'll go through OK, I think, and if it doesn't, I'll get some transferred from my other account. If you can get a bit of cash tomorrow, we can throw it all in together and work it out.'

'Of course. Thanks, Natasha.' I was giddy with all this.

'You're welcome! This is going to be fun, Libby-libs. And – one other thing. You remember how you told those fuckwit men to fuck off at the bar?' I nodded. 'So this is going to be the opposite of that. We need to be as charming as we possibly can. Make everyone adore us. Things become much easier that way. You'll see.'

I told myself that Sean was looking after Mum, that I was seventeen and that my own mother had told me to go and have adventures. I switched my phone to silent. I was with Natasha now. Although I was still unsettled, this felt like the best thing I had ever done.

We sat side by side on the Metro. I didn't feel like speaking and Natasha didn't push it. Every now and then she would look at me, and I met her eyes and then looked away. I was trying to work out who I was, because this was not the kind of thing I had ever done before, but at the same time I had never felt more like myself. It was ten o'clock and the train was quite busy. I wondered where everyone was going, what they were doing, what their lives were like.

The woman directly across from me was tiny and brilliantly dressed, with grey hair that was partly pink. Her silk scarf and trousers were lilac and she was wearing a perfect white blouse with frills down the front. Her shoes were high and lilac, and her make-up was perfect. She was about eighty years old and she looked as if she had stepped out of one of those brightly coloured Spanish movies.

Two men got on at the next stop and looked over at us. Natasha gave them a cheeky smile. They had some music playing out of a phone, and they both started to sing along to the chorus. Natasha started humming it too.

When we got off the train I just followed her. We pushed through the barriers like everyone else, and went up to the street, where I was surprised, although I shouldn't have been, to see that it was dark. We walked along the pavement, with grand buildings on either side of us, in a part of Madrid I didn't know, or at least didn't recognize, because I had only been to the tourist centre. Everything felt like a hallucination.

When Natasha said a polite hello to a doorman and set off up some steps to a grand-looking hotel, I hung back. We couldn't really be going to sleep here. Could we? The doorman saw me hesitating and misinterpreted it. He stepped forward and took my suitcase, motioning me up the stairs in front of him.

'Thank you.' I was paralysed. I wanted my bag back because I didn't know if I was meant to tip him for taking it. 'I mean, *gracias*.'

'You're welcome, *señorita*,' he said.

I caught up with Natasha at the reception desk, where she was laughing and chatting with the man and woman who were staffing it as if they were her oldest friends. I had never been inside a place like this. It was so grand. It smelled beautiful, like oils and perfumes, with a little bit of tapas underneath. The ceiling was high and bookcases went right up to it, like in the library in a country-house murder, except that it had a reception desk and a bar.

I imagined the bad air creeping in here, and everyone dying.

The check-in woman was thin and stylish, with glossy dark hair and deep red lipstick.

'Here you are,' she said. 'We've given you an upgrade as we're not so busy right now. Everyone is at the coast. Not many people want to be in the hot city. It was forty-seven yesterday! So you have a superior twin suite. Enjoy your stay, both of you!'

'Thank you *so* much,' said Natasha. 'You are just adorable and wonderful.' I caught the quick look she gave me and knew it was my cue.

'Yes,' I said. 'Thank you. This is a beautiful hotel.' I said it, and my words came out fluently and I marvelled at myself.

'Thank you!' The woman looked genuinely delighted by our words, though she couldn't have been really. Then the doorman took Natasha's bag too (she was far more gracious about it than I had been) and walked us to a lift.

'You take this one,' he said, pushing a button. 'I will bring your bags. Here.'

I watched as an old-fashioned lift clunked down and stopped inside a grating. The doorman pulled the wrought-iron frame back and ushered us into a strange antique lift with a banquette to sit on and art deco fixtures. 'Press number four,' he said to Natasha, and he closed the grille and clicked it shut.

As we bumped upwards I widened my eyes at her.

'I feel a bit of a mess,' I said.

'You look great,' she said. 'Your make-up is impeccable, remember? You managed to run away from home without crying one single tear.' She was right. 'I *knew* we could get them to upgrade the room. After this we'll go downmarket a bit, but hey. That's fun too.'

Actually, I thought, I would go home. I would just get on a bus whenever I was ready to go back. I wasn't committing to anything beyond two nights in Madrid to give Mum a break.

The lift jolted and stopped at floor four. Natasha yanked the grille open and pushed the door on its other side, and we were out.

We looked for our room, which was 432. It was down the corridor. There was a long way between each door: it was not at all like the Premier Inn, where Mum and Sean and I normally stayed.

I was definitely not thinking about my family. I was not thinking about Zoe, or about the end of the world. I was just thinking about the moment, about Natasha and me, in Madrid, on a hot evening at the end of days.

17. Stay out late in Madrid

Our room was huge. It smelled of perfume and linen. There was one big bed but with two separate duvets. Everything was white. All the linen was white. The walls were white. The pale grey carpet underfoot was soft and luxurious.

I pushed the door to the bathroom, and saw that this too was enormous, with a chequered black-and-white floor and bathrobes hanging up. There was a bath at one end and a shower with a huge showerhead at the other.

Back in the room Natasha sat down on the bed and bounced a few times.

'Oh *yes*,' she said. 'Yes, this will do, won't it, Libs? I have to say, I'm pretty pleased with the way this has worked out.'

'You did it,' I said. 'It was all you.'

I walked to the window and looked out at the city. We were on a corner, so there was a view in two directions, and I could see streets and buildings, cars and people, lit up in the darkness. It was all there, spread out before me. A capital city. Madrid.

'This is amazing.' I was filled with love for the city. It was so beautiful. So many people. So many lives, all hurtling towards the end. When I had ploughed through my Spanish at school I had never thought very deeply about actual Spain. There had been an exchange trip in Year Ten, but I hadn't taken part because there was no way I was going to go and spend a week with a Spanish family. I had learned Spanish from teachers, from lists of words and from YouTube.

Now I was here, with a sparkling city at my feet.

Natasha came and stood beside me. We really were exactly the same height.

'Yeah. That city, Libby? It belongs to us now.'

I looked at her, into her dark brown eyes.

'Madrid belongs to us?' I laughed a bit.

'Yes. Tomorrow we're going to have the best time, the most fun. And we never had dinner! Let's go out for something right now.'

'I'm not that hungry.' What I really was, was incredibly tired, and of course Natasha could see that.

'I know,' she said. 'You're exhausted, and you're a girl who needs her sleep, unlike me. It's been an emotional day. Can you believe this is the same actual day as the one when we went skinny dipping after midnight?'

I smiled, though I really wanted to cry. I had run away from home. Had I fallen out with Mum? Was this awful? I was so confused.

'It doesn't feel like it,' I managed to say.

'Don't worry. Just spend a bit of time in the city. I promise you you'll love it. I think –' She stopped. 'Oh, never mind what I think. Come on. Let's go. You don't need anything except your handbag.'

My 'handbag' was a canvas rucksack that I used for taking a book, sun cream and sunglasses down to the pool. I took the phone out of my bag and left it on the bed.

'OK,' I said. 'Let's go.'

We found a bar round the corner. It was outside, on a green carpet that covered the space between two buildings. It looked like a pop-up, with an outdoor bar and wicker sofas and chairs. There were fairy lights, which I appreciated.

'This is gorgeous,' I said.

'Right?'

The barman said, '*Buenas noches*,' and barely looked up from wiping glasses. Natasha led me to a sofa in the darkest corner and told me to sit.

'I'll get some drinks and see what food they've got.'

I sat in the corner, secretly pleased to be hiding in the shadows, and watched as she leaned on the outside bar and chatted with the barman. He laughed. She laughed. I couldn't have heard what they were saying from here even if I'd been able to understand real-life high-speed Spanish, but when he put two glasses of beer in front of her, I saw her lean forward, frowning slightly, looking at the side of his head. He put a hand up, self-conscious. Natasha leaned further forward and took something from behind his ear, and I realized she was doing the most basic street-magic trick on him. She opened her hand to reveal a note and used it to pay for the drinks.

The barman laughed. He looked delighted.

'How do you even do that?' I said when she sat down.

'You know how I do it. I palmed the money and pretended to find it behind his ear.'

'Not that. How do you make everyone love you straight away? You've got social skills like . . . I don't know. Like, you always know what to say to people.'

'Your mother and Sean don't love me,' she said. 'Well, Sean would have been fine, but he loves Amy so much. He'll go along with what she wants, and that's thinking I'm a bit evil for overstepping the mark.'

'Yes but . . .' I couldn't think about them. 'I mean, like just now. And at the hotel. You say the exact right things to every single person. You never stand around feeling awkward and blushing and looking stupid.'

'You're right. I don't. I never do those things. Because, like I said to you a long time ago when we were messaging, I trained myself out of it. I'm going to train you out of it too. We started it, didn't we? You went to that party. You nearly kissed your girl, until her girlfriend came along and put a stop to things.'

I frowned. I knew I hadn't told her that part.

'How did you know that?'

'You told me.'

'I really don't think I did.'

I could remember how I'd reported it to Natasha. I knew that I'd held back from that detail. It had been a big decision for me.

'Then I must have intuited it. Picked it up from things you didn't say. I'm right though, aren't I? You were getting somewhere, and then the girlfriend put a stop to it.'

'Yes.'

'There you go. Ten tasks and you won't be shy any more. As you know, some of them are really easy. You did the fifth one last night, telling Miguel to get fucked. We'll do more tomorrow.'

I sipped my beer. I did want to be fixed. I wanted, desperately, to be like Natasha, though I also very much didn't want dead people shouting in my head.

'Did you plan to get the money from his ear when you went up there?' I said.

'No. I spoke to him for about twenty seconds and after that I could tell that he'd like it, so I did it.'

I put my glass down. 'Yeah. Teach me that. I can do the pulling out of the ear bit, but not the bit where you have to be confident and chat to someone and judge what they would like.'

We sat there until two in the morning. I had another beer and some tap water, and Natasha drank two cocktails after that first beer. We ate little plates of tapas that the barman brought over. We had *patatas bravas* (my favourite), some little fish in tomato sauce, fried squid, mushrooms. Each time he brought a plate over, Natasha did another piece of magic on him. She produced a second Svengali book that she had filled in with Spanish animals going one way, and with the word LEON going the other, and the barman, who, on my own, I would have found intimidating, brought us free puddings just to get her to do another one. She rewarded him by telling him to look in his pocket, where he found a bunch of flowers we had made together from the contents of the napkin dispenser. He laughed and told her she was *fabulosa*.

The bad things lifted that evening, to the point where I could barely remember what they had been. I was exhilarated, drunk on freedom and Natasha and beer. The night was hotter than any night I had ever known before. I could feel the warmth radiating from the city around me, distorting the air.

We talked about Natasha's travels in Europe, about how I had played Juliet, and how easy I had found it to come out of myself when I was acting. I recited parts of it. I remember doing the 'wherefore art thou Romeo?' speech for her, and I remember Natasha gazing at me as I did it, and that it ended up feeling better even than the real performance had been, even though I had previously thought that that performance was the best thing in my life.

I said that everyone thinks 'wherefore art thou Romeo?' means 'where are you, Romeo?' but that actually it means 'why?'. Why are you Romeo, the person I love, from the family we hate? She must already have known, of course, that *wherefore* meant *why*, but she heard me out and acted as if it were interesting news.

'It's a bit like you and me,' she said. 'I mean, in a different way. We've run away together. Our fathers became enemies for whatever reason. Do you know the reason?'

'No,' I said. 'I do not. Do you?'

'I could easily find out but I don't want to. It should stay in the past and be forgotten. But here we are, friends. And family. I know we're not Romeo and Juliet, but we're here. Against the odds. I found you even though my dad never told me you existed when he was alive, and you came away with me even though you weren't supposed to.'

I smiled at her. Right then, Natasha was everything I wanted, everything I had ever needed. She was my other sister, the one who wasn't three years old, and I thought I had longed for her all my life without realizing it.

We giggled back to the hotel. A different doorman was on duty, an older one, and he called the juddery lift for us and made sure we were shut into it properly.

'A very good night,' he said, and I didn't know whether it was a wish or an observation.

'There are chocolates on the pillows!' I had never seen that before.

'Quite right too.' Natasha passed one to me. Our fingers touched as I took it from her.

We slept well, side by side. At least, I did. I didn't know whether Natasha slept or not.

18. Try new food

I woke at half past ten, and it took me ages to remember where I was. When I did remember, my heart pounded and I had to work hard to keep control of myself.

I was in a five-star hotel, in Madrid, with Natasha, who was still asleep. I got up quietly and went to find my phone.

There were seventeen missed calls, five voicemails and twenty texts, all from Mum. I didn't listen to the voicemails, but I did read the texts, which were milder than I'd expected and mainly concerned with where we'd stayed last night. I replied to them all with one message.

> Mum, I'm sorry. I'm fine. I
> promise. Got here safely, stayed
> in a nice hotel, ate food. So don't
> worry – have some time and
> space. It's fine. I'm finally doing
> something independently. Maybe
> when I come back you can tell me
> what that was about? Libby xxxxx

Then I put my phone on to charge, and had a long hot shower, because the air conditioning was so effective that hot water felt good even though I knew it was forty-seven degrees outside. Natasha woke up, and while she was in the shower I lounged on the bed, trying to work out what I wanted to do. I knew what Natasha wanted me to do, and I also knew what Mum wanted. But what did I want? I had no idea. Today I wanted to be in Madrid. That was the best I could do.

I listened. The shower water was still running, so I picked my phone up again and wrote an email.

Dear Zoe,

So here I am in Madrid. I've left Mum and Sean's for a bit and come to the city with Natasha. She and Mum had a kind of fight and it was all weird, but I'd been feeling for a while that Mum wants a bit of space anyway, and she kept telling me to go off and do things. So I'm in the city with my cousin having an adventure.

So far we've been for tapas, and we're staying at an amazing hotel. No idea what today will bring.

How are you??? I wish I could see you.

xxxxx Libby xxxxx

Natasha and I walked down the road in the sunshine. I was very hungry. The hotel breakfast wasn't included in our room rate and it was spectacularly expensive, so we hadn't eaten yet.

As we walked we passed a religious procession. People were dressed in white robes, following a woman at the front who was holding up a cross. They were all chanting. We stood to the side to let them pass. A smell of incense came with them.

'Mum would like this,' I said, and Natasha nodded.

'She would be right at the front,' she said. 'Doing everything she could to make it all right. I do understand. The mind is a powerful thing. Everything we experience is processed through our mind. If you can get your mind not to accept the CO_2, you won't be able to experience it.'

'It won't stop it happening, though,' I said. I read the leaflet a robed woman had offered me. 'These guys think God's done it as a Last Judgement. They want to go to heaven so I guess they're cool with it all. Lots of people think that, don't they? That it's like Noah's flood.'

'Yeah. They all want to be the special ones, chosen to be on the ark.'

I could see the attraction. It must be lovely to have their certainty, their whole-hearted belief that whatever was coming was orchestrated by a higher power. I didn't think it would take much for me to put on a robe and join them. I wanted to believe in something with all my soul.

They walked slowly and sang their words (possibly in Latin – I wasn't sure) and they looked peaceful.

Natasha took my arm and pulled me along.

'Just down here,' she said. 'Right. This is perfect. This is the place, here at the end of this square. The exact place I was looking for. We'll go in and get a coffee and some food and watch everything. Then I might do something I haven't shown you before. I need to get a feel for it first.'

I walked beside her. It was nearly midday, and the sun was hot, and I was hungry. We were walking through a huge square, a very touristy place indeed, and it was filled with people. It was like the Prado: a pocket of tourism in an otherwise eerily empty city. There were cafe tables round the edge, and people in the middle trying to sell things. A man had a Segway and was offering rides on it for eyewatering amounts of money. We walked straight through and out the other end, past a man in a tight superhero suit for which he didn't have the figure, offering photos with 'fat Spider-Man'. He greeted us as if we were his friends, and we walked past waving.

Natasha stopped and reached for her phone.

'Stay right where you are,' she said. 'The way the sun's on your hair. You look like an angel. I can practically see your guardian angel around you.'

I stopped, self-conscious. Natasha took some steps back and aimed her camera at me. I smiled an awkward smile, pretty sure I didn't actually look like an angel, and that there wasn't a guardian angel around me.

She looked at the screen.

'Perfect,' she said. As she put her phone away a piece of paper fell out of her pocket. I went to pick it up, but a passer-by got it first, a woman in a big straw hat. She handed it to Natasha with a smile.

'*Gracias*,' Natasha said, and she stuffed it back into her pocket. 'Look, Libs! Don't you look adorable?'

It was a nice picture of me; I had to admit that. I decided that I would use it as my profile picture on social media. I hardly ever posted anything anywhere, but it would be nice to have this picture up anyway.

The San Miguel food market was ahead of us. This, Natasha had decided, was where we were going to start. It was a beautiful building made of wrought iron and glass, and even before we crossed the little road to get to it I could see that it was filled with people.

We walked in and looked around. It was clattery and the air smelled of every wonderful thing. There were stalls all round the outside, each one selling something different, and there were people standing drinking glasses of beer or gathered round coffee stands and juice bars. I stood still and stared.

'Not so busy yet,' she said, though it looked it to me, and I followed her to a stall where she bought two espressos and something that turned out to be two tiny custard tarts. I felt more lumpen and useless than ever as I followed her to a long table and sat beside her on a high stool. I had thought I was quite good at Spanish. Now I was terrible at it, and I was getting worse.

There were people on all the stools around us. The other table, behind us, was full, and there were only a few free spots down at the end of ours. It was intoxicating being here. The whole place smelled of garlic and fried food and coffee.

I didn't really know what we were going to do here: unlike that square with the fat Spider-Man, this place was not filled with people interacting with tourists for money. The other customers seemed to be Spanish as much as they were tourists, and it seemed like a place to eat serious tapas, for locals as well as visitors. It was not a place to hustle. All I could really think of, though, was how hungry I was.

The custard tart was wonderful but very small. I sipped the espresso, hating its bitterness, knowing that it would have been too babyish to go and get a hot chocolate instead. Natasha knocked hers back in one gulp and spoke fast, gesturing with her hands, suddenly looking perfectly Spanish. She was wearing a black dress and bright red lipstick, but she looked low-key with it somehow. I was sweaty and graceless in a blue T-shirt and a pair of shorts that had been fine for lounging by a pool, shut off from the world by a metal gate, but which were making me feel self-conscious in a bustling tapas market in the centre of a capital city.

I had looked good in that photo, though. I hung on to that fact.

'So,' she said. 'Watch me. Actually, can you video this? I'd like to be able to look at it afterwards. Continuous self-improvement.'

I thought about my phone. It was in the bottom of my bag. I didn't want to pick it up because I knew there would be another barrage of messages.

Natasha looked at my face and understood.

'Use this.' She took her phone out and fiddled with it. 'Here you go. Pretend to be texting but try to record the whole thing. You won't hear the words and that doesn't matter.'

I sat on the stool and pretended to be scrolling through the phone, even though I didn't dare look at anything apart from its screen (it would have been interesting, of course, to root around a bit). I pointed the phone at Natasha and pressed record, as she squeezed between the backs of people at our long table and the one beside it, and then turned up directly opposite me at the other side of the table beside ours and, without looking at me, tapped a woman on the shoulder and started to talk.

I was so invested in getting the filming right (I couldn't mess up my first job) that I barely even wondered what she was doing. I half expected Natasha to pull something from the woman's ear, or to get out a Svengali notebook, but she didn't. Instead I watched the woman go from annoyed to sceptical to interested, and although I didn't even know what language they were speaking (and even though I was still *really* hungry), for a while the only thing I wanted was to know what on earth you could say to a stranger to have that kind of effect on them. The woman looked around for a stool, and then one appeared from somewhere. Natasha sat beside her and they carried on talking.

Then the woman, looking hesitant, held out her hand to Natasha, and Natasha took hold of it and studied it. She gave the woman a delighted smile and pointed something out. The woman leaned in towards her.

It went on for a long time, and I filmed it all. Occasionally someone tried to take Natasha's stool even though I had my bag on it, but I hooked my leg round it and kept it there.

Then she was standing up and touching the woman on the shoulder, and the woman pulled her in for a hug. She handed her something, and Natasha tried to refuse, but then accepted with a smile. She walked away but not in my direction, and after a few seconds I stopped filming and went to find her round the back of a grilled prawn stall.

'Did you get that?' She didn't wait for me to answer but carried on speaking. 'Let's get some proper food. I'm starving. What do you want? We can get a load of things and go and eat them outside. That was exhausting and I am ready for some serious lunch.'

'I did get it,' I said. 'All of it. Were you reading her palm?' We stopped in front of a stall. Natasha started chatting in Spanish and pointing to things.

'Can we get that tortilla?' I said, because tortilla was my favourite. Natasha added it to the order, and soon we had a collection of dishes on paper plates, all piled into a paper bag.

We sat on a bench, down the road and round the corner, in the full glare of the sunshine.

'Go on then,' I said.

She grinned.

'I told her that I can speak to people in the spirit realm and that I had a message for her. It's amazing when that happens. I was looking around, and this voice came into my head so vividly, and it sent me to her. It turned out it was her mother who died two years ago. Her mom's looking out for her, and she thinks she should apply for a new job she's been thinking about. Also, she doesn't like Conchita's boyfriend. That woman was Conchita. We covered loads of other stuff. It's wonderful when it works out like that. You saw how happy she was. And I'm happy because she gave me twenty euros to get some food. Win–win. Thank you, Conchita's mom.'

'You actually heard her mum's voice?'

I tried as hard as I could to believe this. I longed to accept it, but I just couldn't. No part of me believed it for a single second.

'Yes,' she said. 'Just like I did with Violet the other day. Clear, in my head, but speaking Spanish. Oh, Lib. I know you're sceptical. It's written all over your face. And why wouldn't you be when it's not a thing you've experienced? I might be a sceptic too, if I were you. I promise, though. It's a thing we have in the family. You might be able to do it yourself, if you let go. In fact . . .'

She stopped.

'What?' I said.

'Oh, nothing really. I just wondered about something you said. But don't worry.'

'What?'

'We'll talk about it later . . . So I gave her messages and she was very happy, as you saw. I looked at her palm and gave her a bit of a reading while I was at it. That wasn't anything to do with her mom: it's just a way of bolstering someone's confidence and making them feel good. Let's go over your footage back in the room later. I'll show you how it works. You have to make them trust you, build up a bit of rapport.'

'Yeah.' I speared a bit of omelette with my wooden fork, chewed it, swallowed and continued. I was too hungry not to eat everything straight away. 'How do you begin then? I mean, you can't just look at someone across a food market and decide to give them a message from their dead mum. Not when they're a stranger.'

Natasha grinned. 'You can! That's the joy of it. The spirits know where you are, and if you're near someone they want to talk to, they will go insane until you do what they want. It's easier, when that happens, just to go with it. I knew what to say to her because I've done it a hundred times before, and also because Maria, the mother, was yelling it right at me.'

'And everything you said to her was right?'

'More or less. It's obviously a complicated equation, and sometimes I misunderstand. For one, I was doing it in Spanish. For two, things always get mangled. It's a strange science. I thought Conchita had a child, but she didn't. It was the spirits of the children she hadn't had.'

I looked at her, unsure whether she was being serious, but it seemed that she was.

'I mean it! Her unborn children are with her mother now. She was pleased to hear that.'

'I bet she was. Will she get to meet them when she dies?'

'She will.'

'Are they . . .? I mean, was she ever actually pregnant, or are they the spirits of the children she would have had?'

'Could be either. Not for me to know.'

I didn't know what to say. I felt Natasha was toying with me, but I was also almost sure that she believed it. She was the most convincing person I had ever met, and in spite of my scepticism I was impressed. I reminded myself that I wasn't in any position to be certain about what happened after death. There was no reason not to consider every possibility.

Natasha passed me a plate of prawns and I started on them. She was eating with as much joy as I was, completely energized.

'It makes me feel weird,' I said.

'I know it does.'

'What were you going to say about me?'

She hesitated, then said, 'You know you told me about Carmen?'

'She's not a *spirit guide*!'

'Well,' said Natasha. 'No, she's not, of course. She's a character you assume to make you confident in Spanish. But she is also someone who was alive, who watches over you. She would love to be your spirit guide if you'd let her a bit closer in. Don't worry. We don't need to talk about that any more. Not yet.'

'OK,' I said, spearing a prawn. That bit was just stupid. 'So. What's next?'

'Street magic. We make enough euros for dinner tonight. Partners in crime. It's begun.'

19. Make money from magic

We walked back to the hotel, down the hot roads, past a few parties and some more end-time gatherings, and several drunk people passed out on pavements.

The term 'end times' seemed to have been adopted by everyone, whatever language they spoke. Every party, every religious ceremony, every gathering, was called 'end times' now. The whole world was gearing up for an enormous scream for its last month.

'I'm never going to have to tell anyone I'm in touch with their dead relative,' I said. 'Am I?'

'Libby! You never say things like that. You say: I'm afraid that I don't have a strong connection to the spirit realm.' Her eyes were laughing.

'I don't have a strong connection to the spirit realm,' I said. 'And can you tell Carmen that I don't plan to either?'

'Fine! You do have this gift, you know. I knew you would. But you don't want to use it, and that's up to you. Leave anything like that to me because those spirit bastards are having a mad end-time fiesta of their own in my head right now. Even though it's not *their* end time. Any excuse. I can teach you palm reading, but anything that involves the future just makes people ask about the Creep. And all you can say to that is, we'll all be OK. If we're wrong, they'll hardly be able to find us to complain. How about if I teach you to do tarot?'

I winced. 'Natasha. I really, really couldn't read tarot cards. I have no affinity with that stuff. I'd be useless at it.'

She stopped and pointed at me.

'Your sixth task! Learn to read tarot cards and give someone a reading. Here's a secret: it's the easiest thing in the world because, the way I do it, the only rule is that there are no rules. I'm sure some people do it properly, but not me. Life's too short.'

The hotel room had been made up, and I was astonished all over again at how luxurious it was. I threw myself back on the bed, excited about the fact that I was going to sleep here again tonight.

'This bed is gorgeous,' I said.

'Have a little sleep! I'm going to lounge in the tub, I think,' said Natasha. 'So wasteful. But you know. Life is short. And the AC is amazing.'

I liked that. I took some deep breaths and closed my eyes.

She was shaking my shoulder.

'Hey! Sleepyhead!'

It took me ages to remember where I was and why. I sat up. Natasha had wet hair and was wearing a fluffy bathrobe. She looked lovely.

'I've run you a bath of your own,' she said. 'Tons of bubbles. Not too hot but not at all cold. Very perfect. And then I think we should get a couple of new tricks up and running, as well as the ones you already know, and get out there and see how many banknotes we can magic directly into our pockets.'

I was lying in the bath, my head underwater, when Natasha came into the bathroom and sat on the lid of the loo. I was mortified and hoped very much that the bubbles weren't going to pop, but she was unperturbed.

'So,' she said. 'Oh, here. I got you a drink.' She put a glass of something that looked like champagne on the edge of the bath, and I smiled and widened my eyes. I couldn't actually pick it up without the bubbles falling off my chest, so I didn't. 'Local cava,' she said. 'Cheers.' Luckily she didn't have a drink with her to clink with mine.

'Cheers,' I said back without moving.

'So. I'm going to teach you the transferable cross, and one more card trick. Early evening is the time for tourists. Aperitif time. And, Libby – I wanted to talk to you about tomorrow.'

'Yeah,' I said. 'Me too.'

'What do you want to do?'

I looked away. 'I need to go back and check on my mum.'

'Yes. I thought so. You want to go back to your mother, and I want to go to Paris. Totally different plans. So I have

193

a proposition. Let's meet in the middle: why don't we stay in Madrid for a couple of weeks and hustle for money. Street magic and tarot. When we have enough to fund a trip to Paris you can either come with me or go home. Because I'm going there anyway.'

I put my head right underwater so I didn't have to look at her. When I came up I said, 'I have to see Mum. It's always been me and her. There were years when it was just the two of us, before she met Sean. She didn't have an easy time. I mean, she had to send me off to be a bridesmaid for my dad twice. I can't abandon her.'

'Hey,' said Natasha. 'Of course you can't. That would be terrible. You remember that she does want you to have adventures this summer, right? You heard her saying that. We both did.'

'I know.'

'So – give her a call and see what she says. You're seventeen. That's adult in lots of places. You're safe here with me. You know that. And I think we'll be able to get enough money together to support ourselves. But it's up to you. If I were you, though, I'd do this: speak to Aunt Amy and say you're fine, and she'll hear it in your voice that you really are. Remind her again that she actually told you to do this, to go off and have an adventure, only the other day. I know we can make enough money to rent ourselves a couple of beds in a hostel. Don't worry: I've stayed in lots of them and they're safe. We'll be in a women-only room. And then we take it from there. Paris, or not-Paris.'

'We don't need to make the money to go to Paris, though,' I said. 'My dad gave me a card to a savings account. I could pay. I'll buy you a ticket.' I remembered all the money that her father had left to my dad. Even though it didn't mean anything because it wouldn't arrive in time for us to use it, I felt bad about it.

'No way,' she said. 'We fund this ourselves. Keep your college fund. Assume you're going to need it. I entirely refuse your offer.'

Natasha crossed her legs, far more elegant than anyone sitting on a loo had any business to be.

'It might be fun to stay here a little bit longer,' I conceded.

'Yes. It would.' We stared into each other's eyes for a while.

'Just a few more days rather than a couple of weeks. If I speak to her and explain, and if she sounds OK, then let's do it.'

'That's my girl. Now get out of there and we'll work up a few more tricks.'

I was relieved when she left the room so I could get out of the bath without her eyes on me. I dried myself quickly and put on the bathrobe, and took a gulp of cava, and I felt wonderful. I had never felt before that everyone wanted me, but now I was torn between Moralzarzal, where I was wanted, and Madrid, where I was also wanted. Not only that, but I was wanted at home, in Winchester. I knew Dad wanted to see me before the Creep, and I couldn't let it happen without seeing him and Anneka and the babies. Everyone wanted me. It was a strange feeling.

*

The first table we went to had an English family sitting at it. There were two adults and two children. The adults (who had been out in the sun and were pink and uncomfortable) were drinking wine, and the children (plastered in sun cream but still hot and grouchy) were swinging their legs and looking bored. My heart thumped as we approached the table.

'Come on, Libs,' said Natasha. 'Smile, smile, smile. Energy and charm! We're doing the parents a favour.'

She took my hand and yanked me over to the table.

'Hey there,' she said, talking to the children (a boy and a girl, aged perhaps eight and ten). The mother looked at us sharply.

'It's OK,' I said to her. 'We just want to try out a magic trick or two, if that's OK? We're not after anything.'

'Do you like magic?' Natasha was talking to the boy, the younger child, and I knew she would be locking eyes with him, making him feel like the only special person in the world.

He nodded.

'Do you?' She turned to the girl.

'If it's good.' The girl was older and sceptical. 'Not if it's bad, though. Normally I can see how they do it.'

'OK,' said Natasha. 'You'll tell us if it's good or bad, right?'

We launched straight into the tricks. Natasha had a set of squishy foam balls and doing the tricks with them was just a matter of practising the moves. She got the girl to hold out her hand and put two balls into it.

'Now close your hand,' she said. She talked and distracted the girl and got both parents and the brother to agree with her that there had been two balls there. Then she said, 'I have a feeling they've been doing a bit of multiplication, just between themselves. What's two multiplied by – I don't know – four?'

'Eight!' The boy was quick to shout that out.

'Open your hand.'

The girl opened it, and eight foam balls spilled out on to the table.

'Yeah,' said the girl. 'That's pretty cool actually. Can you show me how to do it?'

'Sorry,' said Natasha. 'Magic Circle. We're not allowed.'

I turned to the boy, my heart pounding, about to do my very first piece of street magic. I'd had a two-euro coin held in the palm of my hand for ages for this very moment. It was strangely easy to make your hand look normal, because the amount of grip needed to keep the coin between the base of the thumb and the bottom of the little finger was actually tiny.

'Hey,' I said. 'You've got something stuck in your hair. Right behind your ear. Hold on. Stay completely still. Don't move a muscle. I'll get it for you.'

He was suddenly rapt and held himself completely still. I made sure my hand was as natural as possible, and I reached for his ear, pulled a strand of his hair, and said in my most puzzled voice, 'Oh, it's money! What are you doing with money stuck in your hair? You must be a very rich guy if you can do that. Two euros!'

I showed it to him and transferred it to my other hand and put it in my pocket, while actually palming it again. Then I did it again and again and again, and on the fourth time I handed the coin to the boy.

'There you go,' I said. 'Lucky fourth coin. You can keep this one.'

He took it and stared at it.

'Thank you!' he said. 'That's so cool. How do you make euros come out of my hair? I really want to learn that.'

'Sorry,' I said. 'Magic Circle.' I had never felt this confident in my life. I felt myself becoming someone new, saw possibilities opening up in front of me.

'Right,' said Natasha. 'Thank you so much! We just wanted to try these things out. Thanks for letting us practise on you!'

'Do more,' said the girl. 'Please.'

'Yes,' the boy agreed. 'More, more, more.'

I looked to the parents, who looked agreeable.

'Well . . .' Natasha hesitated. 'Do you like card tricks?'

'Yes!' The two children spoke together, and Natasha did a card trick that amazed me too. It culminated with her getting the boy to lift up his shoe to reveal the jack of hearts on the ground under it.

'Thank you,' Natasha said, standing up.

The mother looked awkward. 'No. Thank *you*, girls. I have a feeling this is going to be the highlight of their holiday. Can we buy you a drink?'

'Oh, no thanks. I mean, it's hot and a drink is a lovely idea, but we have to keep moving.'

The dad handed Natasha a ten-euro note. 'Here. Get yourselves a drink when you're finished.'

'Thank you very much!' I said. 'That's very kind.'

Natasha beamed at everyone, and then said, 'Hey, there's something in your mom's hair.'

We left as the children both grabbed at the paper flower Natasha had dropped on to their mother's head. That part wasn't even magic, but it didn't matter at all.

'That went well,' I said. 'Ten euros!'

'Not bad. That's another lesson, right there. Sometimes they want you to sit and have a drink with them. But we never do, OK? Never. Always moving on. If they offer an actual drink, it's usually easy to convert it to money for one later. Like we did, back there. If we have a crowd, one of us goes round with a hat to collect money. Otherwise we just have to nudge them into it.'

'You've done this a lot,' I said. 'You really know what you're doing.' Every time I thought I had an idea of Natasha's life, it changed.

'Sure I have. My mom taught me. And then when Dad passed over and Mom became sick I travelled doing it. I went all over the States and Mexico. Constantly moving on. It was the only way I could distract myself. I followed the voices in my head.' She shrugged. 'It's the only thing I know how to do.'

I hugged her. 'It's really not. You have so many skills. You're amazing.'

There were lots of English-speaking tourists out, and the ones with children seemed to be behaving exactly as they used to do when the permafrost had been nicely frozen. Exactly like Anneka and Dad. They were completely carrying on as normal, apart perhaps from the fact that (unlike Anneka and Dad) they were in Madrid.

The early evening was what Natasha called 'the Anglo time of day' for drinking. I had no idea how she knew all this.

'Locals come out later,' she said. 'Tourists are great anyway. They're away from their normal lives, and they're here specifically to see new things and have experiences, and their money's soon going to be worthless anyway. The Creep thing is a godsend in a very micro way for us.'

I hadn't got the hang of the card tricks yet, except for the one with the corner of the queen taped on to another card, so when Natasha did them I stood back and watched. She was amazing, to the point where even though I knew how they worked, because she had shown me, I was still incredulous every time. It did feel like magic. She picked up lots of money for those. The one I was best at doing was the Svengali notebook. I told people again and again and again that they were thinking of Paris.

We got chased off by waiters from time to time but that made it even better. Running off laughing, round the corner to the next set of pavement tables, was the most exciting part of it all. I felt free, different, new.

'This is amazing,' I said to Natasha when we'd done seven tables and were stopping for a rest. 'How much money?'

She turned inwards towards the wall and counted it out.

'A very acceptable sixty-seven euros and fifty cents,' she said. 'Once we hit two hundred I think we can stop.'

By the time we got to two hundred euros I was exhausted, yet still exhilarated. It turned out that Natasha spoke French reasonably well too, and I was all right at it, and so we managed to entertain two sets of French tourists as well as the English-speaking ones and some people from the north of Spain.

Some people asked us if we were sisters. Every time they did, Natasha said 'twins' and we gave each other a special smile.

It was dark by the time we stopped for the night.

'Two hundred and five, plus a bit of change,' she said. 'Amazing. Back to the food market?'

We sat on hard-won high stools and ate prawns and drank cold white wine and fizzy water. Our seats were opposite each other this time, and I saw that Natasha was watching me, almost scrutinizing me.

'So, all change tomorrow,' she said. 'And you know what? It's going to be *all* change. I'm going to get my hair bleached with some of this cash.'

'I'll get mine cut then,' I said at once.

'Perfect. Two blondes hustling central Madrid. It's going to work. We can get some clothes the same. They don't have to cost much. Does that sound OK?'

I nodded. It did.

20. Worry about your mum

August

At the beginning of August there was a flood of news reports that even reached Natasha and me, though we were very much avoiding such things, that said scientists were working hard on a resolution to the poison issue, that they were cautiously optimistic. I didn't know anything about the science of it and I didn't care, but the people we spoke to started to cheer up a bit.

On August the twenty-first I stood in reception, waiting for Natasha, who had stopped to have a chat with a couple in their twenties who had arrived at the hostel two nights earlier. No one was staffing reception, and when the phone rang I reached over and answered it.

I was still, essentially, shy, but being Natasha's partner in crime had given me the tools that allowed me to appear brave. I answered the phone by pretending to be Carmen, or indeed Ana, who ran the hostel.

'*Digame*,' I said, like Ana did when she answered it. *Tell me*. I liked that.

A man's voice asked in Spanish whether there were three beds for tomorrow night. I took his name and number and said someone would call him back. I wrote it down on a piece of paper and put it on top of the other paperwork on the desk.

Then I carried on waiting, smiling at the people who came past. Everyone knew Natasha and me; we'd been here three weeks now and were part of the fittings. Oddly, these days people found it hard to tell us apart, even though our faces really didn't look alike. It was strange that as soon as our hair had more or less matched people stopped seeing beyond it. We were two white girls, the same height, in the same clothes, with the same hair, and so we were seen as identical. Natasha was right: misdirection was easy. We even had the same mannerisms.

I looked at my phone. There was a text from Mum.

> We're coming into the city
> today. Can you meet us?
> Lunchtime?

I checked the clock above Ana's desk. It was eleven.

> What sort of lunchtime? Twelve
> or three?

> One? 👻

Sure. See you there.

This would be the fourth time Mum and Sean had come
into Madrid to check on me. The previous three times it
had felt awkward, because on the one hand I was doing
the very thing she had wanted me to do, and on the other
I knew she desperately wanted me to leave Natasha and go
home to her. It was nearly the end of August and time was
running out. The city was impossibly hot, and everything
was hurtling towards the end.

And every time I saw Mum she was thinner, tenser, less
happy. I knew I had to talk to her properly, to make a
proposal. I would do it today.

Natasha appeared beside me, practically skipping.

'Those two are so cool,' she said. 'I think they're royalty
or something. They love Spain. They want to meet later for
a coffee. Is that OK?'

'Course,' I said. 'But I have to meet Mum and Sean for
lunch. She just texted. You don't have to come.'

'Thanks,' she said. 'I won't. I'll meet up with Neema
and Kweli, and you can call us when you're done. I don't
think your mother ever wants to see me again.'

She was right. It was much easier for me to see my
parents without Natasha there. That night when they'd
argued, when Natasha had tried to deliver a message from

someone called Violet, had changed their relationship completely.

Ana came rushing back. She had a floaty dress on, and fabulous gold sandals.

'Oh my God,' she said in Spanish. 'So busy! Normally the summer is never like this, and this week it's all gone mad! Why? Why do they do that? Why now?'

'I answered the phone,' I told her. 'I wrote down a message.'

She looked at it. 'Three beds for tomorrow,' she said with a laugh. 'Sure! That's not going to happen, mister. I'll send him a text. Hey, you two? Still OK for the psychic evening? I'm printing posters this morning so it's your last chance to change your minds. Otherwise it's tomorrow night.'

Natasha and I looked at each other. 'Sure.'

'Every time I mention it everyone is so excited. We'll charge to come in and we'll split it, OK?'

'Yes,' said Natasha. 'Split it three ways – two thirds to us and one third to you.'

Ana looked at her, then sighed. 'OK. Sure. The hostel is full, and I think we'll do well. Everyone will love it.'

Everyone else was dashing around so fast that no one stayed anywhere for more than a couple of days. No one said 'bucket list' any more; they said 'end times' – 'I'm doing it for end times'. We had watched the city change from quiet to busy to quiet to busy again. It happened in waves that made no particular sense.

Outside, Madrid was hotter and hotter and hotter, and as August rushed by it began to feel frantic. The human race was panicking. Whatever this carbon breakthrough had been, it hadn't changed that.

People were trying to fit in everything they could while it was still an option. As the temperatures went up so did the pace of life. The Madrileños, as I had learned to call them, had fled to the coast, or to the rest of the world, by train, car and ship, lists in hand. The city was forty-five degrees, then forty-eight, then fifty. It was never going to cool down.

We shared a five-bed dormitory with a shifting population of female backpackers who always wanted us to teach them magic. There were always people around to talk to and I was, magically, able to speak most of the time. Having Natasha at my side made me invincible.

My Spanish was much better now, unlocked by confidence. Lots of people spoke English anyway, but I preferred to speak Spanish because I could summon Carmen to help me. The walls of the hostel were brightly painted, the breakfast was included, and there was always music playing and usually someone dancing.

'*Chau!*' said Ana, giving us a wave as we left the building and stepped out on to the street that, even though I knew what to expect, was a wall of heat. I pulled my hair back and tied it with the hairband that was on my wrist. I didn't miss my long hair at all. It had been like wearing a hot-water bottle.

The street was quiet and residential, and we walked along side by side, carving a path through the heavy air. Natasha looked at me and tied her hair back too. She was much stricter than I was about us looking the same at all times.

We always wore brightly coloured dresses we'd bought for five euros each from a street stall, haggled down from fifteen as they were packing up at the end of the day. They were cotton and floaty, just above knee length, and above all they were cool. We had three sets: they were red, orange and yellow, and we wore them with black flip-flops. Today we were in orange.

I could hear distant shouting. There was a wildness in the air. Sometimes it felt as if the whole city would tip over into riot and burn itself to the ground, but it never quite did. There was as much contemplation as there was excitement. It felt as if anything could happen, when, in fact, the only thing on anyone's mind was the one massive thing that was scheduled for next month.

I had no idea what was going on in the world at large, and I liked it like that.

'Right,' Natasha said. 'I'm going to try to call my own mom. See how she's doing. You meet your people. Keep them happy. Are you going to tell them our plans?'

'I have to,' I said.

We were easily making four hundred euros a day, just by doing straightforward magic tricks at tables in tourist areas. Sometimes we entertained little groups of children and took a hat round their parents, but most of the time we only asked for money indirectly. Everyone offered to buy us a drink once we'd successfully pulled off a trick, and we were both now experts at converting offers of drinks into money. Drinks were five euros at these kinds of tourist places, then, as August went on, often ten.

Sometimes men harassed and propositioned us, but Natasha gave me ways of dealing with that too. I learned to be as rude to the men who thought we were fair game as I had been to Miguel. We looked out for each other, and so far we had kept each other safe. Some days I had no idea what was me and what was Natasha.

I knew lots of tricks, but far better than the actual tricks, which all involved holding something in your hand or tucking things into other things, or making people look one way while the trickery went on elsewhere, was the fact that I'd had to become confident. It was confidence that made it flow. We had to sweep people into our world and make them delight in being deceived. That was what let us misdirect them and wrong-foot them. It was fun. They enjoyed it too; in the same way people loved films and books with surprising endings, they also loved to be surprised by a thing that didn't seem possible. Sometimes people seriously asked us to use our powers to stop the Creep, and we assured them that we were trying our best.

I had expanded my repertoire to encompass what Natasha called 'psychic reassurance'. I could do palm reading and tarot cards (I had passed my sixth challenge), and I knew we would do that as part of the psychic night. Natasha freely agreed that all that stuff was rubbish, and she had taught me what to say. But I wasn't going to go near the actual spirit realm, because I could only see it as part of the world of confidence trickery.

*

'There she is!' Mum rushed up and grabbed me. She held me tight, rocking back and forth. 'Oh, darling. It's so lovely to see you. How are you?'

'Hey there, Libby,' said Sean. 'How's it going?'

'Good, thanks,' I said. We were outside the food market, at the entrance on the corner. I was dripping with sweat. It really was too hot to do anything now.

'You look thin,' said Mum. 'Are you eating? Are you OK for money?'

'Yes,' I said. 'I'm eating loads, I promise. I guess I'm just sweating it off. We're fine for money.' I looked at Mum properly. 'Actually,' I said, '*you* look thin. Are you eating?'

Every time I saw her I expected her to be back to normal. Each time, though, she was a bit worse. She never asked me to go back with them. If she had, I would probably have done it.

'Of course,' she said. 'Right. I guess we're going in here then.'

We walked inside and it was as clattery and noisy as ever. There was nowhere to sit, so we stood at the end of one of the trestle tables to wait. Otherwise, I supposed, we could eat standing up, or take our food away like Natasha and I had done that first time.

Mum sighed. 'I know this is wonderful and authentic,' she said. 'But actually, darling, couldn't we go to a real restaurant? With air con? This is a bit much. It makes me feel . . . panicky.'

I saw the look in her eyes and agreed. We didn't have to come here; she was right that it was intense. And she didn't look healthy, not at all. I wanted her to be sitting down.

Ten minutes later we were at a quiet table in a random half-empty restaurant that was closing for good the next day, and I had to admit that it was better. The room was air conditioned, and the whole place felt calm. I realized that I had got used to being in the frantic places, the hot places, the places in which people would happily part with their money if they liked a magic trick.

Sean looked at Mum and, before she could say anything, he started speaking fast.

'Libby,' he said. 'I'm glad you're doing so well. And try not to worry about Amy. She'll be OK.'

She looked worse, sitting down. She was jittery, and her eyes were darting all over the place. She had been a bit like this the last time I'd seen her, but it was worse today.

'I shouldn't be here,' she said. 'I need to be at meditation. I shouldn't be missing it. I can't do that. The odds have got better since I started this. We can save it if we carry on.'

Sean put his hand over hers. 'It's OK, Amy,' he said. 'You can do it when we get back. It won't change anything today.' He looked at me and I saw the plea in his eyes.

'But it might,' she said.

I didn't know what to say. I sipped my Coke and waited to see what would happen. Neither of them said anything either, so in the end I said, 'Does the meditation make you happy?' It sounded so lame that I wished I could take it back. 'You don't look happy,' I added.

'It did at first, didn't it?' Sean said. 'I'm not sure it does now.'

'I don't do it to *be happy*,' said Mum in a quiet voice. 'With the power of our minds we can keep the air pure.'

'I'm not sure that's how it works, Mum,' I said, and she flinched.

'It is,' she said. 'And if you'd open your mind you'd see it.'

The waiter was standing nearby, and I turned to him and ordered our food. Both of them had already said what they wanted, so it was easy to do. When I looked back they were staring at me.

'Libby,' said Sean. 'You're like a different person.'

'It's been good for me, being here,' I said. 'I know Natasha seems difficult, but she makes me feel I can do things.'

'She does seem to have been good for you,' said Sean, looking nervously at my mother. 'Confidence-wise.'

Mum leaned forward and whispered, just to me.

'Do what you like,' she said, so close to my ear that it felt strange. 'But you tell Natasha that if she so much as *thinks* Violet's name again I will kill her. I know what she is. A fraud.'

I stared at her. 'Mum,' I said.

She was looking at the table. Sean reached for her hand.

'Hey, Amy,' he said. 'Let it go.'

Mum shook herself a bit and seemed to change. Her tone became distant and a bit other-worldly.

'I don't like her,' she said. 'She has a negative energy.'

I had no idea how to deal with this, and when I looked at Sean I saw that he didn't either.

'Well, let's go home to Winchester then,' I said. 'Get away from all this. The three of us. Together. Now.'

'No,' said Mum.

I waited for her to elaborate, and when she didn't I was suddenly furious. I had offered her, I thought, an amazing option. She just didn't seem to like anything.

'You know what?' I said. 'I can't even have an opinion on this because you won't tell me what it's about. I have no idea what you and Natasha are arguing about, or who Violet is or was, because I'm stupid little Libby and no one tells me anything. That's fine. You can think what you want and do what you want and keep us all safe by the power of your mind or whatever, but if that's how you're going to be, I'm going to go to Paris.'

We sat in silence for a while. I saw Sean frantically looking at Mum, but she was shut away behind whatever her barrier was about. He turned to me.

'Just give things a bit of time,' he said. 'Sure, go to Paris, but come back to us.'

'We do have return train and ferry tickets, don't we?' I said, just to him. 'I'll be back for that. Leaving on the last day of August, and arriving home on the first of September, right? And college starts soon after that. I do want to go to college. I want to see my friends. I want to see Zoe. I want things to feel normal.' We all knew, though, that nothing would feel normal again.

The waiter arrived and put down the food. I had ordered a prawn risotto. Sean had chicken and potatoes. Mum had a bowl of gazpacho, and she stirred it with her spoon and didn't particularly eat it. She had always loved her food. I hated seeing her like this. The most stable person in my life was cracking up.

After a while she stood up and looked around.

'Libby,' she whispered. 'Can you ask the way to the loo for me?'

She could easily have asked for herself, in English if she'd wanted, but I walked over to a waiter and asked, and then conveyed the information back to Mum, and sat down again.

'What the hell is going on with her?' I said as soon as she had gone. 'She's a completely different person. Is her thing a cult? How can we get her home?'

'I did wonder that,' said Sean. 'About it being a cult. But actually, no, it really is a meditation class. She's thrown herself into it because everything else is so difficult. That thing that Natasha said about Violet. It really upset her, but it's not just that. That is the tip of the iceberg. It's not for me to fill you in, Libby, though I would if I could.'

'Yeah.' I rolled my eyes.

'It's up to her. And also, yes, Amy has decided to channel the power of her mind into saving the world. You know Amy; she's always been a sceptic, but as soon as this business came along she woke up desperate for meaning. It's had the most profound effect.'

'The church,' I said. 'The temples, the mosque.'

'And now you're the one who's thriving, and she's . . . fading away. She feels she's taking action against it somehow, and that's led to her thinking it's all on her.'

'How about you?' I felt very grown-up to be asking my stepfather this question. I didn't think I'd ever asked him how he was before, except when he'd been ill. 'It must be intense with her like this.'

'Oh God, Libs,' he said, with a smile. 'Tell me about it. I agree with you that we have to get her back home.'

'OK.' I knew she would return soon, so I carried on quickly. 'Look. Sorry I snapped at her, but this is so frustrating. The whole *Violet* thing. What is it?'

'I wish I could tell you, but she's made me swear not to. It's . . . complicated. And unresolved. And it's three quarters of her problem actually.'

We had to stop talking then because Mum came back from the loo. She looked so pale that she was almost a ghost herself. If I tried, I could see the ghosts around her, pushing her along, trying to help.

I shovelled away my prawns and rice, drained my Coke, and watched my mother not eating her soup, and drinking three glasses of wine on an empty stomach.

'I'm glad she's got you,' I said to Sean, not even lowering my voice. 'Thank you for looking after her.' I wanted her to know that I appreciated Sean, who had been a far less complicated father figure to me than my real father ever had.

He turned to Mum. 'Libby will be back from Paris in a week. That's great, isn't it?'

'I'm only going for a few days. Just to see it. Loads of people we've met have been heading there, and I want to do it. There are parties there all next week. I'll come back.'

Mum didn't react. She seemed to have tuned out altogether.

'Be safe,' said Sean. 'Have you got enough money?' I nodded. 'I trust you to stay safe, right? Call your father before you go. And keep in touch with us.'

'OK,' I said. I had thought it would be harder than this. I'd expected Mum to beg me not to go, to do everything she could to take me back to the house with her. Instead it seemed Mum didn't give a shit what I did.

It was strange saying goodbye to her. She was so thin, so distracted, so absent. It was the worst she had ever been. When I hugged her she was bony and trembling. I felt guilty about leaving her.

'OK,' I said, because I didn't really know what else to say. 'Anything else?'

'That's all.' I watched her rallying herself. 'I love you. Be sensible. Come back.'

21. Showcase your new skills

The following evening we took over the little lounge at the hostel. We'd draped it in fabric that made it look mysterious, and Natasha had found a cloth and put it over the table that we'd dragged to the front of the room. The chairs were lined up for an audience, and we were ready.

Natasha said we had to make hundreds of euros from this performance, because we weren't going to hustle in Paris. 'That place is already full of hustlers,' Natasha had said. 'But you know what's going on there right now? Parties. Huge, amazing parties. Grand balls to mark the end of civilization. Raves. Midnight concerts in Notre-Dame. Boat parties on the Seine. It's wild. I want us to have money to spend. We need to take five hundred euros from this at least.'

I had tried my best to persuade her to let me pay.

'That money,' I'd said, feeling awkward. 'It was money from our grandparents. It's yours too. Please let me buy the train tickets and pay for somewhere to stay. I'd like to.'

Natasha, however, had refused to hear of it.

'No way,' she said. 'I pay my own way. You'll need that money for the future.'

Now, as I sat behind the table, I wished I had tried harder, even though I knew she would never have let me pay. I thought I was more nervous in this moment than I had ever been in my life about anything. My performance as Juliet had been terrifying, as had the moment in my first GCSE exam when I turned over the paper and thought: *This is it. I'm doing my exams.* I had been scared loads of times (and actually for the Juliet one I'd been sick) but for some reason today was in a different league.

It shouldn't have been. I had been performing for a living for weeks. We were going to Paris in the morning, and I wondered whether my nerves were partly because of that. I felt sure it was the right thing to do because of the look in my mother's eyes: she didn't want me with her right now. She had shut me out. It was just scary to go to a new place, to start again. I loved Madrid and I was going to miss it.

Natasha was excited by all of it. She was manic, delighted, and I knew that 'seeing Paris' was the last item on her end-times list, so I could understand how she felt. When she had seen Paris, there would be nothing left to do but wait.

We didn't mention 'Violet' at all. I wasn't engaging with it any more. Life was too short to worry about secrets. I was worrying about our performance instead.

'So,' said Natasha. 'I'll do all the messages from the spirits. You can do palm readings and tarot because you're great at that. Remember people are here because they want to be. Some just for the entertainment. Some because they're curious. Some of them will be here because they want to know about the future – well, everyone wants to know about the Creep. But a few people will be here because they genuinely want to get messages from people they've lost, and those are the messages we'll give them.'

'I know,' I said, and even though I had watched Natasha conveying messages from dead relatives many times, I still felt weird about it.

'It's real, Libby,' said Natasha, looking exasperated. 'I know you're fighting it. I know you've grown up in a sceptical atheist world. But I hear the messages and I pass them on. If you let yourself, I know you could hear them too, and pass them on as well. Our clients want to know something. We tell it to them. You know? What's wrong with that? I'm just the medium with the message.'

I rolled my eyes at her, smiling. That end phrase was the title of this show. *The mediums with the message*, with Natasha and Olivia. ('Lucky we both already have psychic types of names,' she had said.)

Ana bounced into the room. She was tiny and flexible, always dancing around.

'Hey, ladies,' she said in English. 'Are you ready? We've sold every single seat in this room and some more behind, *and* there's a waiting list. It's a packed house. You already have your five hundred euros.'

My stomach dropped. I wanted to crawl under the table and hide, but I forced myself to smile.

'Bring them in!' said Natasha, and as people started to file through the door she greeted each one of them, kicking me under the table so I would do the same.

'Hey there!' she said. *'Hola! Buenas noches! Bonjour!'* She flashed them a brilliant smile. 'Come in, sit down.'

'Hi!' I said. It sounded pathetic. I took a deep breath and, in a way that could only make sense to me, I channelled Juliet. I pretended to be Juliet Capulet sticking by the boy she loved in spite of everything else, and I used her spirit to help me.

'Buenas noches! Bonsoir! Can you find a seat? Is everyone OK?' I stood up, moved chairs around, settled everyone down. Suddenly I was hyper. I felt, rather than saw, Natasha laughing at me. We were so attuned now. I was starting to believe that we really were twins. If I'd had a sibling, I thought again, I would have grown up to be very different.

Natasha stood up and asked everyone what language they wanted the evening run in. *'Español?* English? *Français?'* Because there was a group of Russians there who spoke English much better than Spanish, and some Americans and Australians, we ended up agreeing to compère in English, but everyone who had a reading could have it in a language of their choice as long as we spoke it. I thought the Spanish people there were extremely gracious about that.

Natasha started it off.

'Who wants to go first?' she said. 'Let's begin with a palm reading. That's good to break the ice. Who wants to do it? We've all got hands, and all of them tell a story.'

Ana from the hostel came up first, as we had secretly arranged in advance, so we could be sure things would start well. Natasha took her hand and did a palm reading. She told her that she came from the countryside, that she loved her job but wanted something more from life, that there was something very exciting just round the corner.

'Forget this creeping thing.' She turned and said it to the whole of the room. 'In fact, can we say that now? Forget. The. Creep. It's going to be OK, and a lot of what we're talking about is the stuff that will come after the scare passes. For the next few weeks we all just need to stay safe and trust in our lungs. Humanity can do more good than bad. It will be neutralized, and good will come from it. Humanity will do things differently.'

'Try not to worry,' I said. 'It's a strange time.'

I listened to myself, a teenager, advising these adults. They listened to us. It was odd.

'You have a particular dream,' Natasha said to Ana, studying her hand. 'Don't you? Something you don't talk about often?'

Ana blushed and nodded.

'It's OK. You don't have to tell us what it is. But let me tell you this. You're going to go for it. You're going to get your energy together, risk rejection and you're going to absolutely go for it. And it's going to work. Not in the way you might expect, but it'll work for you in a way beyond all your imaginings. And your life will be transformed.'

The words in themselves were trite. They were stupid things, the same phrases Natasha had told me to use in every reading I ever gave. It was the way she said them. It was her charisma. She had Ana's hand in hers, and she was gazing at it as if what she was reading there was the most astonishing thing in the world.

I could see that there were only Natasha and Ana, that she had created a cocoon for the two of them.

'Is it true?' said Ana, and her voice was quiet.

'Yes. It takes a lot of resolve from you, but look.' I watched Natasha brushing Ana's palm with her fingertip. 'That. That's your line of determination and success. See how strong it is? In lots of people there are two lines here, but for you there's just one. Determination and success are completely interlinked for you, Ana. They have grown together into one immense character trait that means you can do anything. For a small person you are very strong. No one should underestimate Ana.'

When Ana went to sit down there was a stupendous round of applause. Natasha did a second reading, for a Russian man, and then it was my turn.

I hoped no one would ever know I was doing this in character as Juliet. That sounded madder than anything.

Natasha picked a young man for me, an Australian boy who was wearing a wedding ring. I knew that if I hesitated I would be lost, and so I didn't stop for breath.

'Hey there!' I smiled at him, and then round at everyone else. I projected a personality. I was in control here. 'Grab a seat and let's have a look into your life. How would you like to do it?'

'Could we do, like, tarot cards?' he said. He was skinny and white, with a sunburned face and a diffident manner. I thought he was so edgy that he probably had a particular question.

'Sure we can!' I had been hoping it wouldn't be this, but I tried not to show it. I handed him the cards. 'Right. Think about the issues you're looking for guidance on.' I smiled inwardly at the way my English teacher would have hated that sentence. No one here cared. 'And cut the cards. Cut them nine times and lift up the card on the bottom of your ninth cut. All right? Nine is a mystical number, less obvious than seven, and I think it chimes with your character.' I mimed what he needed to do. 'You have an amazing aura,' I added. 'I think you're a bit psychic yourself, are you? Do you sometimes have odd things happening to you – the kinds of things that don't happen to other people?'

He laughed. 'Yeah,' he said. 'I do a bit. Actually, yeah.' He cut the cards, doing it exactly as I'd shown him, and turned over his ninth selection. 'The Chariot!' I said. 'That's absolutely incredible. Thank you. I had a feeling it would be this.' *I must not hesitate, I must not hesitate.* Natasha had said tarot was so loose you could literally make up anything as long as you did it with conviction. 'Well, it's no surprise that you picked that one on first glance. The chariot. It's about travellers, adventurers. You've come here from far, far away on your chariot, haven't you, Robbie? You're an adventurer, coming such an immense distance from home when there are no aeroplanes. When we all had this deadline imposed on us it was a wake-up call to lots of us to get out there and see the world, but for you it's more than that. It's about not being daunted in the face of the odds. People in chariots are absolutely determined to get to the place they want to go. They smash obstacles out of their way. And even though you're a human being with a gentle soul, you don't get put off by obstacles, do you? You just smash through them, no matter what.'

I went on like that for a while, and he nodded his agreement.

'My wife and I came straight out here,' he said, and he looked around the room. He seemed a bit guilty, so I went with that.

'She's not in the room, is she?' I said. 'But she's staying here at the hostel with you?'

'Yeah. No offence, but she doesn't like this kind of thing. She went out tonight instead.'

'Sure,' I said. 'Some people are more close-minded than others. I'm sensing you're feeling some dilemmas about the relationship. Don't feel bad about that. Every feeling is valid in here, and it's a safe place to talk.'

It really wasn't.

'Oh my God,' he said. He blushed a deep purple. 'Yes. We've been together since we were fourteen, which is ten years, and I suppose . . . I keep finding myself thinking about freedom now at the end times. About what it would be like if I wasn't with Shell all the time.'

'Let's see what the tarot suggests. Cut them again.'

His next card was the High Priest. He looked at me for guidance.

'Oh,' I said. 'Right. Well, this represents wisdom, and what this card is telling me is that you should look inside for the answer. You know what it is. It's in you. You just have to face it.'

I couldn't bring myself to tell this man, who was seven years older than me, with many times more life experience, to leave his wife.

'Right,' he said. 'I just have to face it. OK. I know what that means.' He smiled. 'Thank you!'

His final card was the Five of Cups, and that meant that if he chose to follow his heart he would find incredible things happening to him. But not in the way he expected (that was Natasha's prime rule for this stuff: you give amazing, but vague, predictions, and add 'but not in the way you expect').

Robbie was unnervingly delighted. I was pleased that my first public attempt had gone well, but I was also unsettled. It was, I reminded myself, entertainment.

There was only time for ten readings, seven of them given by Natasha. At least another ten people wanted to book in for private ones at another time, and we told them that we were leaving in the morning so they couldn't.

Then Natasha clapped her hands. 'Can we turn the lights down?' she said. 'By way of an encore I'd like to take this into somewhat different territory. I've had voices of a couple of very insistent characters in my head all evening. They're people who've passed over into the spirit realm.'

'Dead people,' explained an American to her friend loudly, and there was a general nervous laugh.

'Yes, if you like. Though they prefer to talk about the spirit realm, because they very much still exist. They have their thoughts and feelings and loves, just as they always did.'

I pushed my chair back, a little way away from Natasha. I knew that I couldn't play any part in this at all and I wasn't comfortable with it.

'Cool,' said a Spanish boy.

'If this isn't for you – and it's not for everyone, that goes without saying – then you should leave. It's all going to be from me, because I have a spirit guide called Walter, and he is highly insistent. Olivia's guide is Carmen, but Olivia's good at shutting her out because she gets annoying, so they are going to observe rather than participate. Only stay for this if you have someone you think might be wanting to communicate with you or if you'd like to support those who do. Everyone else – thank you so much for coming and I hope you have a wonderful rest of the evening! Feel free to put anything you want into the tips jar! It's by the door. *Muchas gracias!*'

Almost everyone stayed, though Robbie left. The lights were switched off and Ana fetched a little lamp and put it on the table, changing the atmosphere completely.

I didn't want to be a part of this, but I knew I couldn't leave. Natasha had just said I would be observing; to walk out would look very aggressive. I walked to the back of the room and watched from there.

22. Uncover the family secrets

She closed her eyes, and when she opened them again, she was someone different. Her voice had become lower, and her accent had changed subtly.

'Bear with me,' this voice said. 'It takes me some time to get comfortable in this body. Greetings to you all. I am Walter, and I bring you salutations from the world of the spirits. I am Natasha's spirit guide. I lived many years ago. Natasha and I, together, can work to bring you messages from your loved ones.'

I took a step back. I did not like Walter. I pictured him as a little ghost man, collecting messages from all the other ghosts and yelling them into Natasha's brain. It felt wrong, a crack in the order of things. Everyone else leaned forward, desperate to hear what he had to say.

Out of nowhere I laughed. It was so ridiculous. I pretended it was a sneeze and Natasha came out of character for a micro-second to give me a sharp look.

'You people, gathered in this room,' she said, back to Walter, 'have many loved ones. They wish to speak to you, and they are not being orderly about it.' She stood up and held her head. 'No! Stop! One of you, please. Just one of you. Thank you.'

Natasha sat back down. The room was silent.

'I have a message,' Walter's voice said, 'from a very persistent spirit who begins with J. Does anyone in this room have someone whose name began with J?'

Several hands went up.

'And they want to speak to someone with a B.'

A woman was on her feet. 'I think this is me,' she said. She was Spanish but speaking in English; Walter clearly didn't speak Spanish. 'My name is Bonita, and my father . . . my father was Jorge.'

Natasha was silent. 'Yes,' she said, in Walter's voice. 'Jorge. I didn't understand because he was saying he begins with J, but to my silly ears it sounds like the letter H. Exactly that. He loves you so, so much, Bonita. That is what he wishes to say. He says he's sorry, and he loves you. Does that make sense?'

'Yes,' she whispered. 'Tell him I miss him every day.'

'He has regrets about the way he died. He is sorry. So, so sorry.'

'Yes. I'm sorry.'

'He died suddenly. He wasn't ready.'

'He was ill for a long time, but . . . I suppose we weren't ready for him to die on that day.'

'Yes. He wasn't ready either. When it came, it came suddenly, and all this time he has been hoping for an opportunity to get a message to you. That he loves you. He's proud of you. He will be waiting for you.'

'Is he with Luna?'

'Yes. Luna sends you love too. She is happy!'

'Yes! She's my dog. She died just before he did.'

'Exactly. They are together all the time. Luna has a new lease of life now. She is bounding around the place.'

They talked like this for a while, and I was amazed. It was a side of Natasha I had never seen properly: in fact, it didn't seem like Natasha at all. It felt as if Walter was talking through her body, which was exactly how she said it worked. I reminded myself that she was doing this consciously. It was a trick that she had practised. It wasn't real.

All the same, it did look convincing and I found I couldn't look away. For the next hour I watched her giving messages from people in the afterlife, and I struggled with the feeling that, despite everything, there was something real happening here.

I knew there wasn't.

And then I thought there was.

I didn't know what I thought.

I watched her delivering messages to Kweli and a few other people around the room, and although – if you took away the surroundings and the theatre of it all – the messages were bland and reassuring, they reduced everyone to tears. And because the whole room desperately wanted to believe in them I found that I teetered on the brink of being convinced.

After twenty minutes I decided to slip away; I was halfway through the door when Walter/Natasha shouted: 'I have a Violet! She is looking for someone beginning with a letter O or L, but really her message is for A. Does that make sense to anyone?'

I froze. I looked back. Natasha locked eyes with me.

I didn't say anything.

'Her name begins with O or L, and it's a message from Violet,' Natasha said again. 'O's spirit guide wanted to tell her, but she was locked out.'

Everyone was looking at me, partly because Natasha was, but also because she was clearly talking about me.

'I don't know Violet,' I said.

'I know you don't,' Walter agreed. 'She wants to speak to your mother, is that right? She begins with A.'

'Amy,' I said. 'You know that.' My heart was beating very, very fast. I *knew* that Natasha was just making this up, but I couldn't move. I wanted the strength to shake my head and leave the room properly, but instead I took a step back into the room.

'Yes. Amy. This is what Violet says: *Amy – I forgive you. I still love you and I always have done. It wasn't your fault. Please be safe. Olivia, I wish I had met you, my little sister. Your life would have been different.*'

'OK,' I whispered, and when Natasha moved on I left the room.

My little sister.

I was pulled out of myself by a woman who grabbed me and screamed into my face. I could tell by her breath that she had been drinking.

'What the hell did you tell him!' she shouted. 'Robbie. It was you, wasn't it? You told him to leave me! You fucking bitch! He's done it! Thanks for that.'

I stared at her. 'I didn't. I told him to follow his heart.'

She burst into tears and collapsed in on herself, and I walked away. I felt terrible. I went to our bedroom and lay down and cried into the pillow. I was glad we were leaving tomorrow: I certainly didn't want to run into Robbie or his wife again.

'Natasha,' I whispered later.

It was two in the morning and neither of us was sleeping.

'Yes?'

'Robbie's wife shouted at me.'

'Yeah. I heard. Don't worry. You didn't make him do anything. You just told him to follow his heart. It's not your fault that following his heart will lead him to spend the rest of his time going after Spanish women.'

'I feel bad.'

'Don't. Not your circus.'

I nodded, even though she couldn't see. That had only been my preamble anyway.

'Is Violet really my sister? Did I have a sister who died?'

Her face appeared, upside down. She was looking at me from her top bunk. Her hair was falling down.

'Yes. Sorry, Libs. You did,' she whispered. 'That's what Walter and Dad say, and I believe them.'

I nodded, even though it was dark. 'I shouldn't know that. Mum isn't ready to tell me.' I thought about it. Now Mum's collapse made a kind of sense. 'Does she have the same dad?'

'No. Your mom was young.' One of the other girls turned over in bed, and I didn't know what to say. I knew that Natasha had decided to tell me, and had used 'Walter' to do it dramatically in public, and I tried to push the knowledge away. 'Violet is from her past,' Natasha continued, 'and, as you know, she wants to speak to Amy. She's insistent.'

I imagined a big sister called Violet. I pictured my mother going through something horrific when she was young. No wonder she had fallen apart when Natasha said the name.

Natasha's breathing changed, and she slowly fell asleep. I just lay there, on top of my sheets in the hot night. I could hear four sets of breathing, and the odd creak as someone turned over in bed. I felt wider awake than I ever had in my entire life. I thought I would stay awake until the end of time. I cried for the big sister I had never had.

I wrote a text to my mother, but deleted it without sending it. I needed to do this in person, not by text. I needed to look into her eyes. I needed her to be ready. I would see her in a week, and I would tell her, then, that I knew.

I longed to talk to someone who didn't know Natasha. I wanted a break from being her other half, her twin. I'd had two messages from Max and hadn't replied to them (Natasha's instructions to me to ditch him had, somehow, been effective). Instead I wrote to Zoe. I didn't write about Violet. I hadn't sent her a short, breezy message for weeks, so I just wrote a few of the things that I wanted to say.

Hi Zoe – how is August going? I'm still in Madrid and it's amazing. I feel very different from the way I used to be. I've learned to do magic and to read palms and tarot cards, and that's just the start of it. Tomorrow I'm off to Paris.

I know we haven't talked about it since it happened, but I just wanted to say sorry to you if I made anything feel awkward at Vikram's party. Performing as Juliet with you was incredible, and, whatever happens next month, I want to say thank you for that. It was one of the best experiences of my life, and you are very talented and brilliant.

I'm writing this in a bunk bed in a Madrid hostel. It's too hot to sleep, but everyone else in the room has managed it. My cousin Natasha is on the top bunk above me. I'm travelling with her for the moment. We're going to go to Paris tomorrow and then I think we'll go our separate ways from there. She's taught me all the tricks. Where are you?

See you next month. I'm planning to be home on September the first. Can we meet up?

Love,

Libby xxx

I looked over it, and then, in an extreme break with my own protocol, I sent it.

It was almost light by the time I fell asleep, and then I only tossed and turned for an hour or so, dreaming of Violet, before I was up again.

Natasha leaped down from her top bunk in one elegant move.

'Libby!' she said. 'Guess what? It's time to go to Paris! And something absolutely amazing is going to happen when we get there. I've got us on the guest list for a huge party. On the twenty-eighth of August. You know the parties I was talking about? It's the best one out of all of them.'

PART THREE

PARIS

23. Don't trust anyone

Two hours later we were at the station. I didn't want to go. Natasha had said Violet was my sister, and I was being pulled back to Mum. I wanted to know if it was true. And I knew that Mum needed me. I felt that somehow I had stolen her strength.

But I was seventeen, and I had never seen Paris. We were all going to die, and anyway I was only going for a few days.

The station was filled with plants. There were huge trees growing through the atrium and up to the glass ceiling. It felt like its own ecosystem, like an indoor rainforest. I was enchanted.

'Olivia Lewis,' Natasha said, seeing me hanging back, 'the world might end next month. And neither of us has ever seen the city of love. You're going for less than a week. On August the twenty-ninth you can come back and fix your mom, and take her home on the trains and ship you've already booked. There's time. She'll be ready to talk by then.'

She took me by the hand and, as ever, I was swept up. She pulled me, laughing, towards the train.

It was the most seductive thing. A train to Paris in the hot European summer. Everything we had was in our bags (again, free-spirited Natasha was twirling around in her backpack, while I pulled my suitcase like a tourist). I loved it that we were carrying our lives with us.

We changed trains at a place called Figueres, but we didn't leave the station, even though it was Dalí's birthplace and I was sure it would have been cool. We just sat in the cafe and drank Diet Coke and ate tortilla sandwiches. We didn't even really talk to each other. I was a mix of excited about the adventure, and scared, and worried about my mother, but the surroundings made me languid. The sun was shining outside, and the cafe was sticky and friendly, with an older couple drinking red wine, and a few backpackers waiting, like us, for the train to France.

The next train was a double-decker, and it was completely different. I had never been on a double-decker train: I hadn't even known they existed. Our seats were on the top deck. Natasha pushed me into the window seat. I leaned against it and closed my eyes.

I dozed for hours, dreaming of Walter and poisonous air and suffocation and dinosaurs and tiny unknown Violet. Violet became a dinosaur. Natasha spoke to the dinosaur in Walter's voice. Violet kept nearly telling me, and nearly telling me, and nearly telling me her story.

I woke with my heart pounding, but I was just leaning on a window on a warm train, going through the south of France. The train was full, and I could smell people and perfume and coffee and food. I stayed where I was, my eyes closed. Natasha was chatting to a man across the aisle, and laughing, and (of course) she was speaking fluent French. The man was laughing too and leaning closer to her.

I looked at my phone. There was a message from a telecoms company welcoming me to France, and there were a few texts and emails from Mum, but the only message I opened was from Zoe.

Libby! So cool to hear from you. Loving the sound of your summer. Am in Winchester with the fam. Dad wanted to take us to Nigeria to reconnect with the family there, but turned out they wanted to come and visit us so we've done that instead. I'm at home, with loads of cousins here. 'Tis fun, but . . . not as much as doing magic tricks in Madrid/Paris!!!!!! OMG!!!!! Show me everything when you come back and let me know when you're here. I can't wait to see you. Let's meet up as soon as you're back.

And don't be silly about Vik's party. Nothing was awkward. It was fun.

Z xxx

It was a real message. I had sent mine, and I'd got one back. It had happened, in real life.

I smiled, and leaned my head back against the window, formulating a reply in my head while pretending to have drifted back to sleep. I could understand enough French to work out that the man Natasha was talking to was telling her about his bunker, stocked with tinned food, pasta and bottled water and compressed air that would last him and his family for a year. They were going to retreat there before the Creep and hope for the best. Natasha was telling him that talking about it in public was a grave error, because if people knew about his air supply they would turn up in the dystopian future wearing gas masks and bang on the door demanding to be admitted, and then his air would run out much faster.

They stopped talking. I felt the vibration of Natasha's phone in her bag, which was leaning on my thigh. I heard her say, 'Libs?' in a very quiet voice, and then I felt her take her phone and retreat.

I opened my eyes a few seconds later. Natasha had gone. I needed the loo, and so I stood up, took my bag because it had my purse in it, and walked to the end of the carriage.

I stood by the toilet door and heard my cousin's voice. She must have been just round the corner. I stopped, only for a moment, to listen.

'Not a thing,' she was saying in a quiet voice. 'Hundred per cent. Sweet, but *so* stupid. Oh my God. I'm doing her such a favour, you have no idea. Pathetic.'

She was talking about me. I knew she was. No one else was sweet, stupid and pathetic.

'Yeah,' she said after a pause. 'The twenty-eighth. I know. And the Violet stuff. I'm ramping that up.'

I opened the toilet door, slammed it behind me and stared into the mirror. I wanted to be sick.

I thought of my mother. *Don't trust her.* That was what she had said over and over again. *She has a negative energy.*

I thought of the things Natasha had said that hadn't added up. And now I was not going to trust her.

I felt the bond between us snap, just like that.

For the rest of the journey I pretended to be asleep, while going over Natasha's words in my head.

The Violet stuff. I'm ramping that up.

I didn't know who she'd been talking to, but I knew this: if she was going to ramp 'the Violet stuff' up, then I would be looking out for it. I realized that Violet might not be my sister. I only had Natasha's so-called spirit guide's word for that. Whoever she was, whatever 'Violet' actually meant, Natasha was using it against me. Using it to control me.

I remembered how close I had come to believing in Walter last night, and hardened myself. Natasha was toying with me. She thought I was stupid and pathetic; she had said so herself in her own voice.

And I *was* stupid, because I'd known all along that she was a queen of manipulation, but for some reason I'd imagined I was special. I had spent weeks watching her mess with other people's heads for fun and for money. And all along she had been doing it to me as much as to anyone else. Probably more than to anyone else.

I wondered who she had been talking to. Someone else knew what she was doing. I wasn't the person on the inside of her plan – someone else was.

I opened my eyes because the sun was in my face, and there was a city outside the window, and the train was slowing down to stop.

'Is it Paris?' I said sleepily. I was going to mess with Natasha too. I was going to pretend to be more stupid, more naive, more in thrall to her than I had ever been before. And then, when she wasn't looking, I would slip away. Today was the twenty-third, and it was Sunday. That meant the thing she had in mind, for the twenty-eighth, was on Friday. She was expecting me to leave on Saturday, but now I knew there was no way I would still be here on Friday.

'Hey!' Natasha had put on bright red lipstick and brushed her blonde hair, and she looked ready for anything. 'Sleeping Beauty! Welcome back! Not Paris yet. It's Nevers, which means we're not far. Ten hours on trains is a lot, I know, but it'll be worth it. Two hours to Paris from here? Something like that.'

The bunker man across the aisle leaned over. He had dreadlocks and a lovely smiley face.

'Is she your twin?' he asked Natasha in accented English. 'I didn't see because she slept, but you two are the same! Two of you!'

'*Oui, des jumelles,*' said Natasha. '*Tu aimes ça?*'

'Wow.' He laughed. '*Oui, bien sûr!*'

They dropped back into conversation and I tuned out.

I looked out of the window. I'd been to France once on a camping holiday with Mum and Sean, but all I really remembered was croissants for breakfast, and baguettes for lunch, and sandy beaches and books. I had read so many books that holiday that I'd barely looked up at what was around me. I'd certainly never been particularly curious about the country. I knew nothing about what France was like.

I stared and stared, at the houses with shutters, at the unfamiliar words on the shops. Carrefour. Leclerc. Monoprix. It felt so different from Madrid, and different from home. I felt myself drawing back from it all, retreating into my old shell at the onslaught.

Planning.

When we did finally arrive it was nearly midnight and I was steely. I stepped off the train behind Natasha, watching her. Every movement she made was affected. Every second, she was acting. Suddenly it was all clear to me.

The air smelled different here. It felt strange to walk through it. I could hear distant shouting, car engines. Paris felt like a tense place, a city on the brink of something. I remembered news reports about riots. The night was hot and dangerous, but it was less hot than Madrid. Less hot, but more dangerous.

'Come on, Libster!' Natasha called. 'Paris! The city of love! *La ville de l'amour.* We made it!'

I let her take my free hand and pull me along as I wheeled my suitcase behind me, skipping a bit to keep up with her. I didn't know where we were going, or what we were going to do, but, as ever, my cousin had a plan.

She led me down a staircase and out on to the edge of a road, where a couple of taxis were waiting. Natasha opened the back door of one and nudged me in. The bunker man from the train tried to get in too, but she pushed him away and he stormed off.

I stared out of the taxi window. I looked at the street lights, at the buildings that were different from buildings at home or in Madrid. Here in Paris buildings were tall and imposing, like townhouses but grander. We drove along main roads, and there were few other cars, but the ones we did see were driving fast. One was revving its engine and looping around across the road, on one side and then the other, all the way down the street. Another was stuck on the pavement, its wheels half on the kerb. Down a side street I thought I saw a car on its roof, though we were past before I had a chance to focus. I did, however, see a group of people sitting cross-legged round a collection of candles.

The rest of the time, it was eerily quiet.

The car stopped, and Natasha handed the driver some cash (she was, of course, in charge of the takings from last night) and jumped out. She set off into a hotel, and I wondered how, if she'd never been here before, she had managed to book a place for us to stay and get a taxi to take us there.

The hotel was just a door in a wall. A grumpy man let us in and looked us up and down and said the word '*Jumelles?*'

and Natasha agreed that we were, indeed, twins. He led us up three flights of narrow stairs and unlocked a wooden door with the number seven on it. Inside were two narrow beds. He showed us a bathroom off the landing, shared with the other two rooms on this floor, and wished us a good night.

Natasha put her backpack on the bed nearest the window.

'Right!' she said. 'Paris! I'm starved. Let's get some food.'

It was past midnight. I lay on the other bed and closed my eyes even though I was too wired to sleep. I didn't want to go out with Natasha. I didn't want to be with her at all.

'No,' I said. 'Tired.' And I closed my eyes, in my clothes, without caring for once what my cousin wanted me to do. She waited for a while, and I felt her looking at me, and then she said, 'Suit yourself,' and left.

Before the door clicked shut I heard her say hello to someone on the landing.

I didn't hear her come back in, even though I stayed awake for a long time, but when I woke up in the morning there she was, sleeping, snoring gently, with one dirty foot poking out from under her sheet.

24. See Paris

When she was awake she was moving all the time, planning, fizzing with energy. Now she was still and she looked like a waxwork of herself. It was a rare thing for me to look at Natasha without her distracting me.

We didn't actually look alike at all. Our faces were different. Natasha's was narrow and her bone structure was amazing. My face was wider and my bones were probably in there somewhere, because something was holding my face up, but you'd never have known it.

The twenty-eighth was only four days away. I didn't care what she was planning because I wouldn't be here. I took my phone, joined the hotel Wi-Fi and tried to log on to the Eurostar site. I stared and willed it to open, but it just crashed and crashed and crashed. When eventually it did work there was a message that said, in five languages: *Tickets are no longer available online. Please visit a ticket office at a Eurostar station.*

I could hear the city outside the window: people were shouting, cars were going by, and it felt on the very edge of eruption. It probably wasn't. I was projecting; it was me that was on the edge of something. It was unsettling being in a new place and not having seen it. I couldn't imagine what was out there. I could only picture the Eiffel Tower or a glass pyramid.

It was more unsettling knowing that Natasha wasn't the way she seemed. She sighed in her sleep. I wondered where she'd gone last night. What she'd done. Who with.

Her phone was on the table between our beds. I reached for it; she didn't stir. I eased the charging cable out of it, wrapped the phone in the threadbare towel that had come with the room, and took it to the bathroom across the hallway. I made sure I opened the bedroom door very, very quietly, and left it on the latch so I could get back in.

I couldn't, however, get into the bathroom. There was a woman standing on the landing outside the door, which was locked. She looked at me, at the towel in my hands and smiled.

'Sorry,' she said. She had long black hair tied on top of her head in a topknot. 'We seem to be a queue. To be honest it's been like this each morning. You'd think a bathroom shared between three bedrooms would be OK, but the person from room eight does like to take her time.'

'I don't mind waiting,' I said quietly. I took out Natasha's phone and looked at it idly, like people always did. It was an iPhone. Obviously my fingerprint didn't work, and I knew I was unlikely to be able to guess the code. I realized I didn't know her birthday. I put in 1709 for the end of the world, but it didn't work. I had no chance of going through her phone, unless . . .

'Maybe I'll go back and wait in the room,' I said, looking up.

'Sure. If you like, I'll knock when she finally comes out. I'm Meera,' the woman said. She extended a hand, so I shook it. Her hand was small and her grip was strong. It felt strangely formal. I didn't feel like someone standing on a Parisian landing wearing just a big T-shirt and knickers. I felt like a grown-up at a business meeting. This woman was perhaps ten years older than me, but she was treating me as if we were the same.

'I'm Libby,' I said. 'How long are you here for?'

'Three days so far. We're doing one of those rail tours of Europe. We can't afford it but we're doing it anyway. Staying another couple of nights, I think. We like it here. Paris. We might stay longer. I don't know. Once you start to look at the art you just, you know, you find there's a lot of art to look at. I always wanted to see it and now I want to see all of it. And, of course, this week is party week. It's wild. How about you?'

'I'm here with my . . .' I wasn't sure what to say, but then realized I didn't have to tell Natasha's lies. 'Cousin. My cousin Natasha. We came by train from Spain.'

'Oh!' she said. 'You're not with your parents? You look so young.'

'No,' I said. 'Our family is complicated, but mine are in Spain and England and hers are in the US. I'm going to see

Paris today, and then catch a train back to England tomorrow, if I can get a ticket.'

'OK, cool,' she said. 'Sorry, I didn't mean to treat you like a child. So you're British? You have a cute accent.'

'Thanks,' I said. 'So do you. Where are you from?'

'Oh, we're from India,' she said. 'From Goa. I'm here with my husband, Arjun. We flew over just before they stopped the flights.'

'I'd love to go to Goa! I bet lots of people have gone over there for the end times.'

'Oh my God, they have! Everyone who could make it by land. Unfortunately it's a very expensive place to live in now and very, very full of tourists.'

'Maybe one day,' I said, and we smiled at each other.

I walked back into the room, still smiling. I had just had a friendly conversation with a stranger because I wanted to and not because Natasha had told me to.

I shut the door gently. Natasha was stirring, so my idea (holding her thumb on the phone while she was asleep) wasn't going to work today. I put the phone very quietly on the table instead, and then I put my towel on top of it so she wouldn't see it was unplugged.

'Too early,' she muttered.

'Depends what time you came in.'

'I had a great night,' she said with a yawn. 'I sat outside a brasserie and hung out with some guys. I ate cheese, I think. Drank some wine.'

I opened the window. A breeze came in. It smelled of the city, of bakeries and traffic and people and trees.

'What can you see?'

'We don't exactly have a view,' I said, 'but I can see a tree. Mostly it's the back of a building, but there is definitely a tree too.'

I sat back down on my bed and breathed the lovely oxygen that the tree was pumping out. When Meera knocked I had almost forgotten that I was waiting for the shower, but I opened the door and introduced her to Natasha, who leaped into action, putting on her most charming of faces.

'This is my cousin Natasha,' I said firmly.

'I'm so delighted to meet you, Meera,' Natasha said. 'Libby says we're cousins because our real story is so outlandish; we're actually twins.'

I rolled my eyes. Meera was confused.

'You look alike,' she said. 'But you have different accents.'

'Fraternal twins,' Natasha said. 'Separated at birth.'

'Seriously?' Meera looked to me to confirm it. I shrugged. I didn't want any part of this. She looked back to Natasha. 'Sounds like that movie. *The Parent Trap*?'

'Yep,' said Natasha.

'For real? And now you're together in Paris?'

'I know, right?'

'Anyway, twins, cousins, whatever – maybe we'll see you later. I just wanted to say the bathroom is free.'

'Thanks!' I said, and I picked up my stuff and left the room before Natasha could tell me off. I heard a voice from room eight swearing at a stupid bastard hairdryer in English as I passed.

When I came back, wrapped in a towel and with dripping wet hair, Natasha was looking pleased with herself.

'So,' she said, as witchy and Natasha-like as ever. 'This is it. Paris, my sister. We are here for a reason.'

'Do we actually have to pretend to be twins separated at birth?'

'Why not? I like it. I didn't mean to say it. It kind of just came out. Better than cousins, though! The truth is so boring. Don't say cousins again. You saw her reaction! Twins is a narrative everyone loves. Our parents divorced, our dad took me to the States, you stayed behind in England with Mom. We didn't know about each other until recently and now we're making up for lost time. How perfect is that?'

'Like Meera said, it's literally the plot of a movie. And everyone knows that.'

I really did not want to pretend to be Natasha's twin. I didn't have the energy for it any more, and I didn't want to trick people into giving us money. I didn't want any part of this at all.

I got dressed, while Natasha took her stuff and went to the bathroom. Without really knowing what I was doing, I left my hair wet, dressed in the old shorts and T-shirt that were actually mine, rather than a dress that was half of a pair, and slipped away while she was in the shower.

'Bonjour, mademoiselle!' called the man at the front desk as I passed, and I waved but didn't stop, even though he looked as if he wanted me to. I walked out on to the street with no idea of where in the city I was, or where I should be going.

I did have some data on my phone, though, and the 4G network was still working. I knew that I needed the Gare du Nord. It turned out to be a twenty-minute walk away, and so I went there. I just walked through Paris, enjoying the fact that it was about forty degrees compared to Madrid's fifty. The air had a different smell to it, a smell that I hoped was Paris rather than the Creep. The buildings were grand, the roads wide and busy. I watched a bird hopping in a tree and had a sudden memory of the day I went for a walk in the park and was stopped in my tracks by the newsflash. *Actually yes: we'll all die. Don't panic. Have a good weekend.*

Now it was nearly here, and that was almost a relief.

The area around the station felt tense. There was a demonstration going on, and a crowd of people doing t'ai chi, and some sort of food festival, and a group of men in drag drinking cocktails. I picked my way past it all. A couple of men tried to talk to me but I ignored them and that was fine. I found the Eurostar ticket office and stood in a queue behind an older woman who kept sobbing, and waited. I felt my phone buzz, but I ignored it.

When I got to the front, the young man, who didn't look as if he wanted to be there at all, said, 'Bonjour, mademoiselle,' in the world's most bored voice.

'I'd like to buy a ticket for the next train to London, please,' I said in English.

He sighed and stabbed his keyboard.

'Nothing today,' he said. 'Nor tomorrow neither. You can go Wednesday morning. Half past seven. This is all for the week. Only two trains are running every day, because very few people want to go to work, and soon they will stop altogether.'

I agreed and showed him my passport and visa. In a few minutes I had a ticket, paid for with my savings card. The payment went through and I was relieved; it was the first time I had used that account and I thanked my grandparents fervently for bailing me out.

I texted Mum on the way back to the hotel.

> Mum, change of plan. I've got a
> ticket to London for Wednesday.
> I'm going home, without Natasha.
> See you there. Please.

I was not going to tell Natasha what I had done. On Wednesday morning I would just get up and go home before she had even woken up.

25. Make some plans

'Where have you been?' Natasha was annoyed.

'I popped out to see what Paris was like,' I said. 'I got us a croissant. Here.' I passed her the paper bag.

'You were ages! Jesus, Libby. You didn't answer your phone. I was worried about you! What's it like then?'

'Nice.'

'Good to have the inside info! Right, let's go.'

'The man downstairs wants some money,' I said. 'He stopped me on the way in.'

'Yeah,' she said. 'Well, he can't have it. I mean, we do have some saved up – of course we do; it's why we did the psychic night. But I don't want to give it to him yet. We need to get busy today. We've got a lot to do.'

I made myself smile and look stupid. 'What are we doing?'

'Going shopping. The big party is in the Louvre on Friday. Anarchy for the End, it's called. I want us to go as twins. Do the separated-at-birth thing. And just do our

254

act, like we've done loads of times before. It'll be fun. But we're going to need to be much, much better dressed for this one.'

'OK.'

'What's the matter, Libs?'

'Nothing.'

'Seriously. Something's wrong. Have you got cold feet? Are you worrying about your mom? Do you want to go home to Zoe?' She looked searchingly at me and I knew she wasn't going to let this drop. 'It's that, isn't it? You miss your home. You want to get back. You've probably been making plans to get home. That's fine, Libs! You don't need to pretend.'

I picked up my bag and stepped back into my flip-flops.

'I do want to go home, yes,' I said. 'But – I mean, why don't you? It's the end of everything. Why aren't you going back to the States on a boat while you still can, to be with your own mother? Why not? Why do you want to be here, with me, when you've only known me for, like, five minutes?'

Natasha blinked and sighed.

'Oh,' she said. 'Well, that's because I'm a bitch. And not in a good way. Come on. Let's go out. We can eat these croissants on a bench somewhere, and get a coffee and I'll tell you all about it. I know you need to go home, Libs. I do see that. And I wish I could too. I really do. Look, I know I'm all surface, and I know you're starting to see that. I can see it in your eyes.'

I hated the way she could read me. I vowed to be more guarded. I remembered her voice on the train: *So stupid. Oh my God. I'm doing her such a favour, you have no idea. Pathetic.*

I would never trust her. She didn't know I had heard her talking about me, so at least I had that.

The woman who took long showers and swore at hairdryers came out of room eight as we passed. She was older than us, with bright hair and a long green dress, and she tutted as she stood back to let us down the tight staircase first.

'Hi there,' said Natasha.

'Morning,' said the woman, looking annoyed, but not particularly with us. I wondered what was going on in her life.

The hotel man stood in our way and said, 'Now you need to pay for your room, like you said on the phone.'

The woman laughed and pushed past us.

'Good luck with that,' she muttered as she went. She didn't look back.

The hotel man was in his fifties, with a jowly face and sad eyes. Natasha beamed and patted his arm.

'I know we owe you! Don't worry. We'll go and get you the money now. I promise we'll pay.'

He gave a cynical smile with one side of his mouth. 'OK, but today?'

'Sure! Definitely today.'

'No cheating me.'

'Absolutely not!'

He stepped aside.

We sat on a bench in a square and ate our croissants, and it was almost cold. I watched the Parisians walking past. There were a lot of very chic people of both sexes and all ages. I watched a woman waft by wearing a long striped dress and tall shoes with clear plastic heels that had bunches of dried flowers encased inside them. I saw a man in a crisp purple suit carrying a fluffy white dog that was better dressed than I was.

In that sense Paris was exactly as I had expected it to be. I liked this city, I thought. I would have liked to spend ages here, exploring. With Zoe.

'So?' I said, looking at Natasha. It turned out I wasn't as good at acting as I'd thought I was, because I was finding it impossible to go back to the way I had been before I heard her on the phone, and I knew that she could see that.

'OK. Look. I'm going to be straight with you,' she said. 'I can see that you're impatient now, Libby. It's nearly the end of August, and you want to get home. I get that. But will you stay here with me to go to the Louvre on Friday night? After that, then sure. Go.'

'Yes,' I said, though I wouldn't. 'Of course I'll stay for the Louvre. But I'm going after that.'

'I mean, a party in the Louvre to welcome the Creep. It's going to be insane.' She looked at me, a bit uncertain. Her hair had definite dark roots now; we were diverging. 'Also, there's another one tomorrow. The guys in the bar were telling me about it last night and they said there are still tickets. It's a huge ball, really grand, called the Fête du Fin du Monde, the party for the end of the world. At an old palace somewhere. There are more – there are huge things going on every day and every night – but those are the two I really want to go to.'

I leaned back and blew out all the air from my lungs.

'Why, though?' I said. 'There were parties all the time in Madrid too, and you weren't bothered about them. Why do you care about these ones all of a sudden?'

Natasha stood up and walked off. After a while I followed and caught up with her watching some children swinging across a climbing frame in the corner of the square. I should have left her perhaps. I could have left her. If I couldn't go straight to London, I could have gone to Madrid. If I had, things might have worked out differently.

'OK,' she said when I reached her. 'You're right, this doesn't make sense, so I'm going to tell you a couple of things.'

The playground equipment here, I noticed, had age limits on it. This part was for children aged between seven and twelve. How precise. The restriction made me want to go on it myself. I looked at her sideways. I had never felt so cynical.

'Yes?'

'It's a personal thing,' said Natasha. 'Not a hustle.'

We started walking. We walked out of the square and down a small street. We passed a stall with newspapers for sale and I looked at the headlines. They were all atmosphere and riots. I paused in front of one and looked at photos of fires in Paris. This very city. I was scared: there seemed to be unrest and danger the world over. What if there were curfews and travel bans before Wednesday? I imagined being trapped here with Natasha until the end.

I didn't look at her. I started walking again and she kept up with me.

'What kind of personal thing?' I said.

'It's a long story.'

We had arrived at a canal with boats on it. I could see that it would join up to the Seine at the end. There was a cafe and a little park across a bridge, and we walked over there. It was sunny and getting hotter, and I felt that everything was new and also ending. A new city and a new dynamic.

'Coffee?' I said, seeing a little stand.

'Please,' said Natasha.

We sat on a bench in the sun with coffee in cardboard cups. I was still waiting for her to say whatever the personal thing was.

A woman walked past carrying a little dog. I smiled at its cute face, and then I wondered about the extinction. All dogs would cease to exist, and soon. Every single one. They might evolve again or they might not. Something different could evolve. Something as different from a dog as a pterodactyl was.

'Right,' said my cousin. 'All I've wanted has been to be here for these two parties.'

She stopped, and when I looked over at her I could see that there were tears in her eyes.

I wondered why my cousin had no friends. Being alone on a different continent for the end of the world was a strange choice to make. It wasn't the choice of a person who had a network of people she loved.

I wondered whether she actually liked anyone. She had people who commented on her social media, but that wasn't the same as having friends. I knew her family had been ripped apart, and that her mother was in a psychiatric ward and unreachable. But I also knew that, if my mother was suffering like that, I'd want to be nearby, keeping an eye on her.

Or would I?

A pigeon hopped close to us, hoping for food, but we didn't have anything for it.

My mother *was* like that. Not quite, but I remembered the last time I'd seen her, only a couple of days ago. She had not been stable. She'd been struggling. I was seventeen, and I'd run away to Paris. Natasha was eighteen, and she had too. We weren't so different.

On the train she had spoken about me with such disdain. She wasn't really my friend.

'OK.' She took some deep breaths and spoke again. 'OK. So here's the thing.' A man looked as if he wanted to join us on the bench, and we both glared at him. After hesitating, he walked on.

'What's the thing?' I said.

She looked away. 'You know that when my dad died he was in the car with someone? With the woman I hate?'

'Yes.'

'Her name is Deanna. Deanna Glancey. She's in her early twenties. I mean, gross. Hardly older than me, and Mom had no idea. Deanna walked away with barely a scratch. And she never said sorry. Worse than that, she sent us a mean letter afterwards. It made it all much worse. And then we discovered that Dad hadn't left us any money. A tiny bit of money. Nothing like what he actually had.'

'I'm sorry,' I said. 'That's awful.'

I remembered what Dad had said. Andy had left a 'life-changing' amount of money to us. I had assumed that he'd left at least the same amount, and probably a lot more, to his wife and daughter. It seemed impossible that he'd cut them out.

'You're lovely. So, Miss Deanna is also in Europe now, doing her grand tour without a care in the world. That's why I'm here really. I mean, one of the reasons – you're the other. She basically walked away with a little scar or something. I hate her. I hate her more than I can say.'

'Is she going to these parties?'

'I've been Facebook friends with her for ages. I made a fake profile months ago, and friended loads of her friends first, and then when I added her we had lots of mutuals so she just accepted me. That's how I know what she's up to. She's going to the gala on Tuesday, and then the Anarchy for the End on Friday. I want to talk to her tomorrow, and then get a full revenge on Friday.'

'Are you going to hurt her?'

Again, there was silence. Somewhere, far away, there was shouting, then a siren.

'Her feelings. Sure.' She looked at me, her eyes boring into mine. 'I'm going to hurt her *feelings*, Libby, but not as much as she hurt mine. Because she killed my dad.'

'You know . . .' I wasn't sure how to say this, but I thought I would try. 'You know, it doesn't sound like she actually murdered him. It was your dad's choice to be out in the car with her, and he was driving, wasn't he?'

'Yeah. I do know. It was his decisions that led him there. Sure, he was driving. She was a passenger. She didn't do anything to make him crash, apart from letting him drink and drive. But he's gone, you know? So what can I do to him? She's what's left.'

I sipped my coffee. It was black and strong.

'He's not completely gone, is he? He talks to you.'

'Yeah. That's a shadow. Everything that was him has gone. His ashes are scattered in the places he loved most. Yes, his spirit is still there, but it's not *here*. His voice in my head makes it all worse. Because he isn't real. He used to hug me. You know? And now he's a wisp. And maybe I'm just imagining him. In fact, I think I am and I've known that all along, but I've always been like: *no, it's definitely him, one hundred per cent*. And we're all going to die anyway and what's even the point?'

She blinked fast, and I put an arm on her shoulder. I wondered whether this was all part of the act. Even if it was real it was too little, too late. She turned her face into my shoulder and shook a bit. I knew that she didn't want to cry properly, because her *thing* was being in control, but, for the first time since I'd known her, I felt that she might be showing real emotion.

Not that I cared now.

'I don't know,' I said. 'I don't really know what the point is.'

But I saw it all then too. The new atmosphere (which I was seeing at the edges of my vision as green all the time) would seep across the planet, and everyone would choke and drown in poison. The horror of it all. The horror, as life on this planet was extinguished (apart, perhaps, from the cockroaches and the tardigrades). The abandonment of the entirety of human life. People had watched thousands of other species becoming extinct without being particularly bothered about it and now it was our turn and there was no one left to care.

'I hate her.' Natasha's voice pulled me back to the moment. 'And him, sure, but I'm not going to spend my time shouting at a ghost. Believe me, it doesn't work. She's not sorry, though. She's just walked away. We're in the middle of fighting her for his insurance. I think I'm getting it, but I haven't yet because it's all tied up legally. She said he'd left Mom for her, though he hadn't, and the lawyers are fighting it out.

'So here she is, in Paris with her rich friends, going to a grand gala to celebrate the whole of Western culture and civilization, followed by a wild party at the Louvre to stick a finger up at the extinction. And I just can't. I can't let her do that and know that I'm here too, staying in a shitty hotel and hustling card tricks for money. I have to find her.

She's pathetic. She comes across as sweet on her social media but so stupid. I'm doing her a huge favour by forcing her to confront what she's done while there's still time.'

I froze. Those were the words she'd said on the train.

My arm was still round her shoulders.

'But what will you do?' I said. 'What will you actually do, when you see her? I'm not sure it'll make anything better.'

'It will,' said Natasha. 'It will make things better for me.'

Had she been talking about Deanna on the train? Maybe it hadn't been about me at all. I could have got this all completely wrong.

'How are you going to *hurt her feelings*?' I said.

She looked away, and I felt the barrier come down again.

'I'm not going to do anything really. Just remind her of me for a moment.'

'Have you met her before?'

'I've seen her. I've never spoken to her. It was the most awkward and horrible thing. I hate her so much. So, so much. Her story of the crash was that they'd come back from the best night out, and he was going to come home to our house to pick up his things, and then that was it. He'd told her he was only with Mom because of me anyway, and now I was eighteen, so . . . Anyway, they were driving back, he was drunk, they were both laughing and messing around, feeling like nothing in the world could ever hurt them. And then it did. He drove into a tree. And she pretty much walked away.'

If anyone could frame a person so they found themselves caught in the act of stealing the *Mona Lisa*, it would be Natasha. I imagined the *Venus de Milo* toppling on this woman, or a hall of sculptures coming to life and trampling her to death. I imagined Natasha harnessing her fury, and I was glad I was not Deanna Glancey.

'What does your dad say about the party?'

'Oh, Libby,' she said. 'I don't think he says anything really, does he? He never did. He's dead.'

'But what,' I said again, 'are you actually going to do?'

She was quiet for a long time. I watched the people walking past, amazed at the way life did still go on. Lots of people who had jobs still went to work. As soon as the novelty wore off, life had simply continued. It would probably fall apart again next week, when September arrived, but for now about half the shops were open, and most of the businesses seemed to be carrying on. Humans, I thought, were strange. They were still doing the things they had always done.

I wasn't. What I'd always done was stay at home and wish I could speak to people. Now I was in Paris in the sunshine, and I was going home on Wednesday to meet up with Zoe. I supposed I would go with Natasha to tomorrow's party (apart from anything else, I was totally intrigued by the prospect of seeing Deanna). After that I was off. Home.

'Well,' said Natasha, and I realized I'd become so distracted that I'd forgotten I'd asked her a question. 'I'm just going to talk to her. That's all. Maybe I'll throw a drink? Tell her friends and a bunch of strangers what she did. I don't want her to die. I want her to be mortified, and she *will* be mortified. I want to ruin her hair.'

I looked at her closely, though it was impossible to know, really, what she was planning on doing.

'Really?'

'Really.'

'What does she look like? Do you have a picture?'

Natasha fiddled with her phone for a bit. She passed it to me, and I saw a screenshot of a profile picture: a picture of a young blonde woman, laughing. She was beautiful, but I didn't say that. *Deanna Glancey*, it said.

'Right.' We were all running out of time, and nothing I said would stop her anyway. Plus, I was interested to see what was going to happen. 'OK then. Why do you think she's sweet but stupid?'

Natasha shrugged. 'Because of her vapid social media posts, even now.'

'So what do we need to do before tomorrow night?'

Natasha grinned at me.

'Cousin Libby,' she said. 'I knew I could count on you. We need to get ourselves all dressed up, and we need to make the party unforgettable.'

'OK,' I said. 'It's the end times. So let's do it.'

26. Lie on your back under a Parisian tree and feel happy

It half started to feel like fun, like the one last thing we would do together. I felt a bit bad about the fact that I was going to slip away early on Wednesday morning and leave her to do the big confrontation, the Friday one, on her own. I was no longer sure that she'd been talking about me on the train after all, and if she hadn't, then I was being mean to her for no reason.

But she had mentioned Violet on the train. She had said she was 'ramping it up'. However, she hadn't mentioned Violet since then, so maybe I'd misheard. Maybe she was ramping up the *violence*, to Deanna. I didn't know anything any more.

Whatever happened, I would soon be home. I would live the rest of my life without Natasha, and that felt good.

'I think we should dress the same,' Natasha said. 'You know, keep on doing the twins thing.'

'I don't want to.' I looked over at her. 'I don't want to be arrested for whatever you end up doing. Even though we actually look different, people don't seem to be able to tell us apart when we're dressed alike.'

She grinned. We were walking along the banks of the Seine, heading towards the shopping streets.

'You've changed, Libby,' she said. 'OK. Let's meet in the middle. Vintage dresses for tomorrow, and then matching on Friday. How about that?'

It didn't address what I'd said – that I didn't want to be arrested for whatever she was going to do – but since I knew I'd be gone by Friday I didn't care. She could set me up all she wanted.

'Deal,' I said. 'Twins on Friday. Sure thing.'

'Then let's find a vintage boutique.' She stopped, sat on a bench and started googling. I stood at the edge of the water and looked out.

It was unbearably beautiful. The water was green, the stone across the river yellowish sandstone. I could smell the water. I could see the cathedral of Notre-Dame, and feel a breeze in my hair. I wanted to stay here. I wanted to be standing right here, and when the Creep came I would jump into the Seine and let the water take me.

'Right,' she said, interrupting my thoughts. 'I think I've found the place. It's a little walk away but not too far.'

I looked back at the cathedral. It would still be there a month from now, no matter what was or wasn't happening around it. I imagined everyone walking to the riverbank and jumping in.

When we reached the next set of steps we set off up to the street. The stairs were metal and clanged a bit as we walked.

Two hours later we were in our third vintage shop, trying on dresses. I felt like a girl playing dressing-up, even though I had never done that as a child.

As soon as I put this one on, though, I knew it was the one.

'*Voilà!*' said the shop woman, standing back and smiling. I stepped towards the mirror and looked at myself.

I was Juliet again, dressed for the ball. Transformed.

I would never have picked this dress but now that I was wearing it I felt I would never be able to wear anything else. The shop assistant had chosen it for me. It was her last day of work before September the seventeenth, so she was very happy; she was about Mum's age, I thought, with short peroxide hair and a pair of dungarees, and I gladly accepted all her style guidance, particularly now that I was wearing the dress she'd picked out.

It was a cream-coloured dress that had been made in the nineteen forties. It fitted me as though it had been made for me, and I imagined the lady from the forties, exactly my size, trying on her new dress. The body and waist were tight, the skirt loose, halfway down my shins. My new dress (because that was what it had to be) had gathered sleeves, and a waist with a million little pleats in it, and a sash. The neckline was high. The whole thing felt like stardust. It was magical.

It was, I knew, a couture version of the one I had worn as Juliet for the first scene of the play.

'Oh my God, Libby,' said Natasha. 'Right. That's yours. Task seven: wear that to the ball. Now we just need mine.'

I kept it on for longer than I needed to, just staring at myself. My hair was growing, but still shorter than I'd had it since I was about six. My skin was tanned, and I had changed shape a bit, in the way you would expect when you change from a life of eating cake in the sun to running around capital cities doing street magic and hustling to get the next meal.

I was, I thought tentatively, pleased with what I saw in the mirror. This girl didn't look like me, but she was me. This girl was going home to Zoe the day after tomorrow.

I looked up and saw that the shop woman was looking at my reflection too.

She smiled. '*T'es belle*,' she said.

'*C'est la première fois*,' I said.

While Natasha kept trying on dresses, I got changed and sat down, and took out my phone. There was a reply from Mum.

> Good. We're going to go home
> too. See you there. I have a
> surprise for you. Things are
> much better here. Much.

I'm so sorry. I'll explain on
Wednesday.

I was absolutely swamped with relief. I smiled and
started a message to Zoe.

Hi Zoe, I wrote. How are things?

She replied straight away.

Yeah. Not great. News from here is that
Elisha wanted to have a wilder time under
the circumstances. Honestly, Libby:
everyone is going so mad. It feels quite
scary. I just want to wait it out now and
do nothing until it's all over one way or
the other.

You've split up?

Very, very much so. Weirdly I don't mind
as much as you'd think.

What are you up to?

Waiting it out while being single. Family
stuff. Fun! Glamour!

I wouldn't mind a bit of family stuff
right now.

Elisha's been hanging out in London
doing wild things with wild people, and it's
just me here. And there's you, doing

amazing stuff in Europe, emailing me
from trains to Paris. And you are doing
family stuff because you're with your
gorgeous cousin.

So my gorgeous cousin is not so
gorgeous after all.

How?

I don't trust her.

She treats me like a pet.

Like she's the boss. My owner.

Like bc she's so charismatic I have to
do everything she says.

I heard her talking about me (I think).
I didn't like it.

OMG. Ditch her!

I am. I've booked a train home. Back
on Weds. Want to meet?

Yes!

I haven't told her I'm going.

She lies to everyone.

She lies to me too.

Anyway . . .

Can I meet you at the station on Weds?

Yes!

♥

♥

I looked up and beamed at Natasha.

She was wearing a silver dress. It had been made in the seventies and had the same puffed sleeves and gathered waist as mine but there was a punk sensibility that made it quite different. It was perfectly Natasha: she looked amazing. She and the shop owner agreed that she should wear it with statement shoes, big ones, and the woman went off and started bringing some back in her size, while I just stood there and thought about Zoe meeting me at the station.

I had never been a girl who wore vintage dresses, or who swooped in on someone whose girlfriend had just left. I was the skinny-jeans-and-huge-sweatshirt-and-trainers type, a girl who would rather stay at home than go to a party, and that was probably always going to be my style really, if there was going to be an 'always' after this.

The woman had gone out to the back room for another pair of shoes, and Natasha whispered: 'These dresses are amazing. But we have a slight cash-flow problem. I mean, we can go out to the, like, Eiffel Tower and the gardens by the Louvre and whatever tonight and read some palms and stuff. But for now I'm not quite sure how we pay for them. I spent our psychic-evening money on those party tickets. And these dresses are cheap for what they are, and I'm

273

sure we can get the price down a bit. You look like an absolute angel. A real one.'

I couldn't stop smiling. 'You look like an angel too. A punk one.'

'Punk angel of death,' she said. 'That's who Deanna Glancey is going to meet at her fancy party.' She saw the way I was looking at her. 'Oh,' she said. 'Don't worry! I'm not going to kill her.'

'Promise?'

'Promise. If I was going to do that, I'd wait for the day after the end of the world, when she thinks she's safe, and do it then. But I'm not! I'm not! Totally not worth it when the universe is going to do it for me in a couple of weeks.'

'OK.' I thought about it. We could probably get the nice woman to hold on to our dresses until we'd got the money together. On the other hand, she was about to shut up shop, and I knew my savings card worked. 'Look,' I said. 'I can pay for these now. I have access to my college fund, and I think my dad has put some money into my current account too. I'll pay, and we don't even need to earn the money back. It's fine.'

She shook her head. 'We're not going to spend your savings. We're going to have faith in the future and leave your college fund right where it is, because if we start to spend it it's like we're admitting that you might not need it. And you do need it, Libs.' She paused. 'However, if you paid for them, we could earn it back and replace the money by the end of today. Would that be OK? At least it would stop someone else coming along and buying them. And if she's shutting up shop today, we don't want to come back too late.'

'Of course.'

This was not like her. Natasha always made sure we earned the money before we did something. I guessed she had always intended for me to pay for the dresses today, and that she wasn't going to pay me back, whatever she said, but I didn't mind. I minded lots of things, but not this one.

Natasha got the woman to knock fifty euros off the bill, and I paid four hundred and fifty euros for two dresses, Natasha's clumpy shoes and a pair of silky ballet flats for me.

Natasha turned her back while I was putting the number in, making a show of not seeing it. The payment went through, diminishing my funds by a small amount.

Whatever happened next, I had bought a perfect dress. Two perfect dresses. The shop woman told us we would be the belles of the ball, and packed our dresses in tissue paper, our shoes in a separate paper bag, and put in a diamond bracelet for each of us too.

'Who cares?' she said. 'I'm closing tomorrow. I'm going to travel south to spend the last few weeks with my grandchildren. I'm done with the city.'

Now that it was nearly September, everyone was starting to go home to their families. I was part of that too. It felt like that bit in the Bible where everyone goes back to their birthplaces even if there are no hotels free when they get there.

As we walked down the boulevard I wondered why there had been no room at any of the inns in the nativity story. If all those people had been born in Bethlehem, you'd think they'd still have family there they could stay with. Though I supposed that Mary was being taken along, even though it probably wasn't her birthplace, because the world was sexist, so maybe that kind of thing unbalanced it a little. Still, I thought, Joseph must have had an aunt or someone who could have taken them in, particularly under the circumstances.

Then I realized Natasha was talking to me and I had to pull myself back to the present.

'Sorry,' I said. 'I was daydreaming. What was that?'

'Jesus, Olivia! You were miles away!'

'I know. I was . . .' I decided not to explain. 'Thinking how great our dresses are. What did you say?'

'I said, we need to pick up our tickets for tomorrow night, and I'm going to try to get us on the guest list for Friday. OK?'

'Sure,' I said. 'Great idea.'

'We'll go and sit in the gardens by the Louvre and use that as a base.'

I bridled at being told what we were doing, rather than consulted on it, but I told myself to let it go. It didn't matter. Natasha would get the tickets, and I was happy to leave it to her. The party was tomorrow, and the day after I would go home. To Zoe. Zoe who was single, who wanted to see me. Zoe was ready to throw caution to the wind, and so was I. I would get back in touch with Max (if he would have me) and go home to Sofie and Hans-Erik. To Mum and Sean. Mum's message had sounded normal. It was the most incredible relief.

We walked through the centre of the city. Some people rode past on horseback, and they weren't police or anyone who would ride a horse for work. They were people who had decided that they couldn't let the world end without riding a horse through the centre of Paris.

There was a huge queue at the Louvre. It went round all the barriers they'd put up for it, and then on, round and round the courtyard, past the fountains and the smaller pyramids. I would have loved to go there (big signs said that entry was free from now until September the eighteenth), but I didn't want to see the *Mona Lisa* that much. Not enough to stand in a queue for half a precious day.

The Tuileries Garden was shady, with paths that were dusty gravel. The sun was warmer now, but still nowhere near the way it had been in Madrid. We found a patch of grass to sit on, near a hedge, and Natasha started tapping on her phone. After a while she made a call and, although I could mainly follow what she was saying, it turned out she was just telling someone that they needed some street magicians at their party. I tuned out.

I lay on the grass, looking up at the treetops above me, listening to the birds and feeling . . . It took me a while to come up with a name for it, but after a while I agreed with myself that I was feeling *happy*. I was on my way home, and I had found my voice, just enough. I was going to see Zoe.

I added it to my list of things I'd done before the end of the world: I had lain on my back under a Parisian tree and felt happy. The bigger picture receded, and I realized that I could do far more things than I would ever have imagined. I had shared a room with strangers and nothing bad had happened. I had travelled through Europe by train, and now I was lying in the middle of Paris, not really listening to my cousin telling lies in French on the phone.

I turned my head, feeling the tough grass on my cheek. There was a tiny spider walking up a blade of it. The shade was dappled, and sometimes the sun came through and dazzled me, but then it was gone. Natasha had her back to me, and I looked at her tanned shoulders in a blue vest. Her dark roots made her look cool.

I knew she had been through terrible things, and I knew that if I was being super sensible I should refuse to go to the party tomorrow, and try to stop her going too. Nothing good would come of her confrontation with Deanna Glancey. But I didn't try to stop her because it didn't really matter. Not when the air was already feeling noticeably different.

I just lay there and felt Paris all around me. When I reached out, my hand touched the paper bag with my new dress in it.

I heard Natasha get up and walk off, but I didn't look round. I was pleased to have some time to myself. As soon as she had gone, I rolled over and got my phone out and made the call I should have made before now.

'Libby!' Mum snatched it up almost before it had even rung. 'You're going home! That's wonderful. We've managed to move our train and ferry bookings, and we'll arrive on Friday. Is that OK? Can you go to your dad's first?'

'Of course I can,' I said. 'Oh my God. I can't wait.'

'Neither can I. I have some explaining to do.'

'It's fine,' I said. 'I don't even care what it is. You sound better and that's all that matters.'

I leaned back and watched a bird just fall out of the sky. It was flying overhead and then just dropped like a stone. I didn't see where it landed. I looked at the sky again and saw another one falling.

'How is Natasha?'

I was surprised to discover that I was choking back sobs. The enormity of everything was hitting me. The birds, my mother, going home.

'She's plotting,' I said. 'But it's not about me. It's about her dad's girlfriend. It's OK. She doesn't know I'm leaving on Wednesday because if she did know she'd try to stop me.'

'Good. Just leave her to whatever she's doing and get yourself home.'

When we finished talking I switched to messages to continue my conversation with Zoe.

> So I'm going to a party in Paris tomorrow night, because Natasha needs me for moral support. My last night away!

I stopped and looked at the words. Did she? I didn't think she *needed* me. I went back and changed 'needs' to 'wants'.

> And then I'm going home. Mum and
> Sean are coming back too. Maybe we
> can hang out for whatever time is left?

I waited. I waited a bit longer. I looked away, and back at the phone. After three minutes, Zoe replied.

MAYBE WE CAN.

I couldn't stop smiling.

> I wish I could come right now. But
> there weren't any tickets available
> until Wednesday. Train is at 7.30 a.m.
> and gets to London at 8.45, so I think
> I'll be in Winchester at about 11?

> My mum's been in a bit of a state. But
> I just spoke to her and she's much
> better. She hated Natasha right from
> the start. I should have listened.

> I can't wait to see you.

Same. Can't wait to see your magic tricks.

Does that sound suggestive?

I don't care if it does TBH.

> Well, it does a bit.

I took a photo of my view. It had my toes in it, the nails painted yellow.

Tuileries Garden.

Nice toes.

Then I switched the camera mode and took a selfie. I gave Zoe a huge smile and sent it without stopping to worry. She replied with one of herself, which I knew I would keep forever, with the one I'd taken on Vikram's wall. She was looking at me with a definite glint in her eye. Her hair had grown a bit more. I wanted to climb through my phone to her.

It was ages before I started to wonder where Natasha actually was. I looked around, then further afield. I still had the bags with both our dresses and shoes, and I knew she wouldn't be far away. I stood up, and said, 'Natasha,' not quite wanting to shout, but nonetheless pleased that I was in a park in the middle of Paris, using the voice that used to stick in my throat.

I looked up in case any more birds fell out of the sky, but they didn't. I had to step over four pigeon corpses on the ground.

I walked to the centre of the park, expecting to see her in conversation with someone. I went back to where we had been, to check for a note. I crunched along the little pathways, and eventually found her in the queue for the Louvre, reading people's palms for five euros a go.

It must, I thought, be exhausting to be her. She saw me looking and gave me her secret little smile, so I sat on a low wall by a fountain and waited.

'There you go.' She sat down beside me and handed me a hundred euros.

'Keep it,' I said. 'How long have you been doing that?'

'Maybe an hour? I just wanted to get the money back for your college fund. So you have to take it. I know it's not all of it, but it's a start. I never, ever want anyone to think I'm exploiting *you*. The rest of the world, sure. My Olivia? No.'

I smiled and patted her arm. She was so full of shit.

'You didn't need to do this. I *want* to buy dresses for the end of the world.'

'Well, consider this stage one of your repayment. You can put it in your fund or not. That's up to you.' She pushed the money into my hand. 'And I've got us into the party on Friday, and it's completely free. I paid for tomorrow night's ones.' She took two gilt-edged cards out of her bag and showed them to me. 'You *shall* go to the ball.'

27. Drink three glasses of champagne

When we woke up the next morning all the birds were dead.

We got ready without speaking to each other. At one point Natasha was so bored with my silence that she went to hang out with other hotel guests, knocking on doors and chatting to anyone she could find.

All I was thinking was: *tomorrow*. Tomorrow I go home. Tomorrow all this will end.

Late in the afternoon Natasha was blow-drying her hair with a tiny hairdryer she had borrowed from the woman in room eight. It was temperamental, which explained her swearing at it.

This was my last night in continental Europe, and everything was dying. There were dead birds everywhere. People were out on the streets sweeping them into piles. It was the beginning of the end. I didn't want to read about the rest of the world, but Natasha said that people were starting to die too.

'The vulnerable people,' she said, reading from her phone. 'The sick. The people with breathing difficulties –'

'Stop,' I said. I couldn't bear it.

This was the end of the summer of adventures.

I let her plait my hair and set it in place with what felt like a whole can of hairspray. The room smelled like a dressing room, and I felt like an actress, because I was. I was, and so was she.

I turned and looked up at Natasha. 'OK. Maybe it's going to be fun,' I said. I said it as if I meant it, because I was thinking of home. I meant that tomorrow was going to be fun.

'I know! I'm so excited. Honestly, darling, I promise I'll behave. I won't get us thrown out. I won't do anything crazy.'

'I'll have to trust you.'

I didn't trust her.

I stood up. She sat down and let me begin to fiddle with her hair.

'Are you going to stay in Paris beyond Friday?'

She turned round, pulling her hair out of my hands as she did so.

'You know what? I'm not. I'll look at getting a ship back to Mom, like you said. There are some sailings available, and it takes just over a week so I do have time. I just need to get this Deanna thing done. I'm so nervous. Then it's time for me to go home, I think.'

When we left we were made up in the way Natasha had done it back in Spain, except that she had made me do my own make-up under her guidance.

'There,' she said. 'Now you'll be able to do that any time you want. Any time you need to be Juliet.'

We left our phones behind so we didn't need to carry anything, and Natasha tucked the room key into her underwear.

As we passed, the hotel man barred our way. He did a slight double take when he saw how we were dressed, but then doubled down.

'You need to pay for your room,' he said. 'When you call –' he looked from one of us to the other, not knowing which of us he had spoken to – 'you say you pay on arrival, for six nights. I need your money now. Pay on arrival. Like everyone.'

Natasha smiled. 'Of course!' she said, and she touched his arm. She slipped into French and told him that we loved his hotel, that we loved Paris and that he was the best hotelier ever. She gasped and grabbed at his hand; he pulled it back but relented as she started pointing to lines on it. I realized, up close, that Natasha's French wasn't actually very good (like everything, it was smoke and mirrors) and she went back into English pretty quickly.

'See this one here,' she said, pointing to some part of his palm. 'This is your lifeline. I've actually never seen one this strong before. You've had quite a life, right?'

He nodded, widening his eyes for comic effect. 'Right,' he said, nodding slowly.

'And here? See this?' He nodded. 'This is about the odds you've faced. You've faced down some pretty bad stuff, and yet here you are, still smiling.'

'Not always. I cannot always smile.'

'No. Sure. Not always. But often. Very often, for someone who has lived a difficult life. And look: your determination and success lines are completely entwined. That's a rare thing to see. I mean, look at you here! Now! Still running your hotel, when you could have locked up and gone on holiday. Instead you're chasing schmucks like us for money you'll probably never spend.'

He laughed. 'So this is what you do? You're a . . . hand reader?'

'Yes. We do magic. We do lots of other things too. We're very good at it actually. I'm psychic, and so is my sister.'

He laughed and looked from one of us to the other and back again. He was still suspicious, still grumpy. It wasn't as if Natasha had performed some Disney-style transformation on him. He was deeply cynical, but he waved us off without insisting on the money again.

'Have a good evening,' he said, 'and tomorrow you pay me, right? At the weekend I close. I need the money to visit my friend. Otherwise I would maybe not care.'

'Right!' said Natasha. 'We'll get you the money to visit your friend. Promise!'

'Where does your friend live?' I asked, but he didn't answer.

The shadows were long, the light golden. We walked to the party, and I loved every second of it because it was the end of my summer in Europe. My dress was silky, barely there. It was like wearing the mist. My shoes were flat and comfortable, because I knew my limits and would never wear high heels, and I felt like a dancer.

I felt magical. I was wearing a costume: I was Juliet again, and I was flying through Paris, to the party at the end of the world. I felt (regressively perhaps) like a princess. Cars slowed down and drivers beeped at us. Everyone we passed smiled, and I knew that we did look amazing. Paris was our perfect backdrop. Its history was everything; to be here at the end of days was intoxicating.

Natasha's silver dress was strapless, with a silver rose at its waist. She was wearing it with big clompy boots and red lipstick, and she looked incredible: as she had said, a punk angel of death. I was glad I wasn't on the receiving end of her wrath. We walked down the steps to the river again, and along the Seine, and even though we didn't say much we didn't need to. Our hair was more or less the same (we had followed the same tutorial) and our make-up was the same, and our style was completely different. Everyone we passed turned to stare. We were enchanting. I wanted this moment to last forever.

The party was in a palace with a grand hall and a roof terrace with a view. We handed in our gilt-edged tickets, and our names were ticked off a list.

'This is . . .' I said, but then the party took my breath away.

We walked through a hallway with chequered tiles and a ceiling so high I could barely see it. There was a cloakroom, but as we didn't have anything to check in we ignored it and went straight through to the main party in a huge ballroom.

An orchestra was playing at one end. People were dancing and talking and drinking champagne. I stood on the edge and looked at it all, and I felt like Juliet again at the Capulet ball. I found myself looking around, wishing for my Romeo.

I recognized many of the paintings on the walls and wondered whether they were originals, borrowed for this evening, for the Fête du Fin du Monde. The walls themselves were stone, with arches making little alcoves at the sides. The air smelled of cut flowers and perfume.

I looked at Natasha. She smiled back.

'Is this acceptable, madam?' she said, and she took two glasses of champagne from a table and handed one to me. They were wide round glasses with flowers etched into the glass.

'Natasha,' I said, clinking glasses with her and feeling very adult, 'this has been the most incredible summer of my life. I would never, ever, ever have imagined that I'd find myself here, at the grandest party, in Paris, wearing a vintage gown and drinking champagne.'

I forgot all my reservations about her. I forgot everything. I just wanted to live this evening, because the birds were falling out of the sky and the people were starting to die, and whatever anyone said I knew this was going to be the end.

'And here you are,' she said. 'I guess this summer we took charge.'

We walked around the room. The men were wearing black tie, the women all kinds of couture gowns. Compared to some of them, we were almost dowdy. It was gorgeous to see. I wanted to distil the evening and keep it forever. It was the end of everything. I didn't care about my cousin. I cared about seeing an evening like this before I died.

The glasses and bottles were out on tables for people to help themselves. I didn't think many waiting staff were working any more.

After an hour or so, Natasha kissed me on each cheek, like a French person, and said, 'I love you, Libby Lewis. Now, I'm going to scout around and introduce myself to Miss Deanna. I'll save the main event for Friday so don't worry. Here.'

She took another glass from a tray, a third, and handed it to me.

'Have you seen her?'

I followed her gaze, and I saw the back of a blonde woman in a bright blue dress. She looked like the woman in the picture, but I couldn't be sure.

'Is that . . .?'

'I think so.'

'Don't do anything –'

'It's OK, Libby. I won't do anything mad. I mean, you're right not to trust me, but anyway. Trust me.'

She looked into my eyes. I looked back into hers and nodded.

You're right not to trust me. This at least was the truth.

'Be safe,' I said.

'You too.' She walked me into an alcove with little tables and chairs in it and sat me down beside a table. 'Wait here. You can't have any part in any of this. Don't leave without me. I'm going to need you after this. I'm going to need you to help me plan the next one.'

I nodded. I wanted to stop her, but I knew that nothing I said would do that. I would just wait, parked here out of the way, and I would see if anything happened.

I waited.
I waited.
I waited.

28. Run through a storm

I sat there for ages. I exchanged smiles with a couple who came to sit next to me. They were both dressed in gold, and I wished it was Natasha, in her silver, in their place. I finished the champagne, and as I was not at all used to drinking three glasses of champagne at a time, I was dizzy. We hadn't eaten for hours and the bubbles had gone straight to my head.

After perhaps half an hour I realized that Natasha must have done something that went beyond a pointed conversation. Just because there hadn't been a commotion, it didn't mean that she was all right. She could have been ejected from this party silently, easily. She might have been trying to reach me, but banned from coming back in. We didn't have our phones.

I stepped into the ballroom, but I couldn't see either her or Deanna Glancey. Nothing seemed to have happened. Nobody looked any different from the way they had before. I walked round the edges of the room, ignoring occasional approaches from people, and staring at every woman I saw.

It should have been easy to find Natasha, shining in her dress. But she and I were not tall. Most of the people in this hall were taller than we were and they made a hedge between her and me, like in *Sleeping Beauty*.

It might, I realized, take hours to find her. There were thousands of people in this room alone, and the party spread throughout the palace. I went back to the alcove, but she wasn't there either, and now someone else was in my seat.

The orchestra had gone and there was a band on now, playing through the history of popular music. Currently they were on 'All You Need is Love' and I thought it was a reminder to me that I didn't need Natasha. I needed Mum, Sean, Dad, Zoe. Max. We hadn't brought our phones out, so I couldn't call or text. I walked around and around, giddy with it all.

Whatever she had done, I was ready to walk away from her. I was done with Natasha.

I looked in the side rooms. She wasn't in them either. There were nooks and crannies all over the place, and I thought in passing how wonderful some of them would have been for palm and tarot readings and then I wondered whether she might have set herself up doing that, but she would have told me about it if she had because she would have wanted my help.

Halfway up the stairs, I found myself face to face with Deanna Glancey.

She was on her way down. I stopped. I knew I was trembling all over. I stood in her way, as Natasha would have done. Had probably done already.

'Excuse me,' I said. 'I'm really sorry, but are you Deanna?'

She frowned a little, but not in a cross way.

'*Pardon?*' she said in French. She gave me a little smile.

'*Excusez-moi,*' I said, self-conscious about my accent. '*Vous êtes Deanna Glancey?*'

She laughed a little. '*Non, pas du tout!*' She touched her chest. '*Céline.*'

'*Vous n'êtes pas américaine?*'

'*Mais non! Non, non, non.*' She touched her chest again. '*Française, moi. Et toi – anglaise?*'

We spoke for long enough for me to establish that Natasha had got entirely the wrong person, and she must have worked it out before she did anything, because Céline said that no girl had approached her. She had absolutely no idea what I was talking about when I said it in bad French, and then in reasonable Spanish, and then in English. This was not, definitively, the right person, nor had she seen a girl in a silver dress except, she thought, perhaps she had seen someone like that leaving, hours ago.

I started to get a bad feeling.

I looked everywhere until I could see that Natasha wasn't at this party at all. Céline was right – she had left.

The people on the door hadn't seen her go, but also said they probably wouldn't have noticed. It was ten o'clock, and I couldn't think what to do, so I took five canapés from a table and ate them in quick succession, then set off, alone, to walk back to the hotel.

Whatever was happening, I knew it wasn't good.

I didn't feel safe walking through Paris on my own, but I didn't have any money with me, or anyone to walk with, and I knew that if I followed the river I would find my way back. All the enchantment had gone. I just put my head down and set off, in my bedraggled dress. My satin shoes were stained and ripped. The air was thick with electricity, and I felt a storm poised directly above the city.

I walked along the main road rather than the river path because I was scared of people jumping at me from under bridges. I ignored everything. A car stopped and someone told me to get in, but I started to run, and though they trailed me for a while they drove off in the end. I got lost, and the first heavy raindrops fell on my arms, and I was hungry and scared and confused, but then I realized where I was, and I was so pleased I walked faster and faster and then ran, through the storm, to the hotel.

As I hurried up the stairs, the man (who seemed to be awake and on duty at all times) shouted, but I didn't stop to find out what he wanted, but also, of course, I already knew. He wanted money. Our room was locked, and Natasha had the key. I banged on the door, but she didn't answer. She had to be in there, though. She had to.

I ran back down, and when the man started talking I just cut across him and said, '*Je dois avoir le clé pour la chambre numéro sept.*' It was bad French, but he understood. He reached back without taking his eyes off me and took it off a hook, but he didn't pass it to me.

'You must pay your bill,' he said in English. 'I ask Libby and she say *you* have the money and *you* will pay.'

I tried to breathe deeply and didn't bother to correct him about our names.

'I can see from your aura that you've had enough of this,' I tried, but he rolled his eyes.

'You pay,' he said.

'When did she say I would pay?'

'One hour ago?'

'Please, let me into the room,' I said, holding out my hand. 'She has the key. My money is in the room.' I was so tired. I didn't care about his stupid bill. I would come straight back down and pay it with my savings card. 'I'll get the money. And pay you, right now. I promise. It's all in there. But it's in the room. I can't get it unless you give me the key.' I spread my hands, and then patted myself down, demonstrating that I didn't have anything at all on me.

He put the key on his high counter and slid it to me, indicating with his folded arms that he was going to wait right where he was for me to come back down and pay him his money.

My hand shook as I opened the door. I was desperate for her to be in there, even though I knew she wasn't.

I pushed the door. It opened slowly, creaking. She would be there. I closed my eyes and pictured her, sitting on the bed, counting out some sum of money that she had got while she was missing. Ready to tell me everything that had happened. She would be smiling, desperate to share her story. It would be something dramatic and over the top. I wondered if she had found the real Deanna, and what kind of revenge she had got. I wondered why she had come back here without me.

I wondered whether there was a real Deanna. I probably already knew that there wasn't.

I just had to get myself to the station tomorrow morning and I was done. That would be the end of all this, of all Natasha's games. She didn't know I was going home. That was what kept me going.

When I opened my eyes the room was empty.

I closed them.

I opened them.

It was still empty.

The room was not just empty of Natasha. It was empty of everything.

It was almost exactly as it had been when we arrived, except that it was emptier than that. The floor was bare, and the beds were bare too: even the sheets had gone. There were no towels, no bags. Natasha's backpack wasn't there, and neither was my suitcase. She had left the pillows and the blankets that we hadn't used, and that was it.

I walked over to the window and looked out at the building behind and the single tree. When I turned back to the room nothing had changed, except that from here I could see the closed door, and I saw that there was a piece of paper stuck to it. It had words scrawled on it in Natasha's loopy writing in pink pen.

Darling,

I'm so sorry. You don't deserve it. Your family are shits but you're not and I truly have become a bit fond of you and wish you all the good things.

By the time you read this I guess you might have started to work it out. The big thing I needed you for in Paris wasn't anything to do with Deanna Glancey. It was you. I'm not saying you wronged me, because you, personally, didn't, or at least not on purpose. People close to you — people in your family — have wronged me to fuck, and this is payback. You did nothing for that money and you won't need it anyway. Will I need it? Well, I might. I'd like to have it just in case. Be prepared. Also, it's been fun.

Who am I kidding? Of course I hate you. I've hated you from before I met you. I've hated you all along.

You were right: I came over to the UK earlier than I said. I came over as soon as I knew what was in Dad's will. I lived in London for ages. I stalked you around Winchester. I watched you nearly kissing your girl until her girlfriend hotfooted it out of that house to stop you. I liked telling you what to do, and then watching you do it. I felt like God! And I knew (from watching you and from messaging you) that you were my perfect ticket to getting back at everyone. You stand in for your father, my father, Deanna – everyone.

You know perfectly well you were going to run out on me tomorrow morning. I knew it when I saw your face on Monday. I found the ticket the moment you went to the bathroom. I gave you chance after chance to tell me about it but you never did. You were going to sneak off. This is just me doing it first. We're not so different. You're lucky actually, because I was going to do something very dramatic and illegal at Friday's party and leave you to take the blame (twins). You kind of predicted that. You would have been arrested (I would have melted away and left you to see out the end of days in a prison cell). Perfect revenge on you, and on everyone who cares for you!

I'm pretty fucked off that I've had to water it down, so well done I guess.

Still. You've learned enough to find a way out. By the time you read this I'll be long gone.

Task 8: get out of this hotel without paying.

Task 9: hustle for some cash.

Task 10: get home with no money or documents! Hahahaha

Good luck, Libby! xxxx

She had signed off as me. That was the first thing I noticed, because everything else was too much.

It took me a while to realize that the fact that she had taken everything meant that I literally had nothing. No money or documents. I looked again for my suitcase and my canvas bag, but they still weren't there. I had the rain-spattered ballgown I was standing up in, the ruined shoes I was wearing, crunchy hair, and a face dripping with half-rained-off make-up.

It was eleven o'clock. I didn't dare go downstairs because of the angry man, so I bolted the door and closed the curtains and sat on the bed and leaned back on the wall because my legs weren't holding me up. My head was spinning. I couldn't breathe. I wasn't even upset, not yet.

She had my money. My passport. My train ticket. She had just told me that.

I sat on the bed all night, shivering and staring into space. I became catatonic. At one point I jerked into alertness and decided to go to the Gare du Nord, because if Natasha was going to use my train ticket she would be there now, waiting for morning. Then it turned out I couldn't bear to go back out into the storm in the middle of the night in a rioting city in a ruined dress and ripped-up shoes. I slept a bit, waking and remembering and drifting off all night. I had to wait for morning, and in the end it seemed that morning arrived.

My hair was still up, and when I looked, disorientated, around the room, I knew that it had been real. Natasha had, for some reason, taken every single thing I owned.

I had no idea what time it was, but she must have already used my train ticket. Or perhaps she hadn't. Maybe she'd gone somewhere else.

We owed the man downstairs the money for the room, and also, I supposed, for the things Natasha had taken from it. I checked the window: if this was a film there would have been a handy fire escape, but there wasn't, and I already knew that really.

Natasha had, somehow, got past the angry man, carrying her stuff, my stuff and various things from the room that she couldn't possibly have needed, while telling him that I (Natasha) would pay. And she had vanished.

I started imagining ways of getting past him. If I said I was going to a cashpoint, and then never came back, he wouldn't be able to get me. Probably. But I couldn't be someone who lived in a hotel for nearly a week and then ran out in a ballgown without paying. That was Natasha, not me. It was that man's business, his livelihood, his obsession. He had been asking us politely for money for days, and I didn't want to be Natasha. He needed the money to go to visit his friend.

I knew that this was a distraction. I would get money to him and pay for the room one way or another, just not right now. I was puzzling about that so I didn't have to look at the actual truth of what had happened.

I tried to look at it head on, but I couldn't. I was trembling all over. I couldn't even cry.

I had overridden all my instincts. I had known she hated me since I heard her talking on the train. I had known she lied to everyone, and yet I had gone to the party because I thought it would be fun. I had thought I had the upper hand with my secret train ticket. I cried tears of rage and frustration with myself, and they were hot down my cheeks.

Would I be able to use my savings money to get home? Natasha had my bank card. I couldn't travel to London because I didn't have my passport. Did you need a passport to travel between France and Spain? I was pretty sure you didn't. I needed to call Mum, to call Dad, to call the police, but I had no phone. I was alone in Paris with nothing, and my panic was spiralling. Every half-formed plan I made led to a dead end. She had worked it all out, had left me no lifelines.

I could beg to use the hotel man's phone. I couldn't imagine he would look kindly on it but it was the only thing I could think of doing.

She wanted me to make money by hustling with street magic. That was what she had taught me.

I thought for a while that the Creep had already happened. I couldn't breathe. My head was spinning and I needed to run away, but I had nowhere to run to. I thought I might be sick. I made it to the bathroom, but just leaned over the loo and retched.

I stared at myself in the mirror. Make-up was smeared all over my face, and that gave me something to do, so I washed it off with loo paper and soap. The soap got in my eyes, and the paper shredded itself and stuck to my wet face in tiny pieces.

I stepped out of my dress and switched on the shower. I was the girl who looked like Natasha, the girl who had been taken in by someone too good to be true, the girl who had the great misfortune of having a charlatan and a trickster for a cousin.

Everything was unravelling. This was my moment. There were twenty-two days until the end of life on Earth, and I had wasted my last summer. Natasha was a psychopath. I had known that, really, for a while. I remembered what I had heard her saying on the train and wished I had bailed on her right then. I could have got out at whatever that city was – Nevers? And found a train back to Spain. I'd had my bank cards, and I'd had my passport. I could have done anything.

I pulled the pins out of my hair and stood under the water. It was dribbly, but better than nothing. I washed my hair with soap, scrubbing all the hairspray away, and tried to get my face a bit cleaner.

What had she got? I held on to the wall of the shower and tried to work it out.

She'd taken my passport. I wasn't sure how the biometric gates discriminated between people, but if she couldn't use the passport at the automatic gates at airports or the Eurostar terminal, she would manage to show it to a person. She could travel as me if she wanted to, though I didn't know why she would bother. If Natasha was me then that meant, while she was being me, perhaps I had become her.

I didn't think so, though. She was me, and still herself. She had stolen my identity and left me as no one.

She had my phone. That was hardly a coup. She could have pickpocketed a better phone than that in a heartbeat. Though if she could open my phone she had access to my whole life, and of course she would be able to open it. She had watched me put my code in any number of times. I, on the other hand, had failed the one time I'd tried to open hers, because I didn't notice things in the way that she did.

She had the cash she had earned for me yesterday. She had my bank cards. I supposed I needed to call the bank and cancel them, though I was sure she didn't have the PINs.

Her note had said I didn't need the money. That meant she had taken it. If she had wanted half my college fund I would happily have given it to her. She only had to say it. They were our joint grandparents. I would have shared. Also – what was she going to spend it on? Why would she bother now?

There was more, though. I remembered my dad saying that his brother had left him a lot of money. But he didn't have any of it yet. She had said he'd left her and her mother with nothing, but that might have been a lie. I couldn't think straight. The more I thought about it, though, the more sure I was that she had taken all my money. With the passport as ID, and my bank card, I supposed that it would have been easy.

Nobody needed much money, though. Not now.

I didn't have a towel (my cousin had pointlessly stolen them), so I dried myself on the threadbare hand towel that was in the bathroom already, and, in the absence of any other option, put my underwear and gown back on.

My hair dripped down my shoulders, and the silky dress clung to the back of my neck and felt cold and weird, like a jellyfish.

I opened the bathroom door, and a man was standing there. I screamed, but then calmed myself down. This had to be Arjun, Meera's husband. I saw, in his face, how weird I must look.

'Hi!' he said. 'You OK, Natasha or Libby?'

'Libby,' I said. 'I need your help. Please can you help me? Please.'

He stopped. 'Well, sure,' he said. 'But what help do you need?' He looked nervous. 'Has something happened?'

He was, reasonably, not interested in the fact that I was upset. Everyone was upset all the time. Still, he had a nice face, and he and Meera were all I had. They were the only people on my side of the angry man, unless the grumpy woman from room eight was in, and if she was I was sure she wouldn't be interested.

'I've lost everything,' I said. 'My cousin Natasha. My friend. She's taken it all. I have to get out of the hotel but I don't have the money to pay the bill. I don't know what to do.'

He took a step back. 'Sorry, my friend, but we can't pay your hotel bill. Can you just go out and do the things you do – the magic? And I thought you were twins? Separated at birth, right?'

'No. We're cousins. We pretended to be twins.' I shook my head, trying to get some logic into it. 'I don't know.'

'This is all a bit confusing, to be honest. I don't think Meera and I can help.'

'I'm not asking for money,' I said. 'Honestly, I'm not. Could I make one call with your phone? Or send a message?'

He was backing away now, twitching in disapproval. I was ringing his alarm bells, and reasonably so.

'I'll go and talk to Meera.' And he disappeared. I stood there, on the narrow landing, not quite sure what to do. I was still there when Meera came out of their room and put a hand on my shoulder.

'Hey,' she said. 'Oh, Natasha. We are so sorry to hear about your trouble. Don't be angry, but Libby came to see me yesterday evening, and she said this would happen. She explained that she had to go, and that you were having trouble with your mental health. Don't worry. So many people are finding it difficult now. I mean, I find it impossible some days too – we all do – and you're so young.'

'But that's not . . .' I said.

She talked over me. 'Libby told me you might say that you were Libby and she was Natasha, and that you would ask us for help. She said you would imitate her British accent. But it's OK. She said it's OK; you just have to wait here, right here in your room, and help will come. It's going to be fine. She's gone to meet your mother and they'll be back soon. Everyone needs family now. Just stay here and you'll be OK.' She put a hand on my arm and steered me towards the bedroom. 'Just sit it out in here,' she said. 'Truly. We're setting off for home now too.'

'Can I use your phone?'

'I'm sorry.'

I stared at her. Natasha had told her a story and Meera had believed every single word of it. Natasha had said that I was angry and deluded, and that she was bringing me help. She had copied my voice. Weeks ago I had heard her practising that.

'She's lying. *I'm* Libby. She's Natasha.'

'Your mother's coming. Seriously, she is.'

I wished with all my heart that she was right.

'Are you leaving now?' I said. 'You two? Going home, right now?'

'Yes. We have our bags almost ready to go. We're taking the train to Russia and travelling down from there. We'll be home in a week. You see? Even I need my family right now.'

'Can I come with you?'

Arjun was standing behind her with two suitcases. He was using her as a human shield because I made him nervous.

I let Meera usher me into room seven. She patted me on the shoulder again.

'No,' she said. 'Really. You can't come to Goa. You need to stay here. You'll be all right. Your mother is coming to take care of you, I promise.'

For a moment I allowed myself to believe her. Then I remembered that it was Natasha's lie. Of course my mother wasn't coming to take care of me.

I went and knocked on the other door. Number eight. The woman answered and looked at me with raised eyebrows.

'Can you hel–'

'Absolutely not.' She closed the door in my face.

I was destitute, abroad. There was an angry man between me and any help that might be out there. I sat on the bed beside the window and wished I could even cry.

Because I knew that even this didn't really matter. I could just sit here on my own, and it would get hotter and hotter, and the gas would creep around the world and that would be the end. For the first time ever, I stared it in the face. I knew how it would feel to try to breathe air that wasn't there. I felt it sticking in my throat. I gasped, knowing that my body would do everything it could to try to find something to fill its lungs. I saw the things that would flash through my brain as it failed, as this thing we had all known was going to happen actually happened. I felt myself suffocate to death.

And I watched everyone else doing it too. I saw the bodies, everywhere. Earth would be dead, so I zoomed out, into the dying atmosphere, and past it. I went out and out and out, so the planet was just another speck in the distance. Humans had come and gone in the blink of an eye. I leaned my head on the wall and knew that this was meaningless. Love, life, travel, art. None of it had ever meant anything.

I would just sit here and wait it out, and nothing would matter.

Or.

Or I could get out of here. If nothing mattered, then I had nothing to be scared of. The angry man shouldn't frighten me. I came back, down from the stars and through the atmosphere, and back into the air that I could still breathe right now. I jolted back into my body and opened my eyes.

I took a breath, and it felt like the best gift. I jumped up and looked around the room. I picked up the pillow, somehow hoping I might find my savings card, but there was nothing. I tried the pillow on the other bed. I looked in the dusty cupboards, and under the beds.

I found it when I picked up Natasha's mattress. There was a passport on the bed slats, and it had a note on it:

Well done! You found it ♡

It was a black passport and definitely wasn't mine, because it said UNITED STATES OF AMERICA on it. I flicked through the pages.

There were stamps showing that the bearer of this passport had entered the UK in April and left again on the seventeenth of July. On the morning of the eighteenth Natasha had walked into my life, in Spain. This seemed to be her passport, or at least the passport she was using.

I turned to the photo page. That looked like her photo.

She was a few years older than she had said, not a teenager at all but twenty-two years old.

And then I saw it.

Her name was not Natasha Lewis.

I read the words again, and again, trying to make sense of them. The woman who held this passport, whose photograph was right there and who I had known as my cousin, was Deanna Glancey.

I heard Meera and Arjun bumping their bags down the narrow stairs so I snatched up Natasha's passport and notes (the only things I had), tucked them into my knickers due to the lack of any kind of bag, and crept down after them. If they were going to distract the hotel man by checking out, I would seize the moment. On balance I would rather run away from him than ask to use his phone. There were millions of phones in Paris.

My legs wanted to give way but I instructed them to keep going. I had no idea what was going on. But I summoned everything I had. I called in the spirit of Juliet Capulet, and I co-opted Carmen, and I thought of my baby siblings and my dead sister Violet and Shakespeare and Zoe and Harry the tomato and everything that meant anything to me.

I seized it with both hands. I loved people. Some people loved me. I had to do this. And I set off.

I stood at the bottom of the stairs and peeped round the corner. They were standing at the reception desk, talking to the cross man. He was smiling, and the printer was whirring as it churned out their receipt. He looked nice now, but I knew he would change the moment he saw me.

I waited until all three of their heads were down, all looking at the piece of paper on the counter, and then I ran. I was out of the front door before anyone could shout or try to stop me, and I ran out into the hot street and down the road and round the corner. I dodged past people, and just kept running and running, and then I was at the river.

I sat on a bench and tried to quell the panic.

I had no idea who Natasha was. If the woman I had spent the summer with was Natasha, she had a fake passport with Deanna Glancey's name in it. That was exactly the kind of thing she would manage to do.

If she was Deanna, then she wasn't my cousin, but my uncle's illicit girlfriend. Though that was only according to her own story. I tried to make it fit together. Neither way made any sense.

I walked for a long time before I found a phone in a urine-scented phone box that looked as if it had been forgotten in the corner of a square. It felt like the only payphone in the whole city. Once I found it had a dialling tone, it took me ages to work out how to make a reverse-charge call, but I eventually managed to get through to the operator, and she did it for me.

I heard Mum's mobile phone ringing in Spain.

A woman answered, but it wasn't my mum.

'Hello?' I heard her say in a British accent. 'Er . . . Amy's phone?'

The operator asked her if she would accept the charges for a call from Olivia in Paris.

'Oh shit,' she said. 'Amy's not actually here. She would love to speak to Olivia in Paris! So much! Can you get her to call back?'

The operator cut it off. I didn't get to ask the woman who the hell she was or where Mum was. I went through the whole process again with Sean's phone, but he didn't answer, and I banged my head on the side of the phone box and tried not to scream.

Who had that woman been? And where was my mother?

I didn't know my dad's number. Or Anneka's. I pictured some woman in Spain, an expat yoga friend, sitting at my place at the table, answering my mum's phone while Mum was busy trying to repel the new atmosphere with her mind. I pictured Sean's phone on the terrace while he swam up and down the pool or ignored it while he was drinking wine.

I wished I had stayed there.

I called the international operator again. This time I gave them the only other number I had in my head: Zoe's.

I heard the operator say: 'Will you accept a collect call from Olivia Lewis calling from Paris?'

And Zoe said: 'What? Will I what? Libby? In Paris? How much will it . . .? I mean, of course. Put her on.'

I had loved Zoe for a long time, but I had never loved her quite this much before.

'You are connected,' said the operator, and she was gone.

'Libby?' said Zoe. 'Hey, what's going on? I was on my way to the station to meet you. I mean, thank you for all the emails. They were. Wow. I had no idea . . . I mean, I had a bit of an idea. But I'm really overwhelmed. Oh, shall I call you back?'

I looked at the phone box. I couldn't see a number on it.

'What emails?' I said.

'The ones you sent. Look, let me call you back.'

'I'm in a phone box. I can't see any way of getting calls on it. I didn't send you –' I stopped talking as I began to realize. *No. No, not that. It couldn't be.* 'Oh my God,' I said.

'Are they . . . Are they not real?' Zoe's voice changed.

'Was it about, maybe, forty messages? Going back for months?'

'Mmm.' Her voice was very small.

'I'm so sorry. It was Natasha.'

'So not real? You mean, like a practical joke?'

'Shit, no. Real. I wrote them. She's just sent them. I would never have sent them.'

'You said you didn't trust her. What's going on? Why are you in a phone box? Why aren't you home? Are you OK? Safe?'

That pulled me back to my immediate reality. Tears poured down my cheeks. Then I managed to say, 'I'm not OK. Not.'

'What's happened? What else has she done?' When I still couldn't speak, she said, 'Don't worry about the emails. I liked them.'

In spite of everything, that made me smile, just for a moment. 'Thank you, Zoe,' I said shakily, grateful that she hadn't freaked out about them. 'But . . .' I took a deep breath, trying to hold back my tears. 'It's Natasha. She's not my cousin. I don't think. She might be. She's stolen everything. Like, all of it. She's just . . . gone. She took the things from the hotel room. Just everything. My passport. And money. And phone – which is why you got those emails. Oh, Zoe. I'd been writing them for ages but I was never going to . . . And my ticket home. And she –'

'Hey,' said Zoe. 'Libby. Slow down. Where are you? What do you need? Right now? Money? What can I do?'

I tried to think. The sun was hot on the top of my head. I wanted to wear real clothes, not this ballgown. I was ridiculous in it. I didn't want to be a fake twin any more, the one in the shade. I wanted my old life, to be myself.

I saw then that there was nothing wrong with being quiet. Even if the atmosphere was going to turn to poison in three weeks, I could be quiet from now until then (and after that, I supposed, very quiet). It was OK to live whatever remained of my life as myself, the person I really was. I had been good enough before. I hadn't needed to try so desperately to change myself, to go along with everything Natasha had said, just because I wanted to be like her.

She was a liar and a thief. Not a role model.

I wanted to be like myself. I was braver now, and . . . I stopped to consider whether I was right, and decided I was. I was braver, and I could be a better person. I was a better person than Natasha, but I could also be better than the person I'd been for the past few weeks.

I didn't say any of this to Zoe. I realized that I had made her accept an expensive phone call, and that every second I stood there trying to get my act together was costing her actual money.

'Can you go to my dad's house?' I said. 'I don't know his phone number. Get him or Anneka. Tell them I need help urgently. I'm stuck in Paris with no money. No passport or phone and nowhere to go.'

'OK,' she said. 'Look – we'll sort this out, OK? Are there lots of payphones around?'

'There are pretty much none.'

'OK. Then . . . go somewhere. Can you go to a place and wait, somewhere where you'll be safe? And we'll find you. What about the Louvre pyramid, in the courtyard there? Kind of where you were when you sent me that selfie yesterday. Can you just wait? Then, as soon as we find a way to get help to you, we know where you are. I've got the photo from yesterday. What are you wearing? I mean, just in case someone knows someone who can help out straight away. We can give them your photo and description.'

Zoe was springing into action now that she understood the situation. I felt myself starting to relax.

'OK,' I said. 'This sounds insane but I'm wearing a vintage ballgown. It's white. It's like the dress I had for Juliet at the start of the play. I haven't got anything else.'

'Right. OK. Don't worry. Can you get to the Louvre?'

'I can walk there in about half an hour, I think.'

'OK. Is that OK? Are you all right to walk for half an hour? And do you have sunscreen?'

'Yes,' I said. 'I'm OK. I mean, I don't have sunscreen, but that probably doesn't matter any more, does it?'

'We'll sort this out.' She paused. 'I'm going to do this, Libby. We'll work it out. We'll rescue you.'

'Thank you,' I said, and it was not enough but it was all I had.

29. Don't give up

It took me over an hour to walk there. My feet hurt, and I kept having to stop to breathe deeply and to try not to cry. I could see from people's reactions that I had become one of the weird people. I clearly had nothing to steal, and no one tried to talk to me. They pulled children and dogs out of my path. I was glad. I would not have trusted anyone or accepted anybody's help.

The river path was busy, with a cross-section of what felt like everyone in the world walking by the Seine. I walked among them, dodging people on Segways and scooters, people running, people out with their dogs. I passed a group sitting on the ground meditating, and a lot of runners. I had always known how to keep my head down and become invisible when I needed to, and I did it now, ignoring the other lost souls who sometimes called out to me.

The water was choppy, and there was an intense, changing smell to everything. The air was baking hot and close, and the whole world seemed sweaty and slow, particularly me.

I looked at the water again. I really could, I thought, just jump in. If Zoe hadn't taken my call, I might have done it.

She had hated me all along, I thought. She had said it herself, and I knew it anyway. I'd known it since our train journey; before that I had naively assumed that she loved me, simply because she'd said she did. It was too much to think about, and I forced myself to lock it all away. The only thing that mattered was getting home.

When I reached the Louvre I walked up the steps that led from the path beside the Seine to street level and crossed the road to go into the courtyard. I ignored the many people who were trying to make money from tourists and headed across the hot cobbles, pushing my way between the crowds to the entrance to the museum where the pyramid was.

Why did Natasha or Deanna or whoever she was want all my money, when life on Earth was about to end? I didn't understand. I would have given it to her, and she must have known that. I knew her, though; it had been about the game. She wanted to pull off some kind of heist just for the hell of it.

I knew it would be a while before anything happened, so I sat on the low wall of the fountain and watched the queue snaking round, looking out for my maybe-cousin even though I knew she was long gone. People were working the queue, selling bottles of water and bars of chocolate, but no one was Natasha.

I was thirsty, and I had no money. I couldn't see a drinking fountain, and I didn't have three euros for one of the tiny bottles of water that men were selling out of ice buckets.

As soon as I'd thought how thirsty I was, though, I couldn't think of anything else. I considered trying to drink the fountain water, but it felt like a terrible idea. I looked around. Nearby there was a man with an ice bucket (there wasn't actually any ice in it any more – it was just water, and I would happily have drunk that instead). He saw me looking, and called 'Water?' in English. I shook my head.

I could probably have read his palm in exchange for a bottle of water, but I didn't want to. I wasn't going to hustle any more.

I walked down into the park, thinking that there had to be a drinking fountain in the Tuileries Garden, but I couldn't find one. I was scared to talk to anyone, but in the end I saw a man picking up litter (out of kindness, I thought, rather than as a job) and asked him in French if he knew where I could find *eau potable*. The phrase came to me easily from somewhere in my mind. He pointed me in the other direction, away from the museum, and I hurried there, and found that there really was a drinking fountain, and leaned down and drank water for as long as I possibly could. It went down my chin, down the front of my dress.

It was well into the afternoon. I had no idea what I was going to do if night came and nothing had happened. Sleep rough, I supposed. I would have to find a place that felt safe (perhaps in one of the encampments: I knew there were some women's camps around and I thought that if I asked enough women, someone might know where I could find one). I would have to depend on the kindness of strangers.

Yet I knew I could not trust anyone. Natasha had sent my emails to Zoe, and that was utterly excruciating (I kept remembering things I had written), but that was the least of my worries.

When the sun was getting close to the horizon I joined the queue for the Louvre. It was open until ten and I thought I would be safer in there than I was out here. Also, I had been out in the sun all day, and there would be air conditioning inside.

First, though, I walked back to the Tuileries Garden and found a chalky stone. That was easy, because the earth was gravelly, and lots of the stones in it were chalky. The chalk went up your legs when you walked on it. My ruined shoes were bright white.

I took a stone and went back to the fountain. I knew it was a bit rubbish, but I found what felt like the best spot, and wrote LIBBY IS IN THE MUSEUM on the little wall that surrounded it. I wrote it again, abbreviating it to LIBBY MUSEUM and LIBBY LOUVRE. I wrote it in every place I could find. I wrote it all over the ground and on the walls. I hoped I'd written it in enough places, so that even if someone rubbed lots of them out, one would remain. People stared at me and giggled and I didn't care.

Then I joined the queue. It was long, and I knew I would be there for at least another hour, and that was fine. It was a good place to be, because if anyone did come to try to find me, I would see them. I queued behind a group of people of about my grandparents' age who had travelled from somewhere in central France to see Paris while they still could, and I listened to their conversation in French, managing to work out most of it. I missed my grandparents. They would have helped me. Now Natasha had all their money.

The people behind me were from the Middle East and they spoke English, so I listened to their frantic planning of their itinerary for the next few weeks. They were trying so hard to see everything and still get the right trains home.

I wondered what would happen. Was everything about to break down? Would the trains stop working? Would I ever see my mother again?

Who had taken my place and answered her phone? I hated the idea of her hanging out with some random English woman who casually picked up her phone.

I couldn't cry any more, but I felt so alone. I had never felt like this. I wanted to give up but I couldn't. I had to wait this out.

Zoe was on my side, in spite of everything. That was the bright thing. I kept imagining her, though, answering a call from Elisha, getting back together, forgetting that she had said she'd go to Dad's house for me. Remembering about me tomorrow.

We shuffled forward. Nothing much changed. It started to get dark, and my writing faded away. By the time I got to the front of the queue and told the security guard that I didn't have a bag to X-ray, and stepped through a scanner that luckily didn't pick up the fact that I had a passport tucked into my knickers, I had almost forgotten why I was there.

There was an escalator down to the entrance hall. I went down and took a random route away from the crowds, though there were still crowds everywhere. You didn't need a ticket; once you were inside it was a total free-for-all because only the security staff were working now, and they were, I imagined, being paid handsomely for it. I picked up a map, the one in Spanish because I wished I was in Spain, and decided to start nearby, so I would be easily found. I went up the escalator marked Sully.

As I wandered past paintings of solemn old-fashioned people, I longed to be in the Prado. The Louvre was (newsflash!) enormous, and there was too much art here for me. It was overwhelming. I wanted to see *The Garden of Earthly Delights* but I was in the wrong city. I checked my plan and discovered that there was a painting by Bosch in this building. It was called *Ship of Fools*, and it was in the Richelieu Wing on the second floor. I started to navigate towards it.

It wasn't as mind-blowing as *The Garden of Earthly Delights*, but I stood in front of it and stared. It was a fragment of something bigger, something that had been lost. There was a boat, and it had a bunch of people on it, and a few more in the water, overboard. Someone was rowing with a spoon. Someone else was being sick. A nun was playing an instrument. It was, essentially, a group of people who were adrift, being stupid, with the church on board. The more I looked at it, the more I liked it. It was less showy, but it was cynical and funny and amazing. I forgot myself, for a while.

Then I realized that it would take anyone days to find me here, so I set off to find the most obvious place in the museum to wait.

Ten minutes later I was standing at the edge of the crowd by the *Mona Lisa*, watching people looking at it, taking selfies with it, literally ticking it off lists in some cases. I looked over their shoulders into her face and thought that she wouldn't have panicked.

I stood there and my legs hurt. I stayed there because I didn't know where else to go.

I stood there for a long time. I wanted to sit down because my vision kept going strange and I heard ringing sounds that no one else seemed to be noticing, but I stayed where I was.

I was sure I was hallucinating when someone tapped me on the shoulder and said, 'Libby?'

30. Order Orangina

I had never been this pleased to see my father. As soon as I saw him I wanted to throw myself on him and cry, but this was my dad and so I didn't.

'Libby,' he said again, and at that point I actually did burst into tears, and he hugged me tighter than he had ever hugged me before, and we walked away from the *Mona Lisa* together and took the escalator down into the entrance hall. My legs weren't working very well and he had to support me some of the way.

'You found me,' I managed to say. Dad had hardly said a thing. Some things didn't change.

He spoke, after a few minutes.

'I am so relieved,' he said. 'I need to text Anneka.' He sat me on a bench in the empty ticket office and tapped out a message on his phone as he spoke. 'Zoe appeared on our doorstep. Very upset. She said you were alone in Paris and you'd been robbed. I went to London but I couldn't get on a Eurostar today, so I caught the fast train to Dover, and the ferry to Calais, and then the train from there.

That's why it's taken me all day to get here. I'm so glad you were here.'

'You came to rescue me,' I said.

'Yes,' he said. 'And you're going to need to tell me what's happened. Zoe was sketchy on the details. She was focused on rescuing you above all else. She said you were at the Louvre in a ballgown, and if one of us didn't come to get you, she was going to do it herself. And here we are. She was right. Are you hungry?'

'Yes,' I said, and as I said it I felt more hungry than I ever had in my life before. 'Starving.' I hadn't eaten anything, or even thought of food, since I took the canapés off the tray last night.

'You probably need some new clothes.'

'Yes.' I looked down at myself. 'This is all I have.'

'Food first, or clothes?'

'Food.' I was dizzy now I had thought of eating. He put a hand on my arm and guided me through the underground shopping mall and up to the street.

'Anneka's replied.' It was dark outside. He looked at his phone and said, 'Ah, yes. She's booked us a hotel. It's not far from here, I think. We were waiting until I found you here to plan what was next. Excuse me a moment.'

He put his phone to his ear and said, 'Yes, I've got her! Yes. Yes, exactly. She'd written messages in chalk outside the Louvre, and I followed her trail and found her. Yes, it's a big place but I thought I'd start with the *Mona Lisa*, and there she was. I'm not sure who was looking the more enigmatic. She's OK. Fine. Well, not exactly fine, but she's safe. I know. Yes. All OK there?'

I listened to him chatting away and wondered how Anneka had done it. How had she got my dad to be talkative like this? I wished she were here too.

'Right,' he said, and he turned to me with the warmest smile I'd ever seen from him. 'Libby. Let's get you some food, and everything else you need, and we can exchange a few stories. Does that sound OK?'

'Yes,' I said. 'Yes, it does.'

I ended up getting the everything-else first because we walked past a branch of Monoprix that was about to close forever, so I came away with a bag that had a toothbrush, a pair of shorts and some T-shirts, and new underwear (which was more embarrassing for Dad than it was for me at this point). I had retrieved Natasha's passport and her two notes from my underwear in the changing room, so they were in the bag too. I had changed into a second pair of shorts and T-shirt, and was debating throwing my poor ballgown away before deciding that it wasn't its fault, so I kept it.

'Now. Food?' said Dad, looking over at me with a smile.

We sat outside a brasserie on a corner. It was a warm night, as ever, but there was a bit of a breeze.

'Order anything you want,' said Dad, and I looked down the menu and ended up asking for a mushroom omelette and chips and a salad. That was, for some reason, the thing I wanted most in the world. Dad asked whether I wanted a beer or wine, but it turned out I didn't. I just wanted a carafe of water and an Orangina, which turned into three Oranginas. The sugar was the thing.

'So,' I said when it had arrived. 'We need to talk about . . . our summer visitor.'

'If you feel up to it.' His voice was gentle, understanding. Different.

'How sure are you,' I said, 'that that was Natasha? I mean, do you even *have* a niece called Natasha? Because her passport belonged to Deanna Glancey, who was your brother's girlfriend. I don't think that was Natasha Lewis at all.' He didn't say anything. I let it hang there for a bit, then gave up. 'So she arrived in Spain, straight from your house,' I said. 'I liked her. I thought she was amazing. She made me feel different. I felt that I could do so many more things. I believed in myself, I suppose. I could talk to people. She showed me how to do magic tricks and read palms and things like that. I suppose I was swept up in it.'

'She contrived a fight with your mother and took you off to Madrid,' he said.

'That's right. She told Mum she had messages for her from beyond the grave, from someone called Violet.'

I wasn't expecting him to react to that, but he did. He drew his breath in tightly.

'Well,' he said. 'That would, indeed, infuriate your mother. Did she tell you why?'

'No! Mum wouldn't say, and then she went to pieces and Sean had to look after her and she didn't really care what I did. But Natasha said Violet was my sister, who died. Was she?'

'No. It's not my thing to tell, darling. Your mother can tell you all about it. I would, but I can't. Don't worry, though. Natasha had it all wrong.'

I sighed. Maybe one day *someone* would tell me. Was Violet going to turn out to be Mum's first pet or something? A sledge?

'Fine. So she got us to look alike, mainly through hair. And she copied my mannerisms, I think. I saw her doing it once, when she thought I was asleep. We pretended to be twins, and we went around making money doing street magic. We stayed in a hostel. I saw Mum and Sean from time to time. Have you spoken to Mum? Is she OK?'

'Yes,' he said. 'I've spoken to her. She's OK, or she will be by now because Anneka will have told her you're safe. So then?'

'Natasha, or Deanna, said she had a spirit guide, but it was all lies. She did some weird psychic stuff. I never believed in it. I actually really wanted to, but I never could. Maybe there is life after death, but I never felt Natasha was accessing it. She did some shows where she said she gave people messages from beyond the grave. She tried to tell me I was psychic too, but I never went for it.'

'That,' said Dad, sipping his red wine, 'is because you are a sane and grounded young woman.'

I smiled. 'Thanks. So. Your brother. You know the accident, when he died?'

'Yes.'

'Natasha said he was with a younger woman. He was cheating on his wife, and he was drunk and they crashed and the woman was fine, but Andy died. Natasha said the woman was called Deanna Glancey, and that's who this passport belongs to.' I put it on the table, and he picked it up and flicked through it.

'Yes,' he said. 'Peggy said there was another woman involved.'

'Natasha said she hated Deanna. Completely hated her. She told me, eventually, that we were in Paris because she'd been stalking Deanna's social media, and she knew she was going to this grand party last night, plus another one on Friday at the Louvre. Natasha wanted to go to both of them, and, like, do something terrible. I didn't know what exactly, but she promised me she wasn't going to hurt her. She was going to throw a drink all over her. Something like that.

'Also, I heard her talking to someone on the train saying I was stupid, so I wasn't trusting her anyway by the time we got here. But we got these dresses, and she got us tickets for last night's party, and we went. I had a train ticket home for today, so I wasn't going to the Friday one. She knew. I didn't tell her, but of course she knew.'

I told him how it had gone from there. It was hard, reliving the dizzying realization that nothing had been what I'd thought, and that she had taken everything I had, and then left a passport with the wrong name in it. I had thought I'd been a step ahead of her, but I hadn't.

I sipped my Orangina. It was very hard to say this part.

'And she's . . . I think she's got my bank cards. Well, I *know* she's got them because she's got everything, but I had the card from Grandma's money in my purse. And the money you sent me in my current account. I had access to tens of thousands of pounds. And she's got it now. She took it.' I passed him Natasha's note, the one that said I didn't need the money.

He read it. 'Did she know the PIN to your savings card?'

I remembered us in the dress shop. I remembered Natasha making a point of turning her back and not seeing the number. It was only the second time I'd ever used the card, and I'd never written the number down.

Looking away had been her distraction. I knew it had. She had done it to make me think that she wasn't watching. Somehow she had been watching. That kind of stuff was what she did for a living. It was no different from making your target look at one hand while you hid a coin in the other. The dress shop was full of mirrors. She had been watching.

'I used it once in front of her.' I pointed to the bag. 'To buy that dress, and her dress, and our shoes. She paid me back for some of it. I just paid because . . .' I tailed off. 'Because we had a cash-flow problem. I didn't think she saw me put the PIN in, but of course she did.'

'I imagine so.'

'I haven't cancelled the card.'

'I nearly did when we heard from Zoe. But I didn't know if you had it, and thought you might need it, because we were very unclear on what had happened, and we couldn't contact you, so I left it just in case it was your lifeline. I'm sure that even if we'd managed to cancel it straight away, it would have been too late. Anneka's stopped it now, but, again, I expect she will have taken the money, darling.'

'I suppose she thought it should have been her money too. If she was Natasha. Which . . . I don't think she was.'

'We need to call the police. Did you not think to do that?'

'Not seriously.' I considered it. Natasha had trained me, I thought, not to see the police as allies. 'Also, I ran away from the hotel without paying.'

'Right.' He sighed. 'OK. We'll go back in the morning and pay for the hotel, of course. That problem will go away in an instant. We need the police. I'll get the British embassy or consulate or whatever to sort you out with a passport, but I'm afraid we might be here for a few days.' He laughed. 'A couple of days with my eldest daughter, in Paris in the sunshine. It might not be so bad, once we get the admin done. And if she's cleaned out your account . . . well, it's only money. And who even knows . . .' He didn't finish his sentence. He didn't have to.

'I'm really sorry,' I said. My voice came out very quietly.

'Hey.' He reached out a hand and almost, but not quite, touched mine. 'If it's anyone's fault, it's mine.'

'How do you work that out?'

'Because I sent her to you, without verifying that she was who she said she was. We have a lot to untangle, and to be honest she was very much like Andy, in that she was a spiky character, always shifting, never quite herself. And she's like Peggy too. I could see traits of both of them, but maybe I was just projecting and seeing what I wanted to see, and maybe she was no relation at all. She was probably playing me like she was apparently playing everyone else. In fact, I was the first to be taken in. I was the gatekeeper and if I'd done my job properly you'd never even have spoken to her.'

'I didn't know you even knew Peggy? Mum said she never met her.'

He sighed. 'I need to tell you a bit of family backstory, Libby. I clearly should have done this years ago.'

'Don't take this the wrong way, but I really wish I hadn't inherited that part of you. The bit that wants to say things but can't.'

'Tell me about it. Right. Here we go. You know that I was married before I met your mother?'

'And after!'

'Indeed. My first wife. Margaret as she was known back then. She was all those things you just said. She lied, she faked things, she pretended to be things she wasn't. She would absolutely have pretended she could talk to ghosts. She tricked people. She tricked me. She was charming and she swept you up in her charisma.'

'*Margaret?* In my head she was a kind of staid, old-fashioned person. She looked like Margaret Thatcher.'

'She wasn't. So Margaret did a midnight flit. And took everything she could, just like Natasha did to you. She left me as thoroughly as could be. For . . . Well.'

I realized I knew what he was going to say, and when he didn't say it I filled it in for him.

'For your brother,' I said. 'She left you for Andy, and that's why you never spoke to him again. Margaret is Peggy.'

'She claimed half the house, and off they went to the States.' He was smiling and looking sad at the same time. 'Obviously it was no loss in the long run, though I did keep hoping Andy would turn up saying she'd done the same to him, and he never did. I'm afraid too that it made me mistrustful of your mother when I shouldn't have been. Amy's completely different, and I messed up there, I really did. I owe her a huge apology. And you too, of course.'

'Your first wife was Peggy.' I was still trying to get my head round this.

'Yes. Margaret. Peggy. It was very *her* to have picked Peggy as a new American variant of her name.'

'So . . . she's not American?'

'Oh, God no. She's from Surbiton.'

'I had that all wrong. So Natasha's completely British?'

'By parentage. Though she'll have US citizenship, having been born there, and of course she grew up there. All I can say is that her mother trained her expertly. If it's her. Oh God, what a mess.'

'But she's Deanna. Or she's using Deanna's passport.'

He poured himself more wine. 'If she's actually the person her passport says she is . . .'

'Then she's your brother's secret girlfriend, and the real Natasha is someone completely different. If there even is a real Natasha.'

We sat there for a while. I yawned. Once I started I couldn't stop.

'He might not even be dead,' said Dad. 'Though I think he must be, because he left us that money. According to lawyers. I haven't seen any of it yet. It might yet be smoke and mirrors.'

I really wanted to go to bed, but my dad was talking to me, and the relief at being safe and knowing I had a bed to go to gave me energy.

'What was he like?'

Dad shrugged. 'Well, he wasn't a great brother, what with him running off with my wife and all that. I don't know. We weren't close. Margaret always said she hated him, until it turned out she didn't. He was older than me, but shorter. I was quite pleased with that. Not that it counted for much.'

And just like that, at that moment, I realized that I could talk to my dad. We had an understanding. We were OK. He had dropped everything and run to Paris to rescue me.

His phone, which was next to him on the table, started to ring. I saw the display: Amy.

He answered and passed it over to me without saying a word.

'Hi, Mum,' I said. 'Are you OK?'

31. Sleep

I slept the best sleep of my life that night, and I am someone who has had a lot of good sleeps. I woke up knowing exactly where I was and what had happened, texted Zoe from Dad's phone, ate a huge breakfast, drank a coffee and a hot chocolate and two glasses of orange juice, and Dad and I caught the Metro over to the other hotel.

At that point, in spite of the sleep, the food and the drink, my strength failed. My legs wobbled and I wanted to sit down, but I didn't. I was completely rooted to the pavement. I was too scared, too shaky, to be able to go in. I could not bear to see the furious man, who couldn't tell me apart from the Natasha/Deanna person.

'Can you just do it?' I said to Dad. 'Please?'

He put a hand on my elbow and steered me in. 'You don't have to say a word,' he said. 'I'll do the talking.'

When the man saw me he pointed and drew in a long breath.

'You!' he said.

'Don't worry,' said my dad in English. 'We've come to pay the bill. Pay. Bill. Yes? *L'addition?*'

The man stared at me for a long time and then said: 'Good.' While he was getting it together, and adding extra charges for the things Natasha had stolen (he thought it was me, I could tell), plus a late-payment fee that he clearly invented on the spot, I looked around.

It wasn't the hotel's fault. I told myself that again and again. It hadn't been the *place*. It had been the person.

My dad bought our way out of trouble. The man was mollified and shook his hand, and he and Dad discussed the fact that it had all been the other girl, and finally the grumpy man turned his smile on me and agreed that it must have been the other girl, because this one had come back to pay, and now he could close the hotel and travel to see his friend.

He shook hands with both of us and, as I turned to leave, someone came down the stairs.

I looked around, just in case, but it was just the woman from room eight, with newly dyed orange hair, wearing tight jeans and a frilly white blouse, coming down the stairs with an enormous suitcase. I gave her a little smile and turned back round to leave, when I realized that Dad had frozen. I saw that he was staring at her. She paused on the stairs, then turned and went calmly back up them again, lugging her suitcase with her.

'Excuse me?' he said. She kept going. He called louder. 'Excuse me. Could you come back a second?'

She kept going. Dad set off after her, running up the dusty stairs. She left the case as a barrier and ran back

334

towards her room. Dad jumped over it. The hotel man shouted and went after them and I didn't see what happened next because all three of them were out of sight, and the case toppled down the stairs, thudding as it went, but staying closed.

When they came back down, Dad was holding the woman by the upper arm, and the hotel guy was looking as furious as I had ever seen him.

'Dad?'

I had never seen him like this before. His face was set in an odd expression. The room eight woman shook herself free.

'Get off me, Benjamin,' she hissed.

I stared. She knew his name. That was impossible.

'Not until you explain,' he said.

The hotel man shouted at him, and Dad let go of her arm, but stood between her and the door.

'Oh, fine,' said the woman. She smiled sarcastically. 'Hello, Benji. *Quelle* delight.'

'Indeed,' said Dad. 'I believe you've met my eldest: Libby.'

'We have met,' she said. She turned to me. 'Hi, my dear.'

'You slammed the door in my face when I asked for help,' I said.

'I *closed* it. I didn't slam it. So, I knew your father before he met your mother. There are some sheets and towels from your room in mine. I left them behind. They're no use to me.'

'I've just bloody paid for them!' Dad almost seemed pleased. This was a small, tangible thing and he was furious about it. 'Jesus Christ, Margaret. Libby spent a night sitting up crying in that room with nothing. And you were on the other side of the wall all along? What kind of a psycho are you? We need to sit down and talk through a few things.'

She laughed. 'Absolutely no way, mister. And we're all psychos now.'

'For Christ's sake. You and . . . whoever that Natasha woman actually was – you did your thing. Again. I'm not going anywhere until you explain. I'll call the police. I will *happily* call them.'

She refused. Dad refused to accept her refusal. It went on for a long time. I walked around the lobby looking at things. There was a dusty table in the corner with a visitor's book on it; for a moment I had a crazed idea that Natasha might have signed it, that there could be a clue in what she had written, but, in fact, no one had signed it since 2006. Meanwhile Dad and Margaret got more and more heated with each other. Dad actually did call the police. The hotel man told us all to get out. Margaret said she'd come with us if Dad hung up the phone. He did, and she did.

And so I ended up sitting outside a cafe on the corner of the street, at a little round table with my father to my right and the first of his four wives to my left.

A waiter arrived, and I could see that we looked like a family. A very fucked-up one, with parents who, the man clearly felt, shouldn't stay together for the sake of the child.

I looked at Margaret. I had paid her very little attention on the few occasions I'd seen her, but now I remembered her in Spain. She had been drinking a cocktail in Moralzarzal. She had handed Natasha a piece of paper in Madrid. I thought I might even have seen her in Winchester, outside Vik's house. I could see now that she was about my parents' age, that she was, in an odd way, comfortable in my dad's company. I tried to imagine them married. She could almost have been my mother. She was very glamorous, and very well made-up. She had looked out of place in the run-down hotel, but the world was full of people looking out of place right now.

'Oh, fine!' she said when the waiter had put our drinks down. She had ordered a Kir royale, which was something dark red that came in a champagne glass. Dad had a beer even though it was still morning, and I was back on the Orangina. 'Fine. Put your phones on the table. I'm not having you recording this.'

Dad put his phone on the table. Margaret looked at me.

'I don't have a phone,' I said. 'I did, but your friend stole it.'

'Oh yes,' she said. 'Fair enough. If you're recording this on a burner or something, though, I will find you and you will regret it.'

'Whatever,' I said.

'I'll tell you and then I'm going to leave and we'll never see each other again.'

'Fingers crossed,' said Dad, and I laughed because it was so unlike him.

'Right. Listen up because this is a ten-minute-only offer with full deniability. Andy and I were very happy together. He was like a much cooler, more loving, just *better* version of you. We moved to the States. We wanted to live in Manhattan and settled on New Jersey because money. Very quickly we had Natasha. Everything was great. We cut every single tie to the UK and life was wonderful. Andy moved into finance and ended up making a lot of money, which you would know about. We had a fabulous life, and we stayed in New Jersey but moved to Princeton. It's nice there. You should check it out. Years passed. Meanwhile I became interested in tarot and palm reading, and I made a bit of money doing that. It was fun.

'I met Deanna through that. I actually introduced her to him. Then, before I know it, Mr Midlife Crisis and my young friend are cavorting together under my very nose. I threw him out. Twelve-twelve happened. He crashed his car and died. She had an abdominal injury, but after a quick surgery she was fine.'

She stopped talking abruptly.

'Right,' I said, because she paused for so long that someone needed to say something.

'Yeah. So that was shit. And then it got worse. We discovered that he had left all his money to you. To his estranged brother, and his family, in the UK, who he'd cut off without a second thought two decades earlier. With a note saying it's because of some guilt he's been carrying all these years, yada yada yada. He left enough for Natasha to go to college, and then millions. Millions. To you guys.

And nothing to me, because apparently he didn't like me any more. I mean, no. There was no way that could happen. He owed me. The bastard.'

'And?' said Dad.

'I would have let it go, under the circumstances. We're all going to die anyway. Half the animals have gone – did you notice? I saw a woman earlier with a handbag dog, but it was dead. Head poking out of her bag. Weird times. I would have just damned him to hell and left it at that, but Natasha wouldn't.'

'Natasha?'

'She's a tenacious girl. She was so furious that in the end I said: *Fine! Let's just do it then*. I told her to make a plan, but that wherever she went I was going too, and she did. We spent the paltry sum your brother left her for college, and we came over here by ship months ago. Natasha's a clever girl. I just went along with it. It was nice to see the UK again, and then Spain, and of course Paris. It was nice to keep an eye on you from a distance, little Libby. As soon as she discovered you existed, you became the key to it all. Close enough in age, close enough in looks. It all started there.'

'So that *was* Natasha?' I said.

Peggy smiled, looking smug, and shrugged.

'Or was it?' she said. 'The passport says it was Dee.'

'You've set her up,' I said. 'This is revenge on her too. You're going to blame Deanna for stealing my money.'

Peggy turned a huge, insincere smile on me. 'That's my girl,' she said. 'Natasha has taught you well. Everything points to Dee.' She leaned back in her chair and smiled at both of us.

'Why are you here?' I said.

'Support. I wanted to be where my baby was. I've been helping Tash when she needed it. And for fun. Also, I've got fuck-all else to do. My husband left me, died and gave away all my money. All I've got is my Tash. I feel a bit like Miss Havisham, you know? I taught that girl every fucked-up trick in her arsenal. What else is there for me to do but see Paris and die, darling?'

Dad signalled to the waiter for a second beer.

'You're not with her now, though,' I said, and I looked around, half expecting to see her.

'I still had some Paris things to do,' she said vaguely. 'Tash went and did her bits and pieces. I was on my way to meet her when I stumbled upon my first husband and my . . .' She looked at me, frowning. 'Semi-stepdaughter? Fucked-up niece? Whatever you are.'

'But you've only got Libby's college fund,' said Dad. 'You don't have Andy's money, because I don't have it yet. You only have the college fund.'

'Do we?' she said.

'Do you?'

She was bluffing.

It would, it turned out, be ages before there was any actual money distributed from Uncle Andy's will. It might be a year, and of course there was unlikely to be a year. What actually happened to the inheritance was something we would only begin to untangle on September the eighteenth. If that happened.

'So,' I said. I just wanted to check this. 'You weren't in a mental health facility, shut away for your own good and barely able to communicate with anyone? Not at any point?'

'Should have been,' said Dad.

'Do I *look* like I was?'

'Yes,' said Dad.

I stood up. There was no way I was staying here any longer than I absolutely had to.

'Bye,' I said to Peggy.

'Bye, darling.'

'I hate you,' I said, and Dad laughed.

'I don't hate you,' she said. 'Tash became really rather fond of you, you know. You're a sweet girl. Cute. Naive. A bit of a darling. We'll miss you.'

32. Get yourself home
before it ends

We left Paris four days later. I had a temporary passport, and the police had all Natasha's details, as well as Peggy's (she had, of course, left the hotel straight after our visit, and the hotel was closed and its records unavailable). Neither Dad nor I thought they had the slightest chance of catching either of them, but they said they would try.

My savings account was empty. All my money had vanished and, even though the police and bank were apparently trying to get it back, the fact that she'd seen me putting in my PIN was probably going to mean that I was technically liable. We had tracked down the lovely woman at the clothes shop, who backed me up, but apparently that didn't count for much.

Natasha had caught my train to London and then taken all my money, in cash, from various banks. With my bank card and photo ID, she had trawled around different branches and taken the maximum amount allowed from each, then transferred what was left into a different account and withdrawn that. It had disappeared, like Natasha herself.

I wished she had actually been Deanna. I didn't want my cousin, someone from my own family, to have done this to me. I wanted it to have been a mad stranger.

Her plan had worked, and now she had the money. I couldn't put into words how that made me feel. It wasn't the money (although it was a little bit the money). It was the fact that I'd been entirely and completely taken in by her. I felt dirty and used. I hated her, and I would find some way of getting revenge.

However, Dad was taking the unrelenting view that it was only money and didn't matter, and I had learned to enjoy his company. I was wearing new clothes, and I felt like myself again. Although Dad had grandly said I could buy whatever I wanted, I was too aware of the fact that I had lost my entire inheritance to be able to enjoy shopping in Paris. I was wearing the basic clothes I'd got on that evening when he'd rescued me. My hair was growing, and I thought I might try to change its colour because I didn't want to look like that woman any more.

It took me ages to get through security at the Eurostar terminal. My passport wasn't a normal one, and both sets of border people spent ages looking at it and asking me about it. By the time I was through, Dad was sitting on a wide windowsill by the cafe with two coffees and two croissants next to him.

I sat beside him.

'I've done it,' I said. 'Crossed the border.'

'Cheers,' he said.

I picked up the other cardboard coffee cup and we pushed them together. 'Thanks for the rescue.'

'It's been a pleasure,' said Dad. 'I mean, it really has. It was about time we did something together.'

'Yes,' I said. 'It was, wasn't it?'

The Creep was less than three weeks away. I didn't want to think about it, but it was lurking all the time. Things were dying. I was staying away from the news, but there were no birds left, as far as I could see, and Peggy had been right about the small animals.

Those creatures had died, and people swept up the birds and buried their pets (or carried them in handbags). One day soon there would be human corpses lying everywhere, and no one would be left to clear them away.

However you chose to look at it, the process was underway. It made me feel sick to think about it and I knew that I could be friends with Dad now, and write off the money, and go home to find Zoe, and do all the things I had to do, and I had to do it fast because the days were numbered. We were the dinosaurs in the days before the comet.

The odd thing was that I thought Natasha had been right in one of her early messages: I still couldn't focus on what was going to happen. I couldn't think about it. My mind protected itself by swerving away every time I tried, and I thought it was the same for most people, and I was glad. I was always a bit surprised at how polite most people were. The train was busy, and if we'd wanted to, we, the passengers, could have stormed the driver's compartment and seized control of it, but no one did. Everyone carried on following the rules. Though perhaps there's no point in seizing control of a train, because it can only go where the rails will take it.

I knew that after a mad hot summer of adventures and tricks and lies I was going home. I stopped thinking about the things I should do before the end of the world and started to think beyond it.

My imaginary list of Things to do After the End of the World went like this:

If things are somehow the same, on September the eighteenth –

Do not waste a moment.

Go on mad, wonderful dates with Zoe.

Apply to drama school.

Audition for plays.

Be confident when you need to be, but also own the fact that you're quiet and that's all right.

Work hard.

Have fun.

Be the best person you can be; help people who need help.

Go back to Madrid one day.

Go back to Paris one day.

Learn more languages.

Go to galleries.

Listen to music.

Read books and books and books and books.

Be happy.

No need to hide.

And if you wake up on September the eighteenth, you will go after Natasha and you will find her, and she will be very, very, VERY sorry that she messed with you.

I was trying to hold on to it. It might be all right. I was trying to believe that it would be, because I could not believe otherwise. I didn't want to know the statistics. I most certainly didn't want to think about breathing apparatus and bunkers and things.

Dad and I sat together on the train and I stared out of the window. There were fires in Paris, and demonstrations and groups of people, and then the train went faster and faster and faster and we were passing through the countryside.

I knew that people all over the world were doing their best to prepare. It was a leveller: I had always felt like a child, but now I knew that all the adults were no more prepared, no more sensible, than we were. My own father, previously the most impermeable person, had said that he'd never stopped feeling like a teenager and he didn't think anyone else really did either. Everyone was in this together.

They weren't really, of course. There was aggression, and murder, and war, but there was also peace and love, because humans are complicated. People were preparing bunkers, but the bunkers weren't going to work for long and, even if they did, what kind of a life was that? Was it just that people were so programmed to find a way to carry on living that they would do anything?

I knew that some people were making their own missiles filled with oxygen, to try to kill the pollution. People in countries with big gun cultures were planning to shoot it out of the sky. That was beyond unhinged. There was nothing any of us could really do but wait.

'Strange times, hey?' said Dad.

'Yes.'

'It'll be OK,' he said. 'We have to believe it, no matter what. We have two tiny children in the family, don't we? They have no idea. Sofie heard about it but thought it was something that went creak. It took us ages to work out what she meant.'

'Cute.' He was right: thinking about Sofie and Hans-Erik somehow made the bad things fade a bit. 'Yes. I think it'll be OK.'

'They say you should live every day as if it were your last,' he said, 'but when it comes down to it that's not really it, is it? Live every day as if it might *not* be your last. That kind of works better.'

'Live every day as if you had a future.'

'I'm going to the bar,' he said. 'Want anything?'

'Chocolate, please,' I said.

I stared out of the window at the dark of the Channel Tunnel, and then it went light and I was back in Britain. I'd been away for over two months and it was strange to be here again. I had expected the countryside of Kent to be staid next to Paris, but there were tents and festivals and banners and fires just as there had been in France and

Spain. As we came into London the train slowed enough for me to look in through people's windows, to see that, in spite of everything, they were mainly just living their lives and hoping for the best, and quite a lot of them were watching *EastEnders*.

We got off at St Pancras, walked down a ramp and came out through some sliding doors into the station concourse.

'Libby!' I had known Mum would be there, but I hadn't expected her to yell like that. She had not previously been the sort of person who would shout at the top of her voice across a crowded station. But now she bellowed. I dropped my bag and ran to her, and we smashed into each other like bulls.

Then she hugged me, and I hugged her, and I knew that, whatever was going to happen, we would face it together.

She felt more substantial now. She felt dependable.

We caught the train back to Winchester, me and my two parents, and that was, of course, mortifying, and, in spite of the bond Dad and I had forged since he came and found me in the Louvre, I sat there between the two of them with nothing at all to say. I kind of flipped back into being my old self, and I didn't want that, but I *even more* didn't want to relax into this particular situation. I didn't want to have to start plotting to get my parents back together.

But they spoke to each other, filling each other in on things, and I was glad they were there.

'Can I use your phone?' I said to Mum, and she handed it over. I started a text to Zoe.

> Hi Zoe. It's Libby, on Mum's
> phone this time. I'm nearly
> home. Can I see you soon? Thank
> you again SO, SO MUCH for
> saving me. I need to say thanks
> in person and I also need to give
> you the money for that reverse
> charge call. Thank you, thank
> you, thank you – you are
> amazing, my Romeo xxxx

I sent it even though I knew it sounded mad. We'd been texting every day, though I had always deleted the messages straight away from Dad's phone. Oddly, Natasha sending all my old emails to her had fast-forwarded our relationship to a new place that felt full of possibility. I had no need to pretend any more. She replied at once.

> Don't be silly about the money.
> My parents pay the bill and they
> say don't you dare attempt to
> pay them for it. Get your dad to
> give them some wine if you
> want! Yes, we have to meet up.
> Later today? xxx

I leaned back and smiled.

> Perfect.

At Winchester station I said goodbye to my dad. It was the very first time I could remember being sorry to leave him. He gave me a hug and kissed the top of my head.

'Come over and see us all,' he said. 'As soon as you can. Please. Anneka and the kids can't wait to see you.'

'I will,' I said, and Mum and I walked home to Sean.

It turned out, though, that we weren't just walking home to him.

'If you're ready for it,' said Mum, taking my arm and steering me into the park, 'I need to tell you something before we get home.'

'Can't you tell me *when* we get home?' I was desperate for the comforts of my own bedroom. In fact, I was longing for them with all my being.

'It's about Violet,' she said. 'And, no, I have to tell you now. I've spent your whole life not telling you about her when you should have known.'

'Oh,' I said. 'Finally! I thought no one was ever going to tell me about Violet. I thought there was some rule that said I was never, ever allowed to know.'

'Sorry,' said Mum, and she took me into the same park where I'd been walking back in December when I'd heard the news. 'Let's walk and talk. I think it'll be easier this way.'

I had no idea what to expect, except that I knew Violet was dead. I knew that, not because Natasha had told me, but because of Mum's reaction when Natasha had said her name.

'So,' I said. 'Who was she?'

350

'OK,' said Mum. 'Right. This hasn't been easy for me, but it's different now. As you know, I cracked up over the summer, and that's all connected with Vi. It's OK now. And I know it's weird to think of your parents in these terms, but here goes. When I was fourteen I had a boyfriend. He was seventeen. My parents hated him, as you can imagine, but I didn't. To cut a long story short, just after my fifteenth birthday I discovered I was pregnant. Not only that, but I was thirty weeks pregnant. I know. Don't look at me like that.'

'I'm not looking at you like anything! That must have been *awful*.'

'Horrific. Too late to do anything but have the baby. She was a little girl.'

'Violet.'

I waited. The next bit was going to be horrible.

'Violet,' said Mum. 'My parents took charge and she was whisked away. I never saw her again.'

She stopped talking.

'She died,' I said.

'No. No, that's the thing. She didn't die, Libby. She was adopted. It was all right, mainly. I had to get on with life. I messed up my exams and caught up with my education later, in my early twenties, but I just had to hope she was being looked after better than I would have been able to look after her. I thought about her every day, forever.'

'What happened?' I managed to say. I was dreading the answer. Here was another family member – a half-sister – and she was lost too.

'She was fine.' Mum turned a huge smile on me. 'I always thought of her out there, and I always wanted her to come and find me. I left my details on the register for her, but she didn't contact me. After twelve-twelve I knew I had to try harder. The only thing I wanted to do before the end of the world was to find my other baby. I tried to track her down, but without much luck. I wrote messages to her and sent them off to the adoption people, so she might be able to get them if she looked for me. Then, this summer, she did. She decided to look for her birth mother, and she found me.' She took my hand and we started walking towards the house. 'It was difficult. I was very up and down, because when she found out that I had another daughter and that you'd always lived with me, she found it difficult to process. She was very angry and said she didn't want anything to do with me. Honestly, darling, when you went off with Natasha I really wasn't myself. I thought you needed some time away from me to grow, and I'd told you to travel so I could hardly turn round and forbid it. I loathed Natasha but I could see how she was helping you come out of yourself. I don't know what I was thinking when I let you go off with her. I stupidly thought I could use the time to build something with Violet, but then she told me she didn't want to meet me after all. Suddenly I had neither of you. I felt I'd pushed you away to make space to get to know her, and then she didn't want to know me. I wanted you to come back, but I felt so shabby. I suppose it wasn't Peggy who had the massive breakdown. It was me.'

'What?' I couldn't keep up with all this. 'So she's alive? Why did Natasha say she was dead? Natasha said she was a little child talking from beyond the grave!'

'I have never been so angry in my life as I was then,' she said. 'I didn't realize it until later, but she had been through my laptop. I only discovered that last week, when I saw that some documents had been opened more recently than they should have been. She'd found the very private letters I'd written to Violet and misinterpreted them. She thought I was writing to a dead baby, rather than a lost one. Oh my God, that girl. At the time I just thought she'd eavesdropped on Sean and me talking, and picked up the name. I thought it was a shot in the dark. Anyway, I kept on bombarding Vi with messages, and she came round. She understood that I'd had her at fifteen and hadn't been allowed to keep her, whereas when I'd had you I'd been a married twenty-eight-year-old and it was entirely different. I told her all about you and she started to accept that she had a little sister. To be honest, she only felt able to come to Moralzarzal because you weren't there – one thing at a time. But we got to know her and it was . . .' She grinned. 'It was incredible actually. I know I was in a bad way, and I didn't just pull myself back by magic. I went to a doctor, in Spain. He gave me antidepressants, and they took a couple of weeks to work. But they do work. A combination of medication and having both my girls back. It's got me back on an even keel.'

'She slept in my bedroom,' I said. I imagined her, this unknown older sister, sleeping in the room I'd shared with

Natasha. I wondered whether she slept with my flamingo lights on.

'She did, darling,' said Mum. 'Yes. Is that OK? Would you like to meet her?'

As we turned the corner I saw there was a cluster of people near our house, and when I got closer I began to see who they were. There was Zoe and her family. There was Max, who I'd thought was in Singapore, who I'd dumped because he'd told me Natasha was talking shite. Max turned towards me and galloped down the street, and I gave him a little hug, which was the most physical contact we had ever had.

'I thought you'd uploaded yourself to the . . . mainframe?' I said.

'Didn't work. Came back. I thought you weren't talking to me any more.'

'Sorry. I do want to talk to you.'

'Then we're cool. Sorry about what happened. I would have sorted her out for you!' He made fists like a boxer.

'Yeah,' I said. 'If only I'd thought of that.'

Then there was Zoe. She hugged me very tight, and I hugged her back, and nuzzled her hair a bit. I pulled far enough out to look into her eyes. She was looking right back, and her gaze was full of everything.

'Thank you so much,' I said. 'You saved me.'

'You saved yourself. We've brought you a cake.'

'I don't want any fuss.'

She laughed. 'That's why you're so brilliant.'

'But I *could* eat some cake.'

She put her arm through mine, and we walked up the road to have a little party.

'Did you say,' I said, knowing that I had to tackle this first, 'that you were OK with my emails? I mean, I know you said that, but did you just say it because I was in a state? Or did you mean it?'

'I did mean it,' she said, and she smiled. 'In a strange way it was amazing to get to know you.'

I imagined Natasha going through my phone, reading all those drafts, and sending every one of them just out of spite. I had the strangest feeling that, in that respect, she had done me a favour.

Then there was a woman who looked about thirty, hanging back and smiling shyly. She had thick black hair, and brown eyes, and I knew she was my big sister.

'Hello, Libby,' she said.

I grinned at her. 'Hello, Violet.'

We looked at each other, and then I took two steps towards her and hugged her as tightly as I could.

17 September

We were standing on the grass in a crowd of people, and the sky was getting darker. The riots had all migrated to the cities, and here, in the park, it was calm almost to the point of spookiness. There were bonfires, and people were singing old and new songs, together and separately. In the distance I could hear a band. People were dancing, running, just standing there. They were doing whatever they wanted.

I stood with Mum and Sean, with Dad and Anneka and the babies, with Violet, with Zoe, and with her family. The children had no idea, of course, of what was about to happen; they ran around giggling, and Hans-Erik clung to my legs and said, 'Libby!'

I remembered babysitting them that night just after I'd played Juliet. We had stayed up and eaten chocolate. Although he'd been one then and he was two now, I thought that I had changed, since then, even more than Hans had. I leaned down and picked him up, held him close and hoped that he would grow up. He was squishy and perfect in my arms, brimming with possibility.

Violet had fitted into our world as if she had always been there. Her parents had died, one after the other, a couple of years ago, but it had still taken the impending apocalypse to prompt her to trace her birth mother, and when she did meet Mum she realized that her mother had been a terrified teenager and she found that she could understand and forgive at last.

I was being brave tonight, because there was no other way to be. We had all stepped into a different realm, and there was absolutely nothing to do but wait. Giving up, right now, would have been the same as being brave, just as it had been when I was in Paris. Either way, there was nothing to do but wait and breathe. The atmosphere had been notably shifting for weeks. It had been shifting more throughout the day, and we all had gas masks, but no one was wearing them. I thought I wouldn't put mine on, but then I supposed that when it came down to it I probably would.

I was standing with my family and waiting for the atmosphere to change so much that we couldn't live in it any more. Zoe was right next to me, holding my hand. Zoe and I had spent the past three weeks together, and now we had run out of time. I couldn't think about the future. No one could because it was impossible.

I was here with the people I loved. I had a lot of life left to live. I was longing to live it.

I took a deep breath in.
I breathed out.
I breathed in again.
I breathed out.
I

breathed.

Acknowledgements

Thank you first of all to Ruth Knowles for being an incredible editor, as always. This, our fourth book together, has been a wonderful experience, and your ideas and guidance have been amazing at every point. Thanks to Wendy Shakespeare for everything you do to make the manuscript come together (apparently effortlessly) into an actual book. Huge thanks to Marcus Fletcher, Sarah Hall, Jennie Roman, Bella Jones and everyone else who worked on this book.

Steph Thwaites: you are the BEST agent and that is a fact.

In 2017 I went on a course in Newcastle run by the brilliant Ian Rowland. It was called 'Anytime, Anywhere Psychic Readings' and, alongside Ian's book *The Full Facts Book of Cold Reading*, it gave Natasha and Libby lots of their street skills and entertained me enormously. Thanks to my husband, Craig, for coming on the course with me, as it was quite an intimidating prospect.

Thanks to Craig, Seb, Charlie, Lottie and Alfie for all the lovely support and distractions at home, and to Gabe, Tansy, Brendan, Agnes and Ted for giving me lots of excellent reasons to visit Winchester.

ALSO BY EMILY BARR

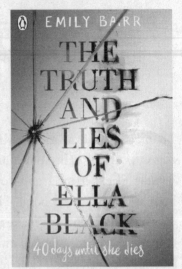

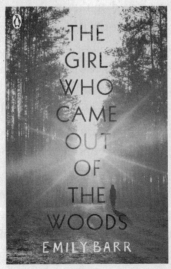